Ambitions

AMBITIONS

The Life and Love of
John and Susannah Morrissey

A Novel By
Frank Baillargeon

FRANK WRITES

HISTORY

AMBITIONS

FRANK WRITES

HISTORY

Bibliographical references and index.

Identifiers

Digital 979-8-9866040-0-8

Paperback 979-8-9866040-1-5

Hardcover 979-8-9866040-2-2

The series Ambitions is dedicated to Francis Joseph Baillargeon, Sr. (1920-2004). My father was devoted, for decades, to researching and sharing the extraordinary life of John Morrissey. For years he would gather and mail new bundles of research he'd pull from newspaper and library archives and forward them to me wherever I was living at the time. The most touching gesture was the box of twenty-four audiotapes of him reading Jack Kofoed's 1938 bio of Morrissey, Brandy for Heroes.

The gift of your voice, Dad, will live with our family forever.

Susannah's Pledge

"When alone again, she leaned close, whispered words of love, recited poems, and spoke of a world of shared happiness and success that awaited them. It was her declaration of devotion to her chosen partner and her new self. He would no longer need to rely on his fists in the life she imagined. He would become a great man, and she would be his muse. She released his hand and rested hers over his heart. She closed her eyes and felt the steady beat and whispered forever."

Prologue

THE CROSSING

1833

Something was very wrong. Judith Morrissey's eyes shot open. She drew her nursing son close and shifted painfully to touch her husband's protruding hip. Tim had been feverish and unresponsive for days. Finally, he was cool to the touch. She strained to see into the blackness. Their daughters, Mary and Bridget were nearby. Judith listened carefully, rewarded with the sound of their rhythmic breathing. *What's wrong?* she wondered as her heart raced.

Fully awake, Judith realized the intense pitching and rolling of the *Albion* had ceased, and voices and movement were discernable on the deck above. She shook her husband as daylight burst into the hold. "Tim. Tim, be quick. Take Johnny and the lasses!"

Tim saw the sudden shaft of light flooding the cargo bay and realized the implications. He leaped into the rat-infested water, turned, accepted his son from Judith, and helped his daughters jump down. Judith adjusted her tattered dress and joined them. The family raced the short distance to ascend to the deck. Other passengers shouted and struggled out of their berths, desperate for sunlight, fresh air, and hope.

1

Ninety-four impoverished Irish emigrants had been secured in the hold of the *Albion*, an aging sailing ship, for six horrifying days and nights. The last and worst of a series of relentless storms had overwhelmed the *Albion* a month out of port. Devoid of light, awareness arrived via touch, smell, movement, or sound, each delivering unspeakable and mounting misery.

The survivors had been forsaken, terrified, and starved. The voyage's provisions, which included a single pound of food per day per passenger, and water enough for a thirty-day crossing, were long gone. Pleas for mercy from the sick, those dying of typhoid and dysentery, grieving loved ones, and suffering children never ceased. Suddenly, deliverance appeared at hand.

The *Albion* had departed Queenstown in County Cork, Ireland, on March 29, 1833, bound for Quebec. She would carry precious lumber from Canada's boundless forests to Britain. The early and dangerous North Atlantic crossing could make three profitable trips possible during the year. The Irish emigrants supplied a convenient source of revenue and ballast.

Master James Isaacs captained the *Albion*. He knew the risks of the dangerous early departure and had objected. "We'll find another captain if that suits you," responded the proprietors. Isaacs relented.

The Morrissey family, including Tim, Judith, twelve-year-old Mary, and eight-year-old Bridget, traveled for seven dollars each. Infant son, John, traveled at no cost. The family's allotted space was six-by-six feet in the middle row of rough planks suspended along the starboard side of the cargo hold. A mere three feet separated them from passengers crammed above and below. Time above deck was rare because of frigid North Atlantic temperatures and continuous storms.

On the *Albion*'s swaying deck, the Morrisseys wrapped arms around each other, gulping fresh salt air as their eyes adjusted to the brilliant sun. Passengers continued to climb out, weak, emaciated and blinded. Crew members pulled and shoved to create more room on deck. Sailors carried buckets of seawater to wash away stench and filth. Others carried buckets of rainwater for drinking. The officers did their best to keep order and ensure that everyone, the infirm included, had time to draw from the lifesaving water.

Holding John to his chest, Tim led Judith and their daughters across the deck to an uncrowded position near the mainmast. Sailors worked their way between the passengers, offering water. When the water reached Tim, he accepted the large wooden spoon and pressed it to Judith's lips, then to each of his children before closing his eyes and taking a gulp.

When the last survivors finally climbed out of the cargo hold on May 9, forty-two days had passed since their hopeful departure. Four deckhands and two ship's officers descended to assess conditions, run the bilge pump, and count and name the dead. While they were below, a bell sounded. Master Isaacs had emerged from his quarters accompanied by the ship's first officer and an armed mate.

"The Good Lord, in His infinite mercy, delivers us this day!" Master Isaacs's voice boomed as he lifted his arms and glanced skyward. "Let us bow our heads and give thanks for His mercy. Let us also pray for those who departed during this crossing. They are children of God and have returned to His loving embrace."

Most of the refugees had long exhausted prayer and abandoned hope for mercy from God or man. Tim Morrissey, however, gazed at his wife with a broad smile. Judith had been a source of steadfast faith. God, she was sure, wanted them to arrive in America. There, her children would be free. "Perhaps," she often speculated, "Johnny will become a priest."

"I have good news for all," shouted Isaacs. "This last great storm has tossed us for a week, but our pilot, Lieutenant Simonson, has brought us within two days of Quebec. Praise be to God!"

. . .

Judith leaned over the starboard rail, shielded her eyes, and stared into the distance, eager to see land as the ship rose and fell. There was none to see; however, circling overhead and landing upon the mizzen crosstrees, Judith saw a tern, then another. She tugged at Tim's shirt and pointed, unable to speak.

Seventy-four emigrants stepped off the *Albion* and passed into Canada. Eight, too ill to enter British Canada, boarded an outbound ship to Ireland, where the poorhouse awaited.

The Morrisseys entered Quebec Province. Tim booked the least expensive passage down the Saint Lawrence River to Lake Champlain. On the open deck of a barge, they passed through the Champlain Canal to the Hudson River. Their destination was Troy, New York, where a community of Irish Catholics, including some from Tipperary, had settled.

Tim Morrissey struggled to support his growing family because he lacked job skills and ambition. He preferred gambling, drinking, and raising fighting cocks to steady work. Five more daughters quickly arrived to add to the challenges of survival. Judith took in work at their apartment, joining thousands of Trojan women sewing collars for its booming shirt industry.

When John Morrissey took his first toddling steps into America, all odds were against him. That he would become America's boxing champion, a millionaire entrepreneur, and a multi-term member of the United States Congress and New York State Senate was unimaginable.

Yet, it happened.

One

J udith Morrissey leaned over her sleeping son, shaking him awake. As he stirred, Judith pressed a silencing finger to her lips. Snow had fallen overnight, muffling the sounds of carriages passing below. Ice had formed on the inside of the room's two windows. Judith placed a ragged wool blanket over John's exposed shoulders. He stood, removed the blanket, and wrapped it around his pregnant mother. It was February 12, 1843, John Morrissey's twelfth birthday.

Judith led her son to an open bedroom door. Four girls huddled under rough blankets strewn across the floor of the eight-foot-square room. "Johnny," she whispered, "See there, your wee sisters? A struggle, it is, to keep their bellies full." A tear slid down her cheek. John tried to draw her close, but she resisted, wiping the rare tear with the back of her hand.

"I'll be expecting you at regular work now, she insisted. "You're twelve this day and strong as a man." Judith turned and walked to the kitchen. She placed three precious pieces of coal in the stove, lifted an empty five-gallon bucket, and went out.

In bare feet, clutching the blanket, Judith descended the exterior stairs to the snow-and-ice-covered courtyard three flights below. There, a pump supplied water for ten families who lived in the overcrowded building on Ferry Street. Jammed in the tiny yard were six privies. These served the sixty-seven occupants of the building and patrons of the first-floor barroom. Judith used a privy, pumped water to fill the bucket, drew a frigid breath, and climbed the stairs back to the apartment.

Inadequate as they were, the three rooms on Ferry Street were an improvement over earlier living arrangements. The Morrisseys' first home in Troy was a crude shelter constructed with scraps of wood and metal. It sat against the steep hillside on the city's eastern edge, where the Morrisseys joined others who'd recently arrived from Ireland. The family had survived the exposure and rampant cholera that had swept through the encampment before moving across the Hudson, where Tim found work as a lumber handler, earning one dollar a day.

Tim squandered portions of his meager earnings on drinking and gambling, just as he had in Templemore. The family was forced to move from one squalid West Troy apartment to another before moving across the Hudson to Ferry Street.

The arrival of new daughters, Mary Ann in '35, Catherine in '36, Ellen in '38, and Margaret in '41, with another child months away, made circumstances increasingly dire for Judith. The thirty-seven-year-old mother of seven remained strong in body but tired in spirit. Her dreams of a better life in America were shattered.

Among Judith's disappointments was her only son. Headstrong and with no interest in formal learning, Johnny stopped attending school after one year, opting for life with the boys on the streets of Troy. He would meet neighborhood boys each morning and await the newspaper-delivery wagons. They'd fight to secure a bundle of papers and scatter to hawk what they could for a penny apiece.

Running wild with his friends, Johnny stole fruit from street vendors and liquor from grocers, played cards, competed in sports, and fought every chance he got. Judith and Tim tried to tame their wild son. "The old man," Morrissey later recalled, could never impress me, except with an ax handle." Of his mother, he said, "She used to take me in hand often, and I was afraid of her."

Twelve-year-old John responded to his mother's demands and began working various jobs, always facing harsh discrimination. Unemployment ran high after the monetary crisis of 1837, with profits, prices, and wages down. Naturally, resentment toward Irish immigrants, willing to work for any wage, was seething. The only jobs available for a twelve-year-old Irish Catholic boy were those that few men would consider.

When not at work, John ran with a group of South Troy Irish lads called the Downtown Gang. Their leader was "Tuffy" Dumbleton, who walked with the aid of a crutch, which served as a weapon in their battles. The gangs fought with stones, clubs, and knives against rival gangs. Individual combat—fists only—were frequent. Here, John excelled. Victories accumulated, and his reputation grew. The Troy police and local courts came to know him well.

The Uptown Gang, led by John O'Rourke, a twenty-two-year-old gang veteran, was the most feared Troy gang. A fight had been brewing between Morrissey and O'Rourke for months. Finally, after a gang clash on the frozen Hudson, Dumbleton insisted upon a match. When the designated day and time arrived, the two met in a circle formed by gang supporters and a host of curious onlookers.

John stripped off his shirt, grinning at O'Rourke. The fighters rushed each other and locked up. O'Rourke tried to throw his much younger and smaller opponent. John, however, anticipated the move, stepped inside, gained leverage, and slammed O'Rourke to the ground. Now, straddling his adversary, John jammed his fingers into O'Rourke's eyes, determined to maim his rival while his gang members struggled to drag him away. The fight was over in less than two minutes. O'Rourke's eyes survived, though his fearsome reputation did not.

With gang pride at stake, eight other members of the Uptown Gang challenged Morrissey. Each time he prevailed. John often suffered punishment early on when facing more experienced or skilled fighters, but it only inspired him. One observer of several fights later recalled, "He never knew when he was licked. Just as you tired of thumping him, he got his second wind. Then you might as well tackle the devil himself as trying to make any headway against him." John asserted throughout his adult life, "I was a tough youth. There was nothing I could think of but to fight."

After defeating all opposing challengers in Troy, he challenged Albany's top bully, Malachi Brennan, and prevailed. The young fighter's reputation spread throughout the region. Drinking in celebration of his frequent victories gave John a taste for liquor. He would never, however, develop an ability to manage it. Sober, he had a pleasant, playful, generous disposition. Drunk, they claimed, "he became a perfect madman." Alcohol fueled his seething rage, obliterated his judgment, and threatened his freedom. It would take years, an improbable and fortunate marriage, and fatherhood to convince him to avoid heavy drinking.

Troy police usually overlooked gang activities as "boys being boys." As incidence accumulated, however, they could no longer ignore Morrissey's more egregious actions. He spent nights in the Fourth Street holding room, with warnings from the court. Finally, a questionable burglary charge sent the teen to Rensselaer County Jail for six months.

John enjoyed his celebrity as an alpha male in a rough riverfront city. He swaggered along the streets with his gang members, looking for fun and trouble. Men learned to give Morrissey and his gang a wide berth. Girls and young women stared at the tall, handsome, self-assured boy and whispered. He and his Downtown Gang frequently concluded evenings paired with bold romantic companions seeking excitement and conquests of their own.

Two

After years as a saloonkeeper and fight promoter in the lower wards of New York City, Aleck Hamilton moved to Troy. Competition in New York was fierce and could be deadly. Hamilton saw greener and safer pastures along the waterfront in the booming manufacturing city one hundred and fifty miles north.

The saloon and brothel at Hamilton's Eastern Hotel catered to a rough crowd of canal and factory laborers. Cheap hard liquor and affordable prostitutes were the principal attractions. Fights were inevitable. The only way to deal with the violence was immediate and greater violence. The muscle needed to keep order never lasted long. Men fought with fists, feet, teeth, and anything they could wield or throw. The price of shattered bones and reduced faculties took a toll on even the hardest men.

Hamilton was down to a single effective brawler named Marcel Archambeault. He was a six-foot-four giant who'd spent years felling trees in Quebec before marrying a thirteen-year-old Mi'kmaq princess and stealing off to the United States with his pregnant bride. Upon arriving in Upstate New York, Archambeault needed work, and the United States Army needed soldiers for its expanding war with Mexico. Marcel left his wife and child at a convent run by the sisters of Charity in Glen Falls, New York, and marched off to battle.

Upon coming home, Archambeault discovered that his wife and child had "returned to her Indian family." Archambeault took his broken spirit and foul mood to several jobs along the Hudson. At Troy, he found his way to the Eastern Hotel. A Saturday night of drinking led to a fight with three locals, who were no match for the giant. Liking what he saw, Hamilton hired Marcel on the spot.

Recently, Hamilton saw that Marcel received as much punishment as he dished out. He would still be good weekend muscle when Hamilton had two stout men at the bar, but he needed someone with the reputation, skill, and bravery to stand in night after night. Hamilton dispatched his janitor and handyman, a free black named Nathan Parker, to find John Morrissey, the young man he had recently seen beating Malachi Brennan.

John knew Hamilton's reputation as a fight promoter, which was reason enough to accept the invitation. He told Parker he would visit after his shift ended the following day.

"Where's Hamilton?" John asked as he entered the saloon the following afternoon.

Near the end of the bar, the proprietor eyed the tall, broad-shouldered brute and said, "You found him."

John walked up to the short, balding man with a cigar stub hanging from his lip. "I'm Morrissey. You lookin' for me?"

Hamilton appraised the ragged young man. John's hair was a greasy mess of black curls. His clothing included a filthy shirt, coveralls held by a single strap, and a worn leather cap. John's hands already bore signs of his battles. A scar cut through his left eyebrow. Still, he stood close and confident.

"Well, young man," said Hamilton, "I hear you're a brawler, but you're young for the job. That handsome mug won't last a weekend."

"How do I show you I'm your man?" Morrissey never broke eye contact.

Hamilton grinned. Bibber McGeehan was occupying a seat near the end of the bar. He was one of the most notorious of a troublesome clientele. Bibber fancied one of Hamilton's younger prostitutes. After one experience, she refused to entertain him. He was now seven or eight drinks in. Both Hamilton and Archie were keeping a watchful eye.

Hamilton turned to Morrissey. "See that ugly buffer at the end of the bar? I want him to leave, and he won't without a struggle."

Morrissey strolled to the end of the bar and stood above the brooding McGeehan. "Time to go," he said.

"I s'pose you're gonna make me?" Bibber slurred as he rose, unsteady. His right hand gripped an empty whiskey glass, ready to strike.

Morrissey's right fist struck McGeehan's throat, forcing him to the ground, gasping in desperation. John grabbed his ankles and dragged him across the floor, out the front door, and down the stairs. People on the street stopped and stared as the young man deposited McGeehan in the muddy ruts. Morrissey leaned over the still-gasping man and whispered, "Come here again, I'll kill ya."

Hamilton had followed the pair and stood watching. When John turned back toward the Eastern, Hamilton said, "Well, you earned a chance. Come upstairs."

John followed the proprietor upstairs into a small, drab office. Hamilton took a seat behind his desk, opened a drawer, and removed two small glasses and a whiskey bottle. He wiped the insides of the glasses with his sleeve, half-filled the glasses, and offered one to John.

"Sit. Please." Hamilton motioned to the unmatched set of chairs facing his desk. John settled into one and accepted the drink.

"Thank you, sir," John said, raising his glass.

"Ten dollars per week," Hamilton told the young fighter. "That's what the job pays. You'll work every day, except Monday, from five until we lock up. You'll help tend the bar and jump in to keep order without destroying my place or killing anyone. You also must help the whores upstairs when things get out of hand. Archie, the big slugger behind the bar, will show you the ropes."

"Fifteen," said Morrissey. "Fifteen a week, a room upstairs, and you make some fights for me."

Hamilton leaped out of his seat. "You're a cheeky one!" He glared at Morrissey. "I never paid nobody fifteen! You won't last a week!"

"Well, if I don't, you lost nothin,' and I'll split my winnings on fights you promote. This place will keep peaceful, I promise it."

John leaned back in his chair, holding his worn leather hat, waiting. Hamilton downed his drink and poured himself another. The lad had just dispatched a very rough customer with ease. Hamilton watched his catlike grace and confidence. Now he saw something else - opportunity.

"Here's the offer, lad. I'll pay you twelve-fifty, and you can bed in a room upstairs. But two conditions; first, I'll give you a month to see how you do; second, I'll stake fights and manage your bets. When you win, I get half the winnings. If you lose, I'll take the stake from your pay."

Morrissey smiled, reached across the desk, shook Hamilton's hand, and asked, "When do I start?"

The arrangement proved beneficial for both. Initially, locals and toughs passing through took the measure of the sixteen-year-old. Hamilton saw that his new hire had devastating punching power, could throw any opponent in a rough-and-tumble fight, and had more bottom than any fighter he had seen. The young man could take a pummeling and grow stronger and more determined. He was a rough fighting gem. All he needed was polishing.

Fights at the saloon reduced. When they occurred, John and Archie responded with decisive force. Saloon business was up, and property losses were down. The prostitutes were safer and happier, provided a richer share for Hamilton, and competed for the favor of their young protector.

John liked a job for the first time. With his help, the Morrisseys could afford a slightly larger apartment in a safer neighborhood. They had more food and better clothes for the girls, though his mother was bitter about his absence from home. Because he worked nights, his gang activity and detainments by the police and courts all but disappeared.

Hamilton honored his commitment to promoting fights for young Morrissey. For a stake of one hundred dollars, winner takes all, he arranged a series of illegal fights that fall and into early 1848. Hamilton knew when, where, and how to schedule and promote the popular fights, often in the backrooms of bars or local cockfighting arenas. Though enforcing rules was difficult, combatants fought under London Prize Ring Rules. Hand coverings were not allowed. Rounds ended when one or both fighters fell to the ground. The fight was over when a fighter could no longer come to the scratch line. These bloody, bone-breaking contests often went on for dozens of rounds and hours.

John's threshold for pain was extraordinary. He would not quit a fight. Often, he returned to the Eastern with a battered face, a body covered in bruises, and swollen, busted hands. Yet, he smiled through the damage and surrendered to the prostitutes eager to comfort him. With fifty dollars for each contest and profits from large side bets, Hamilton considered his agreement to pay Morrissey twelve-fifty a bargain.

Hamilton often stopped at Isaiah Rynders's Empire Club during his trips to New York City. He bragged to the fighters, promoters, and gamblers there that he had a boy at his saloon in Troy who could whip any of them. He even offered to put up a five-hundred-dollar stake to back a fight. "Dutch" Charlie Duane, a prizefighter and promoter, told Hamilton to "send the farm boy" down, promising to teach him some modesty.

Morrissey became more convinced of his invincibility and less patient for his chance to fight the best. If Hamilton couldn't make it happen, he would have to do it himself.

Three

It was almost five o'clock when Morrissey sprinted up the Eastern's rotting porch steps and yanked open the door. Regulars sat apart at the bar, not bothering to lift their heads. Nathan Parker was swabbing the filthy floor. He looked up, nodding.

"Hamilton in?" asked a breathless Morrissey.

"There." Parker pointed the handle of his mop toward the ceiling, indicating Hamilton was in his office.

John rushed to the stairwell. Hamilton's office was on the second floor on the left. The prostitutes entertained in the rooms down the hallway to the right. The third and fourth floors served as cheap accommodations, offered by the hour, day, week, or longer.

Morrissey bounded up the stairs and burst onto the second-floor landing, almost colliding with Veronica. The short, voluptuous madam of the house shrieked as John grabbed her arm and steadied her.

"Sorry!" he exclaimed, removing his cheap leather cap, and smiling down at Veronica.

The women who worked at the brothel were fond of the handsome young lad, none more than the madam.

"Is the devil himself up your ass, Johnny?" Veronica straightened her red day wig. "Where are you off to in such an almighty rush?"

"To see the boss." He could have left it there but added, "I signed on for the *Empire of Troy*. He'll be needing someone to keep the peace here."

Veronica shoved her hands against his chest, her face dissolving into a dark scowl. Her painted lips parted, exposing nubs of stained teeth from years of neglect and poor diet. "You can't go!" she spat, glaring with eyes of fury. You have no idea what it was like around here before you arrived. I couldn't keep any girls for more than a few weeks. They got beat too often. If they stayed, they'd be too ugly for even the likes who drink here to part with any coin."

John removed her hands from his shirt. "I'll be a deckhand when the river's open. I gave my word and my mark. It's done."

He turned and rushed up to Hamilton's office.

"I've news, sir," said John, bursting in. "I took a job on the *Empire*. Start soon as the ice melts."

Hamilton rolled a cigar between his fingers and studied John, wondering if he was looking for another raise.

"How much this time?" Hamilton asked. "You know nobody makes as much as you. You're just a kid. I want to keep you around, but I'm not a rich man."

"No, sir, Mr. Hamilton. It ain't the money. I'll be fighting Tom Hyer for the championship. I'm grateful for what you did for me, but Hyer won't fight anybody from a backwater town. You know better than me. Top fighters and promoters are in New York, where that coward is."

The cigar still dangling, Hamilton glared. "I'll make it twenty a week, but that's more than I should."

John shook his head. "I told you, sir, it ain't money. I need a bigger place to plant my flag."

"When will you be leaving? I'll be needing a replacement, maybe two. My hands'll be full when the animals hear you're gone."

"A few days, maybe a week."

"Well, stay as long as you can, Johnny. Don't spread it around you're leavin'."

Hamilton extended his hand to Morrissey. He, too, had chased impossible dreams at the same age. He sighed and advised, "When you get to the city, call on Isaiah Rynders at the Empire Club on Park Row. Here, I'll write it for you. I bragged about you there." He handed the directions to John. They stood quietly for a moment, unsure what more to say.

Hamilton broke the silence. "Seek out 'Dutch' Charlie Duane. When I bragged I had a fighter who'd take his measure, he promised to teach you manners. Win his respect, Johnny, and he could make serious matches for you."

The proprietor of the Eastern was fond of his young peacekeeper. He was sorry to see him leave for business reasons and genuine concern. He sent John away with a warning; "Trust me, lad, you're not ready for Tom Hyer. I've seen you both. Get fights with experienced prizefighters before you challenge the best, and get a good trainer, Johnny. There are opportunities around the Rynders crowd but be careful. It's a dangerous pack of jackals there. They'll take pleasure in carving you up and tossing you in the river."

"Let 'em try," John responded. "If I gotta beat the lot of them to get to Hyer, I will. They'll have to kill me to stop me, but I don't kill easy."

Hamilton sat behind his battered, old desk as the arrogant young fighter put his cap back on and bounded down the stairs. Opening his humidor, he selected a fresh cigar, cut off the end, and fired it. Hamilton closed his eyes, calming, as the warmth of the scotch-infused tobacco struck. He turned to the window overlooking Second Street and watched as young John Morrissey swaggered toward Canal Street. *Bound for more trouble than the lad can imagine*, Hamilton thought, shaking his head.

Four

The *Empire of Troy* made the night passage between Troy and New York City, with stops along the way. Captain Levi Smith, a veteran pilot, and captain on the Hudson had a reputation for hiring Irish and treating them fairly. Morrissey planned to sleep aboard the Empire in the morning after docking in New York and then chase prizefight opportunities in the afternoons.

Captain Smith was familiar with Morrissey's reputation as a fighter and troublemaker. The last thing Smith needed was a deckhand who would contribute to, rather than solve, disorder on his ship; however, he had listened as John described his current and prior work. The boy spoke of five younger sisters who depended upon his earnings. Captain Smith, though reluctant, hired the lad, knowing he could always put him ashore if he caused trouble.

Though Smith could not match John's salary at the Eastern, he told the youth that he could earn as much with tips for helping passengers with their belongings when the ship docked. John applied his *X* to the papers and appeared, in awe, on deck on March 19.

At three hundred and nine feet, the *Empire of Troy* was the largest steamboat in the world and one of the fastest. She could carry a thousand passengers from Troy to New York City in fewer than eight hours, offering every imaginable amenity, including seventy plush staterooms. Her unique design provided passengers unobstructed views from the grand salon and the covered promenade. Every ticket was sold for the first downriver passage of the year. People in their spring finery roamed the deck, greeting one another while taking in the marvels of the fabulous steamer.

Captain Smith was joined by his bright, strong-willed thirteen-year-old daughter, Susannah, on the season's maiden voyage. His wife, Aldine Buckbee Smith, recently informed their daughter that she would board at Troy Female Seminary beginning in the fall. Susannah reacted with anger and depression. Levi and Aldine hoped that her first trip on the glorious steamer, and a shopping trip in New York City, would help restore peace at home.

Hundreds of spectators lined the pier as the *Empire* threw off its lines and pulled into the channel. Coal-fired boilers powered the twin forty-eight-inch cylinders turning the giant sidewheels. Travel with the speed and agility of the *Empire* was unprecedented and awe-inspiring. Men, women, and children gathered along the east and west riverbanks as the sun slid below the mountains. They waved and shouted as the glorious ship sped by, smoke billowing from its towering smokestacks.

Susannah Smith stood midship, gripping the gleaming brass rail. Her father, beside her, looked resplendent in his formal uniform. She pulled her overcoat close against the spring chill and waved to the crowds, thinking, *this is how I wish to spend the balance of my life. Free as a bird. Off on grand adventures.* Despite her anger, Susannah felt proud of her father. He was the captain of this great ship, the world's largest and most elegant.

"Quite a sight, isn't it?" Captain Smith leaned close to his daughter as the *Empire* built speed as it approached Albany. "In a moment, we'll cross to the starboard rail, where an even larger crowd will wave and shout as we head past the capitol. Suzie, the trip to New York took four days or more when I worked sailing vessels. Today, we'll arrive in eight hours. My dear child, you live in an age of wonder."

"Thank you, Father." Susannah gripped the rail as her heart raced. "I apologize for my recent ill-temper. I'm scared, confused, and hurt. Father, I can't imagine separation from my family and friends. Perhaps you and Mother will reconsider boarding school?"

Levi Smith would not argue with his daughter on the deck of his ship. Instead, he drew close and whispered, "We've made our decision, Suzie, and it's final. Now, I must be about my duties. Please join me." He took his daughter's elbow and escorted her to his luxurious stateroom.

Before closing the stateroom door and heading toward the bridge, Captain Smith smiled at Susannah and said, "Feel free to roam the promenade, but be here and prepared to join me at my table for dinner at seven. If you need help, seek one of my uniformed officers."

Susannah was far too excited and restless to remain in the stateroom. She was upon the promenade within minutes. Passengers were retreating to the comfort of their cabins, staterooms, or the grand salon a deck below. Susannah strolled, stopping to peer through the etched-glass canopy over the grand salon. Dozens of fashionable couples gathered there and presented a tableau of happiness and affluence. She promised herself *that would be my life in a few short years.*

She continued aft, passing two ship's officers, who smiled and tipped their hats. Groups of deckhands busied themselves straightening deck chairs and wiping down wood and brass surfaces. Few were too busy to neglect a glimpse of Susannah as she passed.

Susannah heard an intense argument as she rounded the stern and watched as two gentlemen spilled out of the broad stairway. A third rushed up the stairway and to the deck to intervene. The larger of the arguing pair knocked the newcomer to the deck. "Stay out of this!" he bellowed, pointing at the fallen gentleman. "Mr. Radcliffe here has insulted my wife, and I'll be satisfied."

Both men had raised their fists and circled, looking for an opening to strike.

Susannah froze. She should have retreated, but the prospect of violence transfixed her. An irate crew member rushed past, shouting, "Stop immediately, or I'll have you in irons and ashore at the next town!"

"Stand back," admonished the larger combatant. "This is between two gentlemen. I'll have no interference from the likes of you." Distracted by the crew member, the man failed to see Radcliffe step close and strike him in the mouth, drawing blood. Infuriated, the man attacked. The bosun jumped in to separate the fighters. Susannah backed into the shadows and watched the fight unfold.

John saw the captain's daughter walk past, then saw Bosun Maloney rushing aft. In a flash, John dropped his mop and set out. Reaching the melee, he saw that the bosun had more than he could manage. Two of the three gentlemen were minor threats to a brute like Maloney, but the enraged big fellow was unlikely to stand down. He'd already struck Maloney with two solid punches, stunning and backing him up.

Morrissey stepped in and fired a right hook. It landed with a loud thud on the big man's temple. Susannah watched the man's eyes roll back as he spun around and crashed to the deck. The other would-be fighters retreated to the salon.

John nodded to the bosun and left to return to his duties. Susannah remained in the shadows. She had not moved during the altercation. When John saw her, he approached and asked, "Would ya be needin' help, miss?"

Susannah recognized Morrissey as he drew near. She and her friends often saw him strutting the streets of Troy at the head of his Irish gang. "No," she answered, "I'm fine. Thank you."

Two of the *Empire*'s officers raced toward them.

John smiled and tipped his cap, thinking, *she's a real beauty already; she is.*

When word of the deck-side disturbance reached Captain

Smith, he was furious, mainly because his daughter had been a nearby witness. He summoned Bosun Maloney, the primary witness who'd placed the big offender under restraint. Then, he spoke with his daughter to find out what she had seen and heard.

Unlike Maloney's description of the altercation, Susannah's included a young deckhand interceding and dispatching the aggressor with a single blow.

The captain asked, "Did you learn the deckhand's name?"

"Well, Father, I recognize him. He's a notorious Irish boy from Troy. His name is John Morrissey. He politely asked whether I needed help. I told him I did not. That's when Officers Spencer and Brooks arrived."

Captain Smith thought, *Morrissey, my instincts were right.*

Five

When the Empire docked in New York, Morrissey helped with passenger baggage and collected three dollars in tips. John carried the address Aleck Hamilton provided on a scrap of paper in an inside pocket of his jacket. It was the address for Isaiah Rynders' Empire Club on Park Row. He showed it to a nearby stevedore and asked for directions.

"Go east at the next block. That's Chambers," he pointed south, "You'll reach Broadway in a few blocks. Can't miss it. It's the busiest street in the country, they say. You'll see the City Hall and a big park across the street. Park Row's at the bottom of the park, past the big fountain."

John thanked him, folded the note, returned it to his pocket, and headed toward Chambers Street.

Never had John seen a place like New York City. As he approached Broadway, the sights and sounds of morning traffic and the swarm of rushing pedestrians, carriages, delivery wagons, and omnibuses were thrilling and disorienting. Turning right onto Broadway, he dodged legions of pedestrians, oblivious to him or fellow passerby as they rushed onward. The grand City Hall and its extensive park appeared across the street.

John wanted further directions to find the Empire Club. He spied a police officer at the next intersection and made his way. As he neared, he recognized the officer's look of contempt.

"Is it a handout you're looking for, young man?"

"Directions," John glared at the insolent police officer.

"And where would you be going, son?" The officer turned his attention to three elegant ladies approaching from the south, smiling at them with a mouth full of broken and missing teeth. The ladies covered their mouths, giggled, and moved on.

"Twenty-Eight Park Row."

The officer turned his attention back to John. "The Empire Club, is it?" He appraised the young man, then laughed. "Put some decent clothes on, and you'll fit in with that crowd if they don't tear your Irish heart out first."

"I've business there." John clenched his fists, as well as his teeth. He had lost patience with the contempt and delay.

"Across the street with you, then, along the park," he pointed, "That's Park Row. Empire Club's half a block. You won't miss it, with all the men loitering outside."

When Johnny entered the street, the officer shouted, "Tell Rynders Officer Lansing sends his greetings."

As John made his way along Park Row, a group of men stood on the stairway and sidewalk outside an elegant four-story building. As he approached, they whispered and laughed at his shabby appearance.

"This Empire Club?" John asked, nodding toward the building.

"It is." A mustachioed man in a bowler hat scowled. "If it's work you'll need, the kitchen's back in the alley." This insult brought a round of laughter from the group.

John stepped close to the joker. "I've got business with Isaiah Rynders. He in?"

"Well, I'm sure you won't mind if I ask what your business might be?" said an older, overweight man working his way down the stairs with the help of a cane.

"Aleck Hamilton of Troy sent me." John watched the man for signs he recognized the name.

The man paused, considering Morrissey.

"I'll be back. Wait here."

The man moved back up the stairs and disappeared through the door. The group returned to their conversations, ignoring John.

When the door opened, the old gentleman smiled and motioned with his cane for Morrissey to join him. They entered a barroom, all polished wood, gilded mirrors, brass cuspidors, and paintings of famous trotters. Conversations faded, then ceased as the patrons turned to stare at the ragged young stranger.

John stepped farther into the room, feet wide apart, chin high. He turned to the man who'd escorted him, asking, "Which one's Rynders?"

"He'll be down directly."

John wondered if the braggart who had promised to teach him manners was among the crowd. "Is Dutch Charlie here?" he asked.

Men turned to each other and whispered.

"This must be Hamilton's fighter from Troy," proclaimed a voice from the end of the bar, "Charlie was right. He is a farm boy!"

Laughter exploded.

The same voice added, "The man you look for is at the races. Lucky for you. Now scurry back to Troy, boy." He spat on the floor to emphasize his contempt.

John had had enough arrogance and condescension for one day. Prudence aside, he tossed his hat on the bar and demanded, "There any fighters in this house?"

The laughter and whispers stopped.

Louder still, John taunted the room. "I'll lick any man here."

Those could well have been the last words of the eighteen-year-old. All the men at the Empire Club were hard, seasoned by the constant violence in New York's lower wards. A few, like Mike

Murray and Big Tom Burns, were prominent gang leaders. Their faces darkened at the challenge. They, and four or five others, removed jackets and hats and started toward Morrissey.

From behind, a slungshot crashed into John's right ear setting off an explosion of light as blurred figures rushed him. Before he could recover, the men were upon him with fists, boots, brass knuckles, and any object they could grab. Morrissey somehow fought on, blood flowing from cuts on his head and face. He struggled to keep his footing, pressing his back against the bar. Falling to the floor would be the end of him.

Wooziness from the first blow to the ear eased a bit, and pain from the continued assault receded as adrenaline and rage washed over him. The attackers were growing weary from the sustained effort. John unleashed a powerful left, catching an attacker on his nose. Cartilage crushed, and a fountain of blood flooded the man's shirt and vest. Unfortunately, any satisfaction was short-lived.

Captain Isaiah Rynders had been on the second floor in his office when the commotion erupted. He rushed down to witness six very capable fighters trying to subdue a young man, holding them off in impressive fashion.

Rynders resolved to end the struggle before there was more damage to his club. He grabbed an earthen spittoon behind the bar and smashed it over the young fighter's head. John slid to the floor, and the enraged attackers moved in to finish their work. Rynders rushed to stand over the fallen stranger. He brandished a long fighting knife for all the attackers to see. They knew he would use it without hesitation. They backed off, grumbling oaths.

As John's attackers moved away, Rynders called for Jim Turner and Paudeen McLaughlin, who had not joined the assault, to carry the injured man to a third-floor bedroom. He then sent for a doctor to treat him.

"He's lucky to be alive," reported Doctor Barron, a man Rynders trusted not to report anything to the police, "and he'll live to fight another day."

After adventures out west, Isaiah Rynders had ventured to New York City carrying a resume and an arrogance that attracted fighters, gamblers, and politicians. More than anything, Rynders was an opportunist. He rapidly became the most prominent influence peddler in the city's lower wards.

Rynders visited Morrissey daily, checking the Irish lad's condition and evaluating him as a potential recruit. To his trained eye, the boy was a brave and resilient fighter. He needed more runners, especially Irishmen, to intercept arriving ships and deliver the precious cargo of voting-age Irish males to his patrons at Tammany Hall.

The doctor examined and rebandaged Morrissey's wounds for three days. His right ear rang, and his head and body ached. Worse were his ribs. The doctor shared that four on the left side had fractures, and there was nothing to do but wrap them and give them time to heal.

On the third day, John stood with difficulty. He studied his reflection in a mirror. His face was a swollen mess, but he knew it would heal. His chest and upper arms ranged from deep purple to a black as deep as his anger. He thought only of revenge. He would not forget and certainly never forgive.

On the morning of the fourth day, John called for Rynders. "I'll return to the *Empire* today," he announced, "I don't see my clothes. I'll be needin' them, sir."

"You shouldn't be leaving yet, young man." Rynders's concern was both genuine and selfish. He was eager to bring the Irish fighter under his control.

"The *Empire of Troy* employs me," John explained. "I'm missing several days, and my family depends on my wages."

Rynders grinned at the bruised, battered youth. "I told you there's work here. Better than deckhand work."

John shook his head. "My clothes?" He stood naked before the man who had saved him.

"We burned them. Those clothes were torn to shreds and

covered in blood and filth. My wife bought a new set for you. Someone'll bring them directly." Rynders turned to leave.

"I had a bit of money in the trousers. Was it found?"

Rynders turned to Morrissey. "Nobody mentioned money. See me before you leave. I'll advance you. Pay me later."

"I'll accept no charity, sir. What you've done is already too much; it is. When I collect my wages, I'll pay for the clothes, the doctor, and the loan. You'll see John Morrissey's word's his bond."

After Rynders left, a housekeeper knocked on John's door. John opened it, pulling a blanket around his nakedness.

"Your clothes, sir."

The girl reminded John of his sister Hannah.

She averted her eyes, handed him a bundle of clothes, and fled. John watched her walk away and thought, *I'd run too if I saw this face.*

Opening the bundle, he found new trousers, suspenders, a shirt, vest, stockings, shoes, and a hat. Each was of a quality better than anything John had owned before. The clothes fit well enough, and the reflection in the mirror, at least from the collar down, pleased him.

John left 28 Park Row at midday, reversing the direction taken three days earlier. The fractured ribs caused agony with every step. At City Hall Park, John paused on a bench near the fountain. His first days in New York had gone poorly. He had been rash. To go back now would signal weakness, and that wouldn't do. John eased himself upright and continued toward the waterfront to determine if he still had a job aboard the *Empire*.

The walk was a blur. Arriving at the bustling docks, John scanned south, then north. To his relief, the enormous *Empire of Troy* was at a pier only two hundred yards north. His spirits lifted.

Drawing near the steamer, Morrissey recognized deckhands scrubbing the promenade above. At the boarding ramp, he gripped the rail and ascended, step by painful step. Midway, he rested to catch his breath, checking the bandages wrapped around his broken ribs. A familiar figure, arms akimbo, stood at the head of the ramp, watching him approach.

"Well, what have we got here?" growled Bosun Maloney. "A swell has come to visit. Why would such a gentleman be sporting such a battered mug?"

John pushed back his new leather cap and looked up at the bosun. "It's me, Morrissey."

"It cannot be," Maloney jeered. "John Morrissey is a strapping, handsome Irish lad in rags. He left my ship days ago. I see before me a dandy claiming to be my deckhand. Am I to believe this?"

"I'm Morrissey. Got lost when I left the ship." John caught his breath and explained. "Six men beat me. Someone jumped in and saved me, gave me a bed, got a doctor, and these clothes."

"I know it's you, Morrissey. Captain asked me to watch for you. Sure, he thought you walked out or were floating in the river. Follow me. Let's see how Captain Smith reacts when he sees that ugly mug."

John followed Maloney, trying to keep pace. His vision blurred with his unsteady steps. Reaching out, he found nothing to grasp and fell, unconscious, to the deck.

When he finally surfaced from a troubling dream, John heard voices whispering. He opened his eyes to find the source, only to panic in the darkness. His hand flew to his head, and he felt a cool bandage covering his eyes. When he pulled it off, he was relieved to see light under a nearby door.

A male voice spoke, "He's taken a horrific beating, Captain, three or four days ago. The right ear and neck worry me most. Cuts and bruises will heal. So will the ribs. I've changed the bandages on his open cuts, placed a cold compress around his head, and administered laudanum to ease the pain and encourage rest. I also put new wrapping on his ribs. He should keep them bound for two or three weeks. They'll heal fine if he lets them."

"Thank you, Doctor Meade," John recognized Captain Smith's deep voice, "and forgive me for imposing upon you and Mrs.

Meade. I'll keep the lad in my quarters until we arrive at Troy. His family's there. We'll leave him with them. Can I offer you a drink?"

John tried to rise, but the pain, exhaustion, and medication prevailed. All went black again.

During the trip up the Hudson, John regained semiconsciousness from time to time, but each time the laudanum, the hum of the engines, the gentle rocking of the ship, and the darkness of the room lulled him to sleep.

"Wake up. Wake up, Morrissey." A hand shook his shoulder. "Wake up, young man. It's Captain Smith."

John opened his eyes. The captain had fired a lamp at a nearby bedstand. "There you are," he said, leaning closer. "We've nearly arrived at Troy. Two of our mates will escort you to your family home. Drink this water, please."

John pushed through the pain to sit and face the captain. He took the tall glass and downed it. Swallowing was difficult. "Thank you, sir," he said, "I came back to explain and to ask for my job."

"You'll be no worth to me in your condition, lad. Go home and recover. I'll not hold this against you. I've not forgotten you flew to aid my daughter. New York's a dangerous place. If you return to my service, be more cautious during shore leave. Here's the money we owe you for your day of service. See me when you're able to work."

Instead of proceeding to his family's apartment, John asked the deckhands to take him to the Eastern Hotel. Even with their support, the short walk was exhausting. As soon as Marcel Archambeault saw his young friend, he rushed to help. The giant lifted John with ease and tenderness. He carried him to an empty room on the fourth floor as Nathan Parker ran to inform Hamilton.

"Please let my father know I'm here," John whispered before passing out.

John knew there was neither room nor extra food at his family's apartment. He also could not face his mother's ridicule and anger. The Eastern had, in truth, become his home.

Under the watchful and compassionate care of Hamilton, Parker, Archambeault, Veronica, and her "girls," Morrissey soon recovered. By the end of March, the superficial damages had healed. The blinding headaches he'd suffered for weeks were fewer and less debilitating. Swallowing and speaking were still tricky, and his ribs remained tender, but he needed to resume work and ached for vengeance.

Six

Wearing the outfit Rynders's wife provided, Morrissey headed to the Empire, where he presented himself to Lieutenant Brooks. Captain Smith was busy reviewing the manifest for that evening's trip.

Brooks announced, "A Morrissey to see you, sir."

Captain Smith reviewed the manifest for minutes, not bothering to acknowledge Morrissey's presence. Then, without lifting his head, he said, "If it's your former job you're looking for, see the purser. He'll make the arrangements."

John couldn't suppress a smile. "Thank you, Captain Smith," he said as he headed to the nearby hatch and down to the purser's office.

When docked at Troy, John stayed at the Eastern. Hamilton supplied a quiet room on the far end of the fourth floor for twenty-five cents a night. When docked in New York City, he slept little while systematically pursuing his Empire Club assailants. Whether alone or in pairs, John made sure they recognized the "farm boy" from Troy. He left them all battered, some near death. By the middle of August, he had gotten revenge on everyone who'd laid into him. It was time to visit Captain Rynders. Not, however, at 28 Park Row.

John observed the Empire Club from a safe vantage point during the last weeks of August. On Wednesdays, Rynders always left his establishment before midday and proceeded up Broadway to an ornate four-story building at 170 Nassau Street. John remained there for more than an hour, watching dandies and poor laborers entering and leaving the building. He would intercept the captain as he left the following Wednesday.

On August 30, Rynders climbed the stairs at the Nassau Street building. John watched him enter, then found a seat with a view of the building at a pub several doors south. He looked around, noting that high-back booths ran along the opposite wall. Even at lunch hour, half were empty.

When the clock over the bar showed one o'clock, John paid his tab, took the newspaper he had bought earlier, and stood outside, pretending to read. Rynders came down the stairs, as he had the prior two weeks, and started toward him.

Lowering the newspaper, Morrissey spoke as Rynders passed. "I believe I owe you money, Captain."

Rynders slowed, cautiously turned, and eyed the man. Then he stopped.

"Morrissey? I heard you're around. Six of my best patrons are out of service because of you." Rynders glanced around, looking for help—or escape.

"Let's go inside and settle up." Morrissey placed his hand against the small of Rynders's back and encouraged him toward the pub.

Rynders considered his options as they entered, glad there would at least be witnesses. Morrissey led them to a quiet booth deep inside. Rynders slid across from the young man, who looked far better than the last time he had seen him.

John reached into his vest pocket, withdrawing a small stack of paper currency. He placed it on the table and slid it across, saying, "I believe this ought to cover the doctor and the clothes, plus interest."

Rynders didn't count the money, instead sliding it inside his vest pocket. "I'm glad to see you settled all your accounts, Morrissey. The men you beat deserved it. I bear you no ill will, though they and their gangs will. Young man, you'll need the right friends if you wish to survive in this city."

"I thought that was you." Morrissey smiled.

Rynders forced a laugh and signaled the bartender. "Two whiskeys, please." He offered his hand to Morrissey. "We can do business, young man. Meet me at my office at Park Row tomorrow morning. There's someone I'd like you to meet."

"Can't meet tomorrow. Steaming to Troy tonight and back on Thursday night. How's Friday?"

"Sure. Friday morning's fine, and there's no need to worry about getting assaulted this time. Friends of Captain Rynders enjoy certain protections, at least under my roof."

The men toasted each other's health, then parted.

When the *Empire* tied up in New York early Friday morning, John helped passengers collect their luggage, then returned to the crew's quarters to sleep. When he woke, he shaved and wore his same work outfit. Despite Rynders's words, he considered the Empire Club a dangerous destination. There was no point ruining his only decent outfit. John dropped a heavy slungshot in his pant pocket and tucked a holster with his fighting knife inside his frock coat.

This time there was no trouble at 28 Park Row. John recognized two of the dandies gathered outside among a group of a dozen or more. They ignored Morrissey as he ascended the stairs and struck the brass door knocker. The cane-bearing man who'd led him into the club on his prior visit opened the door and motioned for John to enter. No one followed as they went up the stairs to Rynders's office.

Rynders's enormous desk faced the wide-open double doors.

"Come in, lad. You don't look quite the swell I saw Wednesday. You're ready, I suppose, for another rude welcome?"

A man, seated across the desk from Rynders, studied Morrissey.

Rynders motioned Morrissey to join them. "Meet Shang Allen. I told him about you, and he was curious enough to join us. Come, sit."

Morrissey kept his eyes locked on the man seated next to him. He appeared slightly north of thirty. A wide scar divided his left eyebrow and extended into his hairline. Allen shifted toward Morrissey. "Rynders says you're a slugger. I usually trust his word. He hates England as much as I. Thinks I could use a fighter like you. Stout-and-true Irishmen rally to our flag. We fear no one and fight and die for our neighborhoods and pride. Would you be giving up your life for your Irish brothers-in-arms?"

Morrissey looked at Rynders before leaning toward Shang Allen, almost touching heads. "As a lad of twelve, I joined an Irish gang in Troy. By fifteen, I was the leader. I've fought and beat the toughest fighters upriver. Born, was I, at Tipperary, baptized Catholic. The English drove my family out. My blood burns with Irish pride. I'll rally to it if Rynders thinks you carry the right flag."

Allen continued to lock eyes with Morrissey as he stood and offered his hand. "They call us Dead Rabbits. We're Just a bunch of Irish gangs, fire brigades, and brave Irishmen that come together during troubles. Ask where to find me anytime at Belson's Livery. It's where I work."

Shang Allen turned to the captain, nodded, shook his hand, and left.

Rynders said, "I trust Allen and his Dead Rabbits when I call on them. You'll see that Captain Rynders is a good friend, lad. Let's enjoy lunch, but not at that filthy pub where you shanghaied me on Wednesday."

They headed down the stairs and toward Broadway and Barclay Street.

"Power equals opportunity, and opportunity equals money,"

Rynders bit each word off as he slid across the narrow table at an oyster bar. "You'll understand that in time. You're a smart young man. I can see that."

Rynders introduced Morrissey to "One-Eyed" Daly, another Tammany surrogate, who paired him with Orville "Awful" Gardner. The two, Daly thought, would make an excellent team. Gardner was a veteran prizefighter and vicious brawler. He'd gained wide fame in 1847, defeating Allan McFee in thirty-three rounds, then helped train Tom Hyer for his victory over Yankee Sullivan. What mattered to Rynders, however, was Gardner's success as an immigrant runner. He and the Morrissey lad would make an exceptional team on the docks.

From that day on, when the *Empire* docked in New York, Morrissey would meet Gardner, and together they would stalk the ships arriving from Ireland. John enjoyed the challenge and added money. He was also satisfied that the hungry and confused Irish he met were better off with Tammany Hall's help than otherwise.

John was eager and ready to meet with regular threats from competing runners. Besides his fists, he brandished his ten-inch fighting knife and, in time, a butcher's cleaver. Since ships were arriving in endless numbers, the thought of dying for human cargo was a flawed calculation, even for tough and proud fighters. Unless they enjoyed an advantage in numbers, competitors usually backed down from Morrissey and Gardner.

Seven

Steamboat navigation on the Hudson stopped when the river froze on November 20. Morrissey bid farewell to Bosun Maloney, his fellow deckhands, and the *Empire*'s staff. He'd decided to spend the winter in New York City. If Captain Smith would have him, he'd return when the river reopened the following year.

Staying in New York City was no easy decision, but the Hyer-Sullivan fight was months away, and John needed to be next in line to fight the winner. He could only hope to fulfill that dream if his name was constant and prominent among the promoters and sporting newspapers of the city.

Since his reception at 28 Park Row, Morrissey had made a quick impression on the sporting crowd. His revenge against his attackers, success as an immigrant runner, and his rise among the Dead Rabbits impressed Rynders and others. Nobody, however, believed he was ready to challenge either Hyer or Sullivan. No one, indeed, would put up the outrageous ten-thousand-dollar stake Hyer demanded. Therefore, the Sullivan-Hyer match was the only fight anyone talked about in the nation's sporting circles. It would generate the largest betting on any event up to that point in

America's history. It would also make a national celebrity of Tom Hyer.

Winter was brutal. The months-long lull in immigrant arrivals left John without dependable income. He was arrested for burglary and attempted murder before the new year arrived. Only the influence of Captain Rynders kept him from serving time. When drunk, John often needed little provocation to fight. When the calls came, he would joyfully join the Dead Rabbits on raids into enemy territory or in defense of theirs. He said of this initial time in New York City, "I was so tired I could barely lift food to eat when there was any."

John lodged at cheap hotels near the docks for a time, often sharing a bed in an icy room with strangers. One aging sailor coughed up blood for a week before expiring. John liberated the dead man's oilskin coat and four precious dollars discovered in his boot. With money nearly gone, hotels were no longer a possibility. John searched for shelter in the crowded tenements and cellars of Five Points. He combed the filthy streets for hours, desperate to escape the deadly cold.

John passed group after group of skeletal children with swollen bellies and haunted eyes, huddled wherever there was a respite from the wind, snow, and freezing rain. The bolder of these urchins would rush to him, a hand or cap extended, begging. He remembered the joy of stealing apples with his youthful friends in Troy and pitied the forsaken children. *If only I had even an apple to share.*

Boys hawked newspapers everywhere and raided grocery stores or street vendors for food scraps, precisely as he had a decade earlier in Troy. Girls in threadbare rags sold hot corn to passersby. They jealously watched as older neighborhood girls in fancy clothes and makeup disappeared down dark alleys. Furtive men, hats pulled low and collars high, exited carriages stalking cheap sexual gratification. *It could be my sisters,* he knew. The very thought haunted John.

With daylight and hope fading, John still had no place to stay.

Descending into one of the pubs on Centre Street, he ordered a whiskey, placed two bits on the bar, and asked the bartender if he knew where he could find shelter. The bartender looked Morrissey over as he poured the drink. "When you leave here, go right. Cross Street is a block from here. The big building on the corner is the Old Brewery. Now, it's just dozens and dozens of rooms for rent. You'll find something there if you can stomach it."

John swallowed the drink, thanked the bartender, and headed back out.

The surge of European refugees and a constant stream of escaped slaves made finding shelter almost impossible. A thousand or more would crowd the Old Brewery on the worst winter nights. There could be a dozen—or more—crammed into a single eight-foot-square room where age didn't matter, nor gender, nor race. Police estimated a murder happened every day at the Old Brewery. No one knew for sure. A nearby pauper cemetery and unmarked graves awaited the unidentified bodies discovered in the morning.

Almost out of cash, John paid two dollars for a room for the week. He handed the cash to a burly clerk, who glared at him behind a barred window. Then, with a key to room 308, the exhausted young man groped and stumbled up the pitch-dark stairs. His feet struck bodies as he ascended and were met with a grunt, a curse, or silence.

The last light of day fought through a single filthy window at the end of a long hallway. John strained to see hand-painted numbers on the doors. He started right, discovered the numbers were increasing, then turned back until he found 308. The door was ajar, hanging askew from a single hinge. He pushed it open, delighted to see a window, albeit one with a broken pane.

Scanning his room, John saw a soiled straw mattress, a candle holder with the nub of a candle, and a washbasin half full of urine and filth. He lit the candle, dragged the mattress into the hallway, and watched as scores of cockroaches scampered. The window could not be opened, so he dumped the filth in the washbasin out the broken pane. In his canvas bag were personal possessions and articles of clothing, including the outfit Mrs. Rynders had provided. The bag would serve as a pillow. He removed his outer garments, folded them into the bag, wrapped himself in the dead sailor's oilskin coat, and extinguished the candle. Morrissey eventually fell asleep to a chorus of human misery.

John was sure he could find work in a city with thousands of brothels and gambling houses. He had experience, yet he was turned away repeatedly. He could read well enough to understand the window signs everywhere: "Irish Need Not Apply." New York City, it was clear, was no better than Troy.

As December advanced, the weather grew worse. Finally, after another futile day of searching, John knew he had to resort to bullying and burglary. Anything was preferable to starving. He marked three businesses as vulnerable. Tomorrow, he would strike. Without money, his only choice was to crawl into a cellar along Centre Street, where the most hopeless of humanity cowered in the dampness and perpetual gloom among rats and vermin.

When John turned onto Broadway, a frigid blast stopped him dead. He looked for any public house to enter, hoping to steal a moment of precious warmth. Two men burst out of a doorway on John's left, leaning on each other and laughing as they headed up Broadway. Heat spilled out of the building. Before the door could close, John wedged his shoulder inside and entered.

Unlike the seedy place run by Aleck Hamilton, the house of prostitution that Morrissey stumbled into was quiet and refined. John stood in the foyer, rubbing his frozen hands together and gawking. Ahead, a broad stairway covered with rich, ornate carpeting led to a landing where bronze statues of two candle-holding nymphs flanked an enormous, gilded mirror. The parlor to the right offered a huge blazing fireplace. John drifted toward its warmth.

Kate Ridgely, the madam of the house, greeted all new clients. Her office and private suite stood to the left of the foyer. She had just recorded the payment and departure times of Mr. Wellington and Mr. Langdon. After securing her ledger and cash payments within her office safe, she heard the bell over the front door. She glanced into the foyer, where a solitary man was moving toward the fireplace. Ridgely left her office and crossed to meet the newcomer.

"Quite a wretched night."

John turned. "Not fit for man or beast," he answered, removing his ice-crusted cap.

The madam, who remembered every client, didn't recognize the young man. "I don't believe we've met. I'm Kate Ridgely, proprietor of this establishment. May I help you?" The man was Irish, no doubt, and impoverished. She looked around for Mr. Saunders. The madam expected him to be nearby for situations like this. But, instead, he was missing, and not for the first time.

John was acutely aware of his wretched appearance. "I thought this was a pub when I saw men leaving. Then, I saw the fire. I needed to warm myself." He bowed his head, replaced his cap, and started toward the door.

"No need to rush away." Ridgely felt no threat from the young man. "It's a horrid night. Warm yourself. I'd not wish to feel responsible if the police find your body in a snowbank in the morning."

"That's kind, Mrs. Ridgely." John turned to face her again. "Name's John Morrissey. I'll only stay a bit."

"*Miss* Ridgely," she corrected. "I'm a widow. You should call me Miss Ridgely." She followed John's gaze as a young Asian girl floated down the stairs. Ridgely turned to a gentleman seated across the parlor. "Mr. Hensley, I believe Jen is eager to visit with you."

Hensley rose, nodded, and hastened to the staircase to wrap an arm around the diminutive girl. They whispered and laughed as they moved up the stairs. John watched. *Not like the Eastern at all!*

A disheveled man staggered into the room. Ridgely turned and addressed the new arrival. "I've warned you, Saunders. You had one last chance. You used it. I don't care who your brother is. Take your things and leave this place. Tomorrow, after you've sobered, we'll settle."

Saunders looked from Ridgely to Morrissey and back again, muttering, "Cheap whore," as he wobbled away.

Morrissey catapulted toward the man.

"Stop right there!" barked Ridgely. "There is no violence in this house. Never!"

He stopped and turned back to the madam. "I'm sorry, Miss Ridgely. No man ought to address a lady like that."

"He'll be no more trouble, Mr. Morrissey. I hired him as a favor to his brother, a very influential man. This Saunders is a worthless drunk, and his brother knows it. It will be no trouble replacing him. I have someone here for those rare times when a lady might need help. We have a distinguished clientele, and I have friends in influential places."

John looked again at the fine furniture, art, and appointments. He listened to the house's silence and considered what he had just heard. "You don't know me, Miss Ridgely, but would you figure me for the job? I kept the peace for two years at the Eastern, upriver at Troy. Aleck Hamilton owns the place. He can speak for me. Here in the city, Isaiah Rynders knows me. I need work, and you'll find no better man than me."

"Well, you are quite the opportunist, aren't you, Mr. Morrissey? While I don't know you, I am acquainted with Mr. Rynders. Perhaps." Ridgely studied him. He was tall, broad-shouldered, and carried himself with confidence. If Rynders approved, she would give the young man a chance. She would just have to keep her girls away from him, worrying that they might kill each other over someone so handsome. "Come around tomorrow afternoon. We can discuss it further." She retreated through the foyer into her office, closing and locking the door.

John pulled his hat as far down as possible, buttoned his overcoat, and left into the blowing snow.

Kate Ridgely called her brothel Pétale de Rose. While working as a prostitute for a wealthy madam in New Orleans, nineteen-year-old Kate Meadows married a client twice her age. George Ridgely brought his stunning new bride home to New Jersey, where he took ill and died. She was without a husband, money, or connections.

What Kate had was experience, striking looks, and huge ambition. She made her way to New York City and a brothel with a clientele that included many of the city's most prominent men. Kate quickly developed a loyal customer base, saved her money, and opened Pétale de Rose near City Hall.

Within two years, Pétale de Rose was a thriving business. With sex for sale everywhere, from alleyways to opulent brothels, Kate needed something unique to attract and keep a wealthy clientele. She did this by providing uncompromising quality and discretion. The young women Kate selected represented ideals of beauty from various races and cultures. She offered these carefully chosen young women a safe and luxurious home, protection from abuse, tutoring, discrete medical care, financial counseling, and a dignified and generous clientele. The high price for Pétale de Rose prostitutes helped ensure that clients were people of means. In addition, Ridgely offered a covert entry via an adjoining haberdasher for those who preferred to keep their assignments private, and she preserved their identity under pseudonyms. Clients included judges, ministers, newspaper publishers, leading political figures, and women of social standing.

The morning after John's impromptu arrival, Kate sent a message to Rynders: *John Morrissey, a young Irishman, said you might supply a positive recommendation. I let Saunders go. Would you approve of Morrissey? KR.*

The same messenger returned with Rynders's reply. It read, *Yes. Handles himself well. I have my eye on him. IR.*

John arrived at Pétale de Rose the next day at two o'clock wearing his one good outfit. A young woman with lustrous red hair piled atop her head arose from a velvet-covered chair to greet him. She smiled at the tall, handsome boy through a tiny gap between her front teeth.

"Good day, sir. I'm Eloise. May I help you?"

John smiled back, struck anew by the contrast with the Eastern Hotel. This young lady wore a pink, low-necked satin waistcoat over a matching petticoat. Freckles dotted her pale cheeks and traced down her neckline and over the top of her small breasts. Her midsection was bare. John could not take his eyes away.

"I'm here to see Miss Ridgely."

"Is the madam expecting you, sir?"

"Yes. Morrissey. John. She's expecting me at two."

"I'll announce you, sir." Eloise looked up into his mahogany eyes and smiled.

"Ask for me, Mr. Morrissey. Anytime. Remember. Eloise, or just L."

Eloise sashayed to the door of her madam's suite, knocked, and waited. Finally, Ridgely called for her to enter. After minutes passed, the door opened, and Ridgely strode out. Her ensemble was sapphire blue, except for a pure-white ruffled collar that ran from neck to waist. Both her patterned velvet jacket and skirt emphasized her long, shapely body. Ridgely approached with a broad smile.

"Good of you to return, Mr. Morrissey. Forgive my appearance, I must leave soon, but this won't take long. Please follow me."

Ridgely led John back to her suite. She did not invite him to sit as she searched her desk for something. Finding it, she skimmed it, then looked Morrissey up and down. "You look like a gentleman today, Mr. Morrissey. I'm relieved."

"Thank you, Miss Ridgely."

"Rynders supplied a recommendation. I hope he's right. You've seen, I don't tolerate incompetence. If you accept the terms, the position is for six days weekly. You'll have Mondays off. There is a comfortable room for you on the fourth floor. You'll be available from seven each evening until the last client leaves. The compensation is fifteen per week. The room is included and is serviced by my housekeeping staff. Feel free to enjoy breakfast with the help."

John couldn't believe what he was hearing. When she finished, he said, "I'll take the job, Miss Ridgely. You won't be sorry."

"Good," she said. She slid a two-page contract across the desk. "Sign this, and you can start tonight. Here is your first week's pay. Eloise knows which room is yours. She'll show you. Now, I must leave. My coach is waiting."

John reached for the agreement and the pen lying next to it. He bent to add his mark to the document. From the door, he heard Ridgeley. "Mr. Morrissey, the women here are valuable employees. They are not here for your pleasure. I'll immediately dismiss you and the foolish woman if I discover you with them."

Eloise had already received a similar warning from her madam. She avoided looking at Morrissey. "Follow me," she said and started up the broad stairway. Despite Ridgely's warning, John could not take his eyes off the young prostitute as she ascended the stairs. She stepped aside when they reached the fourth and top floor to let him pass.

"This is where the servants live. Your room is the last on the right. If you need anything, please ask in the kitchen for Mrs. Dolan." Eloise turned and started down the stairs.

John's face flushed with the word *servant*. He walked to the end of the carpeted hallway, where the last door on his right stood open. The room was awash with sunlight from a single multipaned window. A large poster bed was in the middle of the sizeable room. Beside the bed sat a nightstand with an oil lamp. An ornate chest of drawers stood across from the bed, topped by a large mirror. A small desk and cushioned chair sat in the far corner. *Can't be my room. It's fit for a lord, not a piddly servant."*

John felt elated as he walked out of Pétale de Rose. He had entered less than an hour earlier with the dim hope of securing any work. Instead, he was leaving with fifteen dollars in hand, a job that began that day, and a place to live of a quality he could never have imagined.

Kate Ridgely's decision to hire John Morrissey benefited all. As the madam had promised, trouble at the Pétale de Rose was rare; however, there would be conflicts when men, women, sex, and alcohol came together. John proved quick to respond and respectful and efficient in restoring order. Ridgely noticed this and the young man's dependability, pleasing demeanor, and improved appearance. She ignored his cuts, bruises, and damaged hands. What the young man did during his own time was not her business. Besides, she liked fighters.

Tom McCann had been Ridgely's lover since the last winter. McCann's father owned buildings in Five Points. He converted these to accommodate as many individuals and families as possible. Tom collected rents from the poor, evicted those who couldn't pay, and filled the space with anyone who could make a deposit.

McCann often ran immigrants for waterfront businesses that wanted the first crack at any money in immigrant pockets or young women desperate enough to sell their bodies in one of the thousands of brothels spread throughout the city. Morrissey and Gartner had frightened off McCann and his associates on occasion.

John watched the swaggering dandies as they arrived and left Pétale de Rose. He remembered Rynders's words: *Power equals opportunity, and opportunity equals money*. If Kate Ridgely, destitute upon arrival, could secure a place of wealth and influence in this city, *why not John Morrissey?*

It wasn't long before Kate Ridgely jettisoned Tom McCann and invited the handsome young brawler into bed. The relationship was entirely on her terms. It had to be. When beckoned, John went to her, stayed if she wished, and treated her with deference. Unlike his prior experience with prostitutes at the Eastern Hotel, the time spent with Kate Ridgely focused on her needs, not his. John learned important lessons about women and power from the indomitable Kate Ridgely.

Tom McCann had retreated from Pétale de Rose with bitterness and a vengeful heart, resenting his replacement by the young man from Troy and bragging he would have vengeance. Word of McCann's blustering reached Morrissey. He told Ridgely he intended to track her former lover and *shut his gob for good.* A public altercation between her lovers would serve neither her reputation nor business. Kate forbade her employee and current lover from pursuing that course of action.

The respect and gratitude Morrissey had for Kate Ridgely were significant. Despite that, his resolve to silence McCann prevailed. A favorite hangout of McCann's was the nearby St. James Hotel at Broadway and Leonard. John was himself a regular patron. Downstairs, Sandy Lawrence ran a shooting gallery and bar.

Morrissey visited Lawrence's establishment, hoping to find McCann. When a bartender informed him that he expected McCann that afternoon, Morrissey waited, shooting at wooden ducks with a rented pistol and nursing a brandy.

When jilted lover arrived and met his friends at the bar, one pointed a scruffy chin toward the shooting gallery and said, "Morrissey." McCann uttered an oath and ordered a drink. He bantered with those near him, ignoring Morrissey.

As soon as John spotted McCann, he returned the rented gun and headed for the bar, shouting for all nearby to hear, "Men, if somebody stole your business any time they wished and then took your girl, what would you do?"

Silence fell over the room. The pistols on the range stopped barking as the crowd expected violence.

"I did those things to Tom McCann." Morrissey continued to shout, "Now, he's been tellin' everybody what he's gonna do to me." Morrissey stripped off his coat and placed it on the bar. "Well," he said, "here I am. What do ya think he'll do?"

McCann had no choice. He removed his coat, handed it to a friend, and advanced toward the young man. Everyone stepped back to give the combatants room. People from the shooting gallery gathered to watch the action as the two circled, looking for an opening. There would be no rules in a rough-and-tumble fight like this.

Morrissey found an opening and sent a straight right into McCann's mouth, drawing blood. He rushed in, wrapping his powerful arms around McCann, trying to throw him to the floor. McCann kept his footing while trying to butt Morrissey and sink his teeth into the brash fighter. The two shoved and slid across the slick floor. Morrissey backed into a potbelly stove that crashed over, spilling its glowing coals onto the floor. McCann planted a foot behind the distracted Morrissey and sent him sprawling. McCann threw himself onto his downed opponent, using every ounce of strength to press Morrissey onto the burning coals.

The young fighter writhed in agony as he struggled to free himself, yet he uttered no sound. His shirt smoldered. The sickening smell of burning flesh drove observers to turn away. Everyone waited for a sign of surrender.

Realizing his business was about to go up in flames, Sandy Lawrence rushed in and emptied a bucket of water over the men and the red-hot coals. The cloud of acrid smoke blinded McCann. When his hands shot up to protect his eyes, Morrissey, enraged and in agony, struggled out from under his adversary. He wasted no time, launching furious blows at the older man's head. Soon McCann was a bloodied, defenseless mess. Even then, Morrissey, blinded by rage, continued his assault, hammering the man's face. It required four stout patrons to pull him away.

On unsteady legs, Morrissey struggled to the bar. He peeled off his burned, ragged shirt, retrieved his topcoat, and wobbled out of the St. James Hotel. From that moment until his death, John Morrissey would carry the moniker "Old Smoke." He wore it like a badge of honor. Those who saw the fight spoke of nothing else for weeks.

Local newspapers shared details of the brawl, and the story gained broad circulation. The event burnished Morrissey's growing notoriety. He had beaten all his attackers from the Empire Club and competitors on the docks. Now he had risen from what one paper called "the torments of hell" to destroy Tom McCann.

At Pétale de Rose, John went to his room, where he removed his topcoat, threw it on the floor, and stepped out of his filthy clothing. The mirror revealed the damage to his back and shoulders. He would need to see a doctor, but now he had to clean up and arrive in time for the night shift. He did his best to remove the filth, sweat, blood, and stink with soap and a sponge. He dressed in fresh clothes, hoping Miss Ridgely would not request his company after the evening's last client checked out.

Kate Ridgely, of course, heard of the struggle between McCann and Morrissey within hours. She knew about the coals, the burning flesh, and the outcome. Yet, she said nothing when she saw the young man appear for work. At two-forty in the morning, Desmond Epperly settled his account and was the last to leave. As John locked the front door and turned to retreat, the familiar voice of Miss Ridgely stopped him. "Would you join me, Mr. Morrissey?"

John entered the outer office. Ridgely was not at her desk. "In here, please?" she called from her private suite. He followed, thinking hard about how to explain his condition. John saw an older gentleman seated in the tall chair where Ridgely often sat to read. John stood in the doorway and looked at the gentleman, then the madam. "This is Doctor Wilton, Mr. Morrissey." Ridgely stared into John's eyes. He saw the fury behind the calm demeanor and felt the bite in the *mister*. "He'll have a look at that back. Please remove your coat and shirt and stand by the doctor."

Ridgely's eyes never left her young lover as he walked to the doctor and undressed. The doctor lifted a lamp close to the injured back and examined the burns. Again, John felt the cold appraisal of the woman who had been so compassionate with a filthy stranger when he had first arrived at Pétale de Rose.

"I can dress this, Miss Ridgely," said Doctor Wilton, "but the dressing needs to be changed twice a day until the risk of infection passes."

Ridgley asked, "How long would you estimate that will require, doctor?"

"Seven to ten, unless the wounds become infected."

Ridgley glared at her young lover. "Mr. Morrissey, please take your clothes and go to your room. You can remain there until you're well enough to depart. I'll have someone dress your back according to the doctor's instructions. Your work at Pétale de Rose is no longer needed. Good luck to you, young man."

That would be the last time John would see Kate Ridgely at Pétale de Rose.

Eight

Once again, John Morrissey was without work and a place to lay his head. He'd saved little during his time at Pétale de Rose. He could return to Troy, but the pull on his pugilistic ambition demanded he remain near the heart of America's prizefighting fervor.

Shang Allen was eager to keep the feared young Irish fighter close by. When he learned that Ridgely had dismissed John, he sent a lieutenant to invite him to a meeting at the Grey Owl. A bartender directed John to a booth near the rear. Allen sat with a small, bespectacled, middle-aged man. Allen slid across the bench and indicated that John should sit beside him.

Shang pointed at the man seated across the table. "I want you to be meeting Thomas Petrie."

Petrie looked up from the menu and over his glasses, nodded at Morrissey, then returned his attention to the day's oyster offerings.

John turned to Allen, who broke the awkward silence. "Mr. Petrie owns the Gem Saloon. I told him we had a friend who might be a useful employee. He's curious enough to meet."

John knew the Gem, a popular gambling establishment. Looking across the table, he said, "I'm needin' work, sir. I've been the muscle for a saloon and bawdy house at Troy and here at Pétale de Rose. Served as a fighting deckhand on the *Empire of Troy*. If I haven't done it, I'm not afraid to learn."

Still no response from Petrie.

A server arrived. Petrie turned to him, handed him his menu, and ordered six oysters and an ale. Allen glanced over the menu and ordered a similar lunch. Embarrassed by his inability to read, John said he would have the same as Petrie.

Petrie studied the young man. "Ever dealt faro?"

"No, sir. Often across the table, but never dealing."

Petrie rested his elbows on the table.

"You said you're not afraid to learn, Morrissey. If that's true, I'll give you a chance. We run square games at the Gem. Your other talents might prove of value from time to time."

The oysters and drafts arrived. Petrie ignored the men and dove into his lunch. He slurped the oysters, washed them down with the ale, counted and left bills on the table, and stood to leave. With his back turned, he said, "Come by the Gem tomorrow morning. On Church, behind City Hospital. We'll discuss our arrangement. If we agree, you can start work."

John and Allen watched Petrie leave.

Shang asked, "Where ya' sleeping, John?"

"Over on Centre. I'll move when I've income; I will."

Shang knew, of course, that John was back at the Brewery. "If you don't mind the noise of four untamed children, you can stay on our couch until your pay starts."

John shook his head. "I'd be a burden, no doubt."

Allen laughed. "If you are, Mary Louise will put you right; she will. I'll need to call you by your given name when you join us, John. Come, at least, for dinner and meet my wife. Her cooking will convince you."

John accepted. As Shang introduced his guest as "a young man from upriver," Mary Louise looked into John's eyes and smiled. She appeared too young to be a mother of four. She was indeed an Irish beauty with thick red hair, cheeks ablaze with a galaxy of freckles, and a smile that crinkled the corners of her eyes.

"I must apologize for the wee ones and the mess," she said. "My husband, bless his kind heart, gave me no warning." She shot a playful scowl at Shang.

Four children delivered the constant noise Shang had promised. The oldest, Ann Marie, a lass of eight, a perfect likeness to her mother, was the Irish brood's self-ordained ruler. Six-year-old twins Robert and Francis raced after each other under, over, and around obstacles in the tiny apartment. The youngest, David, a lad of two, tried to follow his older brothers, dropping to the floor with cries of frustration. All the while, Shang stood near the center of the small kitchen, grinning and shaking his head. "It is chaos, indeed. It's always so, John."

The offered couch sat in the family gathering room, which would be no problem for John. It was how he had spent his youth. It was no Pétale de Rose, but somehow better. The sound of childhood joy, the kitchen's smells, and the atmosphere of profound and sincere affection eased John's loneliness. With a delicious meal in his stomach and sounds of laughter fading, John stared into the darkness and soon fell into a deep and dreamless sleep.

Shang's children embraced the latest guest on their living room couch. After the twins carried their empty plates to the washbasin after dinner each evening, they would rush to climb all over their man-child guest, their toddler brother running to join the scrum while Ann Marie stood, arms folded and scowled.

It was quiet at the Gem Saloon when John arrived. A doorman, short but thick through the shoulders and chest, scrutinized him before pulling the door open to allow entry. John thought him an old buffer, noting the ruined nose and ears.

It didn't take long for John to spot Tom Petrie. He was close to a tall, slim, red-haired man standing between two roulette wheels.

Petrie spun one wheel, stopped it, then started it again, gesturing toward the wheel as he spoke with the man. When he spotted Morrissey, Petrie signaled for him to wait.

After completing his business at roulette, he walked over to greet his new employee.

"Good to see you came prepared to work!" Petrie exclaimed as he appraised the young man and nodded. "I'm short on workers today. Sick, they say. This entire city is sick. It's bad for business, this cholera, Merganser."

"Morrissey," John said. "It's John Morrissey, sir."

"Yes, right you are, Morrissey. We'll make a faro dealer of you today. Follow me."

John almost needed to run to keep up with the owner. Petrie spoke fast, ate fast, and worked even faster. With his back to John, he continued to talk. "Days. That's when I need you here. I'll teach you the basics, and you'll work on the street. We make a little money there when they lose, but when they win, they're likely to take their luck inside where the odds favor us."

Petrie looked around to ensure no one else was in earshot.

"Pays two dollars per day, to start. Keep whatever tips come your way. We don't open on Sundays; my wife won't allow it. You're done if I catch you stealing or cheating our customers, even once. Let's get on with the art of faro dealing, Mortensen."

John didn't take long to repay Petrie's kindness and trust. On the third Saturday of his employment, three unsteady sailors stopped by on their saloon crawl. They placed random faro bets, losing more than winning and growing frustrated. Finally, with three cards remaining in the shoe, John called the turn, and the older of the three watched as the cards appeared just as he had bet. Winning returned five-to-one. The three shouted, slapped the winner on his back, and went ahead into the Gem. John watched them stagger away. He had seen trouble enough at the Eastern Hotel to recognize it in the making.

After the doorman let the sailors pass, he nodded to John. That was his prearranged signal to fold up the faro table and come prepared to help. John rushed to take down his game and bring it in for safekeeping. The doorman, a German immigrant, named Milo Koch, had positioned himself inside the door to guard the entrance and watch over the sailors. John approached Koch, who grabbed his forearm and said, "Wait. Dad's managing them."

"Dad" was Daniel Cunningham, the redhead running the roulette wheel where the sailors settled. As he watched, John evaluated the three men. If necessary, taking out the best fighter was the smart choice. In this case, he was sure it was the older of the three. The fight would go out of the other two when he went down.

John watched as the spinning wheel slowed and the ball found its number. The older sailor cursed, grabbed the table, and looked to overturn it. Cunningham held firm on the opposite side. Morrissey rushed across the room, with Koch trying to keep up. "Stop!" Morrissey shouted as he drew near. The aggressive sailor dropped the table, and all three turned to see the approaching faro dealer. They squared for a fight.

"He cheated me!" screamed the older sailor. "Move a step closer, and you'll—"

Before he could finish the threat, Morrissey flew into him, wrapping him in his arms. As they tumbled over, the sailor's head cracked against the table. He was unconscious before he hit the floor. When Morrissey looked up, Koch and Cunningham had the other sailors in hand and led them toward the exit. Petrie had appeared, it seemed, from nowhere.

"Do you need help moving him outside, Morganson?" Petrie busied himself, retrieving the money spilled from the table.

"Morrissey, sir. No, I've got this," he answered as he lifted the inert sailor onto his shoulder and carried him toward the exit, where the shipmates relieved him of his burden. Morrissey stepped inside, retrieved his faro table, and returned to work.

When the steeple bells of Trinity Church sounded five, John once again folded his table and returned the materials and daytime proceeds to the owner.

"Nice work today, young man," Petrie said as he accepted the folded table, materials, and money from his new dealer, eyes smiling over his spectacles. "Until the morning, then. Be safe out there." With that, Petrie rushed off.

Morrissey sensed someone rushing from behind and tensed. He turned to see Cunningham. "Wanna have a drink? I'm Dad Cunningham; Dad's what everyone calls me. Daniel's my real name." He offered his hand to John.

"Sure. I'm Morrissey. John. Got nowhere to be."

Drinks at the Double Eagle turned into dinner and more drinks as the young men took each other's measure and liked what they saw. Both came from poor Irish-immigrant families and had to fight to survive growing up in upstate towns along the river. It turned out that Cunningham was from Cohoes, a thriving mill town on the west bank of the Hudson, a short distance north of Troy. Cunningham was two years older than Morrissey. He burst into tearful laughter when he realized it was "the famous John Morrissey."

John wondered what Dad found so humorous until he explained, "Why, I imagined John Morrissey to be six-and-a-half feet with knuckles that scraped the floor. It was you who beat Malachi Brennan, right?"

"Sure, it was, Dad. Brennan's a bully. As soon as his ruby was flowing, his courage was done. That's how it goes with bullies. I fought at Cohoes twice. Local guys. One, named Ziggy, hurt me good."

Cunningham described how he'd left Cohoes after beating his father with a bit of lumber. When drunk, which was often, his father worked over his mother. Dad had had enough and surprised his father with the beating, for which his father promised to kill him. It was time to move on, anyway, since Dad's Catholic girlfriend was pregnant, and her father and brothers were intent on vengeance. The Hudson was a short walk from his family's home on Adams Avenue. Escape was as easy as a float downriver. A friend rowed him south to the docks at Albany, where he stowed away on a steamboat and stepped foot into New York City two years ago.

The young men compared stories about how they had survived so far. Gangs beat and robbed Cunningham multiple times after he arrived. Soon out of money, with no job and no place to stay, he sought refuge at Saint Patrick's Cathedral. The archbishop, John Hughes, offered him temporary work helping with church-property maintenance. It paid one dollar per day. It also included a cot in the church's basement and evening meals at the rectory.

Like Morrissey, Cunningham arrived at the Gem Saloon with a stout recommendation. Rather than from a gang leader, it came from a church patron. Though Petrie's true religion was his work, his wife, Eleanor, was a devout Catholic and fervent volunteer. When Bishop Hughes asked, she always tried to accommodate. So, when asked if her husband might consider an industrious Irish lad for employment, she presented that request to Tom. As usual, he agreed. Dad was now a trusted and dedicated employee. John Morrissey and Daniel "Dad" Cunningham found refuge at the Gem. They also forged a lasting and eventful friendship.

Tom Petrie liked what he saw in young Morrissey. Though he was a wild young man, he was dependable and enthusiastic. The gambling business intrigued him, and his appetite for learning seemed limitless. And, unlike former young men Petrie hired, John didn't steal.

Nine

It was time for Shang Allen to escalate the recruitment of John Morrissey. Though the young scrapper had visited Allen at Belson's stables, Shang had yet to introduce John to his Dead Rabbit lieutenants. They were a paranoid bunch and slow to accept strangers, much less one so clearly a threat to their perceived rank in the organization. Allen, however, could wait no longer. The best fighters had left for the California goldfields, and Captain Rynders, who hated all things British, was cooking up a plan that would require all the muscle he could assemble.

A great rivalry had peaked between America's greatest Shakespearean actor, Edwin Forrest, and famous British actor, William Charles Macready. Audiences on both sides of the Atlantic had become more brazen with expressions of support and opposition.

On May 7, Macready was scheduled to perform *Hamlet* at Astor Place Theatre. It was to be his last performance in America before returning to England. Captain Rynders decided to send him home with a night to remember. He asked Shang Allen to deliver a group of Dead Rabbits to dozens of seats he had bought in the theater's top rows. They were to come, he insisted, prepared to disrupt.

As soon as Macready took the stage, rotten eggs, potatoes,

apples, lemons, shoes, and ripped-up seats rained. Morrissey sat beside Allen and joined the assault. Nevertheless, Macready and his troop bravely persevered through the ceaseless abuse. Rowdies won the night, but the battle wasn't over.

The next day, Macready received a petition signed by forty-seven of New York's most prominent citizens. The petition signers included Herman Melville and Washington Irving. It promised that *the good sense and respect for order prevailing in this community will sustain you on the subsequent nights of your performance.* As a result, Macready agreed to stay for one more performance on May 10.

The police chief, George Washington Matsell, knew his community better than the petitioners. Conditions in the lower wards were ripe for an explosion. He was confident that this provocation was the spark that would light it. Overcrowded housing, lack of clean water and sanitation, unemployment, starvation wages, and rabid discrimination drove resentment and anger. An outbreak of cholera in March added to the misery, taking hundreds of lives, primarily Irish, each day.

With fewer than one hundred officers at his disposal, Matsell knew controlling a major conflict would be impossible. So, he took his concerns to Mayor Caleb Smith Woodhull. The newly elected Whig mayor gained office on a promise to maintain law and order. At Matsell's prodding, the mayor called out the state's Seventh Regiment. They mustered three hundred and fifty soldiers, including cavalry and artillery.

Glad to have another shot at Macready, Rynders printed and distributed handbills and posters throughout nearby saloons and grocers. He invited working men and "patriots" to come out to show their feelings about the British. The handbills asked, "Shall Americans rule this city or the British?" British hatred was one thing that would unite both Irish and nativists.

When the play started, an estimated ten thousand people gathered in the nearby streets. Those there to watch events unfold didn't need to wait. Men had arrived armed with stones and bricks.

They started hurling them at the theater, sometimes at each other, as gangs spied nearby enemies.

Matsell had been correct. Outside the theater, his officers were overwhelmed and chased down neighboring streets. The militia responded and marched out of nearby Washington Park. They soon found themselves surrounded and pelted with objects from high and low.

Morrissey stood across the street from the theater with more than a dozen Dead Rabbits. These animated young men hurled barrages of objects at the theater. Shang led a similar group up Broadway and was busy harassing troops arriving to support the outnumbered police.

Hearing a volley of shooting from up Broadway, Morrissey started sprinting. Within a minute, another volley exploded, followed by terrifying screams. Panicked men and women rushed south and into side streets. He pressed ahead through the panicked crowd, looking for Allen.

Less than a block ahead, Morrissey spotted a line of soldiers surrounded by a mob. Most were dispersing, but a handful tried to rush the troops. Another volley crashed into the crowd, not feet away. Morrissey saw men and women drop. Rocks pelted the militia from the roof of a six-story building. *Allen!* Morrissey thought and looked for a way up. Soldiers were positioning a canon to target the rooftop assailants. He found a doorway and rushed up the stairs.

John was determined to get Shang home to his wife and children. Bursting onto the roof, he saw the Dead Rabbits' leader pressed against the front facade, tossing brick after brick. Morrissey crouched and rushed forward. As he drew near, he saw blood pooling around Allen's right leg.

"Let's be going," Morrissey shouted above the noise.

Allen glanced at him, blinded by rage. He continued to hurl one brick after another. An explosion disintegrated the facade to their right. Men lay bleeding, perhaps dead. Morrissey would not wait for the cannon to fire again. He grabbed his protesting friend and hoisted him across his shoulders. They rushed down the stairs with Shang screaming at him. At street level, Morrissey found a rear exit. He shouldered through a service door into a darkened alley. There was frantic movement all around, but no soldiers or police that Morrissey could see.

Through luck and resolve, Morrissey delivered a now-unconscious husband to Mary Louise Allen. There was no panic as she directed Morrissey to the bedroom and helped lower her husband to the bed. She dispatched her daughter, Anne Marie, to bring Doctor McMahon. Mary Louise tightened a section of the bedsheet around her husband's damaged leg, slowing blood loss. She bent and kissed Shane's forehead and whispered, "You can't be leaving me now, my love."

Anne Marie came running, breathless, into the bedroom. "Doctor," she shouted, "is coming up the stairs!" She looked with fear at her mother, who forced a smile.

"You did well, my child. The doctor will fix up your father. Now go, watch over the wee ones."

Anne Marie left, taking one last look at her unconscious father. The doctor advanced to the bed, listened to Shang's breathing, felt his pulse, then lifted his eyelids to check the pupils. He untied the bandaged leg and rolled Shang over to check for an exit wound, which he found. "We'll need water, lots of clean water and cloth." He looked at Mary Louise. "He'll be fine."

The doctor opened a large leather bag and retrieved two bottles. He measured a capful of thick liquid, lifted Shang's head, pressed his nostrils, and poured the content into his mouth. Then, satisfied that Shang had swallowed, he opened a second bottle, soaked a cotton square with disinfectant, and applied it to the entry and exit wounds.

Mary Louise returned with a large water pitcher and long strips of cloth. The doctor cleaned the damaged leg, retrieved a small leather case with a needle and catgut, and stitched the entry and exit wounds. He covered Shang with a blanket after reapplying more topical medicine and wrapping the leg with the cloth. As he closed his medical bag and pulled on his tall hat, he offered Mary Louise a reassuring smile and said, "Watch for signs of infection. Send for me if he becomes feverish."

John waited in the parlor while the doctor treated Shang. As Anne Marie coaxed her twin brothers back to bed and comforted them, he listened with admiration. The baby had remained asleep during the excitement. Finally, Mary Louise entered the parlor to report that Shang was likely to recover. She walked to John, threw her arms around his neck, and sobbed. "I can never thank you enough, John, for bringing him home to us."

Morrissey was back at the Gem on May 11. The saloon was untouched by the riot. Neighboring businesses had broken windows, and fires still smoldered. Everyone had stories about the great riot. Dozens or more were killed and wounded, including innocent bystanders, rioters, police, and militia members. Morrissey kept mum about his role as he set up and staffed his faro table and watched as a city tried to return to normal.

Mayor Woodhull had served on New York City's Common Council and as president of the Board of Alderman. The outrage over the Astor Place riot called for firm action. A comprehensive investigation followed, with arrests and punishment for those responsible for the violence and destruction. Although the rioters included British-hating nativists, authorities focused on Irish leaders and participants. John Morrissey's name appeared on one of the hundreds of arrest warrants. Neither the name of Isaiah Rynders nor Shang Allen appeared, despite their prominent roles. Both enjoyed influence, while Morrissey had none.

John could not risk arrest and jail time. It was time to leave New York City. If Captain Smith hired him, he would spend the rest of the season on the *Empire of Troy*. If not, he would petition other steamboat captains.

John accepted Shang's invitation to join his family for a goodbye dinner and a night on the couch. Mary Louise greeted him at the door, with the twins peeking from behind. She showed John where to leave his bag and escorted him to the table.

Father Finnegan was there, seated next to Shang. He pumped John's hand and indicated a chair to his right. Mary Louise called the children to gather. She placed a large pot of stew in the center of the table and a loaf of baked bread at either end. Shang asked the young priest to offer a blessing.

"In the name of the Father, the Son, and the Holy Ghost. Bless us, O'Lord, and these Thy gifts, which we are about to receive, from Thy bounty, through Christ, our Lord," and added, "Thank you, Lord, for helping John Morrissey deliver your servant, Shang Allen, to his family. Thank you for Shang's swift recovery. Continue to watch over this family during these troubles. Heavenly Father, protect our friend, John, wherever his life leads him. In Your name, we pray. Amen."

"Amen," repeated the Allen family, even the toddler.

After dinner, Mary Louise and the children went about their regular clean-up duties. The children then offered hugs and good nights. The men could hear Mary Louise reading from *Oliver Twist*, admonishing the twins to "be still and pay attention." It was time for the men to retreat to the parlor. With the help of crutches, Shang rose and asked if Father Finnegan would bring the whiskey bottle and three glasses.

John had little to add to the conversation that carried into the early hours of the morning. He knew, of course, that Shang was a blunt instrument who pushed back against threats and violence with the same or more. It was easy for John to understand Shang.

Father Finnegan offered an alternative way. He shared the Jesuit community's command to love and forgive and supported Archbishop John Hughes's efforts to care for the Irish immigrants' material and spiritual health. When Father Finnegan bade Shang and John adieu, the host was ready to join his wife. His wounded leg ached, though he would never admit it. He grabbed his crutches, struggled to his feet, and turned to John.

"I love that man, John. My heart knows he's right, as is the archbishop. I pray often. Do you know Archangel Michael? He led an army of angels against the devil's forces. God needs me to carry His sword here, at least for a time. I know He does. Good night, John."

On the morning of his expected departure, John tiptoed from the Allen home. He warily approached the Gem. Anyone looking for him would start there. When he was confident that no one was watching, he crossed the street and entered, greeting a surprised Mr. Koch before heading to the roulette wheel.

Dad Cunningham had his back to the entry as John approached.

"Won't you be saying goodbye to a friend?"

Cunningham turned. His smile turned to a frown as he took John by the arm and walked him around a corner, out of sight from the entrance. "They've been here three or four times looking for you, John. It's not safe."

"Thanks, Dad. I'm careful. I had to say goodbye to you and Petrie. I don't know when I'll be back."

Dad squeezed John's shoulders and said, "We'll miss you, my friend. Unfortunately, the boss isn't here this morning. He's got a sick child. I'll tell him you stopped. At least you'll be away from the cholera. Six hundred more died last week. Most in Five Points. It's scary and bound to be worse with summer."

"Be safe, Dad."

Cunningham slapped John's back. "I'll be at mass, Johnny, praying for your black Irish soul."

Ten

Every steamship on the Hudson struggled to secure and keep a crew during 1849. Gold fever struck the East Coast hard. President James K. Polk confirmed accounts that "the abundance of gold is of such an extraordinary character as would scarcely command belief." People borrowed money, mortgaged property, and spent their life savings to make the arduous trip to California. Steamboat crews were depleted, including Captain Smith's.

John was unaware of his former captain's plight when he showed up to inquire about renewed employment. Captain Smith welcomed his former deckhand with uncharacteristic warmth. First, he informed John that he could work again with Bosun Maloney. Then, he offered John his hand and sent him to the purser.

Finding Bosun Maloney on deck was no problem. The sound of his booming voice berating deckhands was familiar. John had to smile as he approached. He had been on the receiving end of those tirades. Hearing someone approach, the bosun turned and bellowed, "If it isn't the swell, John Morrissey, himself. To what do we owe the honor?"

John doffed his cap and bowed low. "It's my honor, once again, to be at work with the best sailor on the Hudson."

Deckhands hailing from Troy recognized Morrissey and whispered to the others. Maloney turned his attention to the deckhands. "Get back to the window cleaning, you lazy monkeys! If they're not spotless when I return, I'll put the lot of you off at Athens tonight!"

Loud enough for the deckhands to hear, Maloney addressed John. "Follow me. I'll show you your bunk and put you to work."

Once below deck, Maloney described the onboard situation. The staff and crew were too few and inexperienced. It made the night trips even more hazardous. Discipline was harder to keep, both with the workers and the travelers. Every trip south included overanxious young men beginning their journey to California.

Reaching the crew's quarters, Maloney indicated a preferred lower bunk and said, "Your bag should be safe here, but if you'd feel better, I'll stow it in my cabin."

John threw his bag on the bunk. "I'll keep it here, Bosun. I won't be expecting special treatment. It'll be a pleasure to stand by you. Plus, I can use the exercise," he added with a grin.

Maloney looked John up and down before leaving. "You're still a sorry-looking lad, but it's good to see you on my ship. Welcome back, Morrissey."

The trouble with excited young men heading downriver was predictable. These new argonauts were anxious, often drunk, and quickly drawn into battle. John jumped in to help manage outbursts. He and Maloney determined which fights they could allow to continue, even placing occasional bets on the young fighters.

A storeroom served as a brig. It was large enough to accommodate up to eight men. Though exhausting, Maloney and Morrissey were a potent fighting team, appreciated by Captain Smith and his inexperienced officers.

With alternating Sundays spent at Troy, John stood in for Marcel Archambeault behind the Eastern bar. He accepted no pay from Hamilton. He enjoyed visiting with Nathan Parker, reveled in playful moments with the working girls, and spent time with his father.

On Monday, August 4, John awoke midday, had a leisurely breakfast at the Paradise Hotel, returned to the Eastern, dressed, and packed before stopping at Hamilton's office to offer thanks and bid farewell. He was excited to be heading downriver. As he approached the great steamer, he spotted Captain Smith nearing from the opposite direction with a young woman on his arm. Both were laughing, and neither noticed John.

"Good afternoon, Captain Smith." John removed his hat and nodded.

"Good afternoon, Mr. Morrissey." The captain touched the tip of his cap. "You remember Susannah, of course."

The young woman stared at John with a quizzical expression.

"Of course," stammered the surprised deckhand, "I'm pleased to see you again, Miss Smith."

Captain Smith said, "We should move aboard, Suzie."

Susannah's eyes lingered on John for a moment, then she tightened the grip on her father's arm, and they boarded the great ship.

John wondered why the captain's daughter had such a strong effect on him. They had only that brief encounter the previous year, yet his thoughts regularly turned to her. His first impression had been that she was the loveliest young woman he'd ever seen. *She's even more beautiful now*, he thought.

At five o'clock, Maloney had his customary deckhand meeting at the galley. He looked around at the eight men and sighed. There should be at least six more. More, he knew, would be missing for the return. As usual, Maloney offered admonishments and threats and sent his deckhands to their assignments.

"Morrissey, stay here." Maloney waited for all the deckhands to leave. "The captain's worried. He didn't like the look of the prospectors who boarded today. We've had our hands full with these forty-niners—thirteen aboard today. Most are already in their cups. He wants you to be ready to fly in when needed. Your only duty tonight will be to circle the deck and watch for signs of trouble. Keep your slungshot handy. Use it if you must. We can't allow trouble to get out of hand. There are but two officers on board and, frankly, useless in a scuffle."

"Bosun, a belaying pin might be a good friend tonight. There's a buffer from Troy with that group. Name's Bibber McGeehan. He recognized me too. I laid him out on my first day at the Eastern. He might be looking for revenge, try to even the odds. If they want trouble, the sound of the pin on his noggin should discourage the others. If not, I'll keep slugging."

Maloney laughed and shook his head. "That's what I like about you, Morrissey. You like a good fight even more than me! Be my guest, lad. Carry a pin. I almost hope they're drunk enough to try us. Follow me. I'll get a pin for both of us!"

Armed with the belaying pin and his slungshot, John headed toward the port rail, the most popular location on the deck. The setting sun would be on the backs of those gathered there, with a wind off the bow providing welcome relief from the hot August evening. It would be an hour before the first-class ticket holders moved to the grand salon for dinner.

Couples lined the rail as the ship rushed past villages along Hudson's east bank. A group of young forty-niners elbowed close to the bow. The dandies gave them space and paid them no heed. John moved on.

As he crossed the bow to the starboard side, he spotted the bosun midship, moving in his direction. Another group of forty-niners, in various stages of inebriation, stood close to the bow. Among them was Bibber McGeehan, who scowled and spat on the deck as John walked by.

McGeehan pointed at John. "There goes the son of a drunk Irish whore."

Morrissey stopped and turned. The man was just as drunk as the last time Morrissey had seen him. Members of his group stepped up to support their fellow traveler.

John didn't hesitate. He tapped the belaying pin into the palm of his left hand, grinning as he walked toward McGeehan, who raised his fists. It was too late. The belaying pin crashed into his left elbow. Shrieks of agony followed the sound of crushed bone. Still grinning, Morrissey glared into the faces of the other would-be fighters. None, as John expected, advanced to the aid of McGeehan.

Maloney reached John's side as another group of forty-niners rushed around the bow. They saw Bibber, the big braggart from Troy, clutching a shattered arm and crying in pain. Two crewmembers, armed with belaying pins, grinned at them.

Maloney spoke to the forty-niners. "I'll be asking, men, that you join me in our galley for our chef's quality food. Mr. Morrissey, here, will take this poor, clumsy fellow to our ship's doctor. You won't be seeing him on this grand vessel again. Now, follow me."

The would-be prospectors followed.

Morrissey squeezed McGeehan's broken arm and hustled him, shrieking in pain and cursing, to Doctor Randolph's infirmary. The doctor regularly treated unruly passengers who Morrissey and Maloney had restrained. He asked no questions, and Morrissey did not explain, only instructed, "To the brig with this one when you're done, sir."

It was comforting to see this group of potential troublemakers tucked away. All on deck was quiet. The evening continued to be humid, even as the sun slid behind the Catskill Mountains. Passengers began to retreat to the relative comfort of their staterooms or gathered in the grand salon. Those who chose to remain on deck strolled or watched from the rails as the great ship sped south. John felt the tension leave his shoulders.

Lieutenant Brooks followed Maloney and the forty-niners to the galley. Once he was sure that Maloney had the situation in hand, he visited the cook and ordered more portions to serve the "guests," then reported to the pilothouse to inform Captain Smith that more trouble from the forty-niners was unlikely.

"Morrissey?" asked the captain.

"Yes, sir, and our bosun."

Captain Smith sighed with relief and said, "No deaths, I pray?"

"Just a mauled elbow, sir. Delivered to Doctor Randolph. I'll put him ashore at Athens."

"Thank you, Lieutenant. Please have Morrissey come to the pilothouse before dinner."

Since the bell for dinner would sound within thirty minutes, Lieutenant Brooks set out to find Morrissey. He didn't have to look far. John was leaning across the port rail near the bow.

"Mr. Morrissey, Captain Smith has asked that you visit him in the pilothouse. Please join me, sir."

John followed the officer the short distance, fearing he was in trouble.

"Mr. Morrissey, as requested, Captain, sir," announced Lieutenant Brooks.

"Thank you, Lieutenant. You can go."

When Captain Smith and John were alone in the pilothouse, the captain gestured toward the river and said, "I've been a pilot or captain on sail and steamships for decades. I've been aboard and in charge during accidents. The beauty of this river is deceiving. Dangers are always present, and the faster these ships, the greater the danger., We often have a thousand souls aboard. One cannot afford distractions. You understand, do you not?"

John was now certain he had transgressed. "Yes, Captain Smith."

"There are two things that distracted me on this trip, Morrissey. One was the group of rowdies we boarded at Troy. You helped put an end to that distraction. Thank you, young man."

John replied, "It was as the bosun ordered, sir."

Captain Smith ignored that and continued, "My second distraction is my daughter, Susannah. She has no chaperone. I won't allow her to wander the decks alone during this unusual season, not after last year's incident." The captain paused, alert to another steamboat speeding north off their starboard.

Confident that the ships would pass safely, Captain Smith continued. "My daughter is high-spirited. She insists on free movement, but I can't allow that. It would be inappropriate to ask my staff officers to serve as escorts. Could I impose upon you to escort my daughter? I would limit it to an hour after dinner, weather permitting."

John couldn't believe what he was hearing. "It would be an honor, Captain. No harm will befall her."

"Excellent. I'll advise Susannah that she'll be free to move about the deck for an hour after dinner and that you'll ensure her safety. That, Mr. Morrissey, removes my two major distractions. Meet my daughter at the salon's port entry after dinner. I'll ask Lieutenant Brooks to advise Maloney." Captain Smith turned his attention back to the Hudson.

Be careful, John. The thought kept recurring as Morrissey rounded the deck after leaving the pilothouse.

Susannah, seated next to her father, suffered through course after course and boring adult banter at dinner. Everyone wanted to shake the captain's hand or introduce someone. Of course, as the captain's daughter, she had to exude warmth and charm. It was draining. At least her father was allowing her a bit of freedom after dinner.

Susannah was about to object when Captain Smith insisted that a crew member accompany her. However, hearing that her escort would be the tall, handsome, and notorious John Morrissey, she held her tongue. During the past school year, Susannah had confided to schoolmates how John Morrissey rushed to rescue her on the deck of the *Empire of Troy*. The local students at Troy Female Seminary knew the reputation of Troy's alpha male and claimed to have seen him around town. They all focused their attention as Susannah described the rescue. She could not imagine a more welcome escort.

Susannah could see Morrissey pacing outside the grand salon. He would look toward the captain's table whenever he walked by. She tried to appear indifferent. Finally, after an eternity, dinner concluded, and Captain Smith offered Susannah his arm to lead her to the exit.

John had used the time before and into dinner to wash and change into his best outfit, the one Mrs. Rynders supplied more than a year ago. He considered all that had happened since seeing Susannah Smith the first time. The boy that arrived in New York was naive, careless, and ragged. Now he was only ragged. He had little, if anything, in common with the captain's daughter.

"One hour. Please return to our stateroom as agreed, Suzie. I'll be in the pilothouse if you need me," Captain Smith whispered as he walked his daughter to where Morrissey awaited. "Good evening, Mr. Morrissey." The captain smiled at his deckhand. "Thank you for escorting my daughter." He noted the fine outfit Morrissey sported and suppressed a smile. "It's a good evening to catch whatever breezes one can."

John held his hat in his hands, wringing it nervously while scanning the faces of the captain and his daughter. He had no idea what either expected of him. "Yes," he replied, knowing how foolish it sounded, "'tis a hot evening, sir."

"Well," Susannah exclaimed with a hint of irritation, "I don't wish to waste my hour of freedom standing in this doorway." Susannah dismissed her father. "Be off to your duties, Captain of the *Empire of Troy*." She turned to Morrissey, looking up into his eyes. "Mr. Morrissey, if you intend to be my escort, I will take your arm now." Susannah grasped Morrissey's left forearm and led him away.

After ascending the broad stairway to the promenade, John and Susannah walked silently for ten minutes. She appeared content to stare across the waters. John was conscious of the hand resting on his arm, the awkward silence, and his racing heart. Other couples appeared from the grand salon and made their way fore and aft on the main deck, nodding greetings. All seemed to be in intimate conversation.

"Do you know, Mr. Morrissey, that you are quite a famous man in Troy?"

John struggled to find his tongue. "I doubt I'm famous at all."

"You are the Irish fighter, are you not?"

"Well, some would say."

"My brothers speak of you with awe. They say that you'd beat the champion in a prizefight. So, like it or not, you are famous."

"Fame in Troy is worth little, Miss Smith. If Tom Hyer would fight me in the ring, I'd win. Then I'd be famous; sure, I would."

"Well, someday, I will tell my friends I know the great John Morrissey. I can even tell them I once saw you fight. And won't they be jealous when they hear we strolled around the deck of the greatest steamboat in the world, arm in arm?"

John could feel himself blushing. Was she flattering him, or was she mocking him? He turned to her. She stared up at him with those big dark eyes. As soon as she had his attention, she batted her eyelashes and offered a luminous smile.

"You don't know what to make of me, do you, John Morrissey?"

Now it was John who smiled. "I'm sure I don't, Miss Smith."

"Well, let's start by not calling me Miss Smith. I'm Susannah— or Suzie if we become friends."

At the bow, they reversed direction and walked in awkward silence.

"Do you still call Troy your home?"

They had stopped along the rail to watch the *Rip Van Winkle* speed by as it headed north. Susannah's hand remained on John's arm. She stood close.

John struggled to breathe, and sweat was gathering under his waistcoat. He swallowed hard and said, "Yes, Troy's home, but I need to be in New York." Even mentioning the city brought back a rush of memories he could never share with her.

With a sigh, Susannah said, "I'll live in New York City someday. It is the greatest city in the world, don't you agree?"

John thought of the city he knew, the squalor, the homeless children, the gambling and prostitution, the crime, the deadly diseases, and the recent riot. He could not imagine this innocent young woman alone in that city.

Susannah sensed his discomfort. "You've grown quiet, Mr. Morrissey. Have I offended you? Do I chatter too much?"

John could not shake the thought of the dangers that awaited her. "Can I ask what you'll do in New York City?"

"My father will transport me to the home of the curator of the New York Museum of Art. I will board there with five young women from seminaries around the country. We'll spend the week studying European art. It's quite an honor to attend. Has your time in the city been less than satisfying, Mr. Morrissey?"

"John. If I'm to call you Susannah, call me John."

"Well, John, are you disappointed with New York City?"

Silence, again, hung as heavy as the humidity.

"Well, John?"

"A poor, uneducated Irishman's what I am. I got to New York with no money and no friends. I came to fight. It's all I know. The city you'll see isn't the one I know. Pray you never see that city."

Susannah gripped John's arm with tenderness. Then, still looking out over the river, she whispered, "You'll someday be as famous in that great city as you are in Troy. I have no doubt."

John laughed. "Well, I'm famous enough in certain quarters. They'll arrest me and drag me to jail if I step off this ship."

"Did you kill someone with those mighty fists?"

"No. I threw bricks at a theater and saved a friend. But I've got enemies. They made sure I got some blame for the riot. I can't risk jail."

"That seems so unfair."

"I'm Irish and Catholic. Life's always unfair."

Susannah tugged on John's sleeve. "We should return to my father's stateroom. If I'm late, I might lose the privilege of your future company."

John and Susannah walked forward. Upon reaching the stairs and descending to the stateroom deck, Susannah let her hand fall from John's sleeve.

"It's been a pleasure to have your company this evening, John. I'll look forward to seeing you on my return to Troy."

"It was a pleasure, Susannah. Be safe in the city."

The following days felt like an eternity. John was eager for the safe return of the captain's daughter. He hoped for an opportunity to renew their conversations and to feel her hand upon his forearm, but he was also aware of the risk involved.

There were no significant incidents aboard the *Empire* during the week. Persistent rain kept passengers in their staterooms or steerage berths. Unruly drunks needed locking up, but nothing that needed a Morrissey-Maloney intervention.

On Wednesday morning in Troy, John left the Eastern and headed to Franklin Street. At the corner of Canal, he approached Peabody's, a men's clothing shop. Finding it still closed, he walked blocks before returning. An hour later, John exited with a long, narrow, gray jacket, a pair of white shirts and collars, a silk double-breasted vest with metal buttons, charcoal trousers, a black silk tie, and a new bowler hat. His next stop was a shoe store recommended by the tailor at Peabody's. There, he bought a pair of ankle-high boots with pointed toes. The purchases were extravagant and not without guilt. Three years earlier, he had a single set of worn, outgrown clothes and a pair of discarded shoes he had liberated from someone's trash. With decent pay and tips this summer, he had reason to feel buoyed by life.

Francis Conway's barber shop was a popular destination for Troy's large Irish population. Conway always managed the chair closest to the door. Mickey O worked the middle chair. Rusty LeBeau had been with Conway since he had opened the place and managed the last chair. Since he was old enough to use a pair of his mother's scissors, John cut his hair. After his second week at the Eastern, Aleck Hamilton added two bits to his pay and sent him to Conway's. "Ask for Mickey O," was all Hamilton had said. John now went there whenever in Troy. He liked the camaraderie as much as the haircut.

"Well, there's himself, the famous Trojan fighter," announced

Conway as John strolled in. "Are you being out of our fine county jail for a while, laddie?" Everybody in the packed establishment looked up and laughed. They always did, except the taciturn Rusty LeBeau.

John chuckled, shaking his head. "The merciful judge, bless his kindness, let me loose. Not a bit too soon, ay? Your sweet-angel daughter missed these brawny arms."

A roar exploded across the room, with no one laughing harder than Francis Conway.

Late on a cloudy and windy Wednesday afternoon, John climbed aboard the *Empire* with his stuffed canvas bag, a shaved face, and closely cropped hair. He stowed his bag and joined Maloney on deck. It had become their habit to stand atop the gangway to watch as the evening's passengers boarded. From that perch, they could spot potential troublemakers. Midway through boarding, the skies opened, and the rain and wind became the best deterrent to trouble. John joined Maloney and his fellow deckhands for their five o'clock meeting in the galley.

The steady downpour through the last days of the week reduced violence and work on deck. John could think of little besides a chance to see Susannah Smith one more time.

On Saturday evening, John joined a deckhand group as they began preparing for passenger boarding. He had no sooner started when Officer Brooks approached and asked him to report to Captain Smith. Arriving at the pilothouse, John found the captain in discussions with the ship's pilot. He waited.

Captain Smith finally noticed the young deckhand standing at the door and addressed him. "Would you help, as you did on Monday, Morrissey? After dinner?"

John's tongue felt thick. He cleared his dry throat. "Yes. Yes, of course, Captain."

The captain looked at the nervous man-child. *He's smitten, poor boy. At least she's off to seminary soon!*

The experience at the New York Museum of Art had surpassed Susannah's expectations. The curator, Simon Price, was a sharp-witted, hyper-energetic host and teacher. Though married, he showed a keen interest in the student from Troy Female Seminary. Susannah was flattered by the attention and looked forward to the daily instructions. The art was breathtaking, and the introduction to the artists and methods would be unforgettable. Yet, her thoughts often drifted to the upcoming return to Troy and the hope for more time with intriguing John Morrissey. She enjoyed sensing her strange power over men, especially this famous Irish lad who lived in such a violent, unfathomable world.

Captain Smith had hired a carriage at midday on Saturday and rode the short distance, in light weekend traffic, to the Museum of Art. Simon Price met the captain in the foyer, Susannah smiling at his elbow. The captain and the curator exchanged pleasantries before the father and daughter climbed into the carriage. Susannah was ebullient. The words spilled out. It was, she exclaimed, the most remarkable week of her life. All Levi Smith could do was sit back and listen. He and Aldine had hoped the experience at Troy Female Seminary would anchor their daughter to her studies. Levi Smith thought; *Aldine will be so pleased.*

As they saw the great ship in the distance after turning off Chambers Street, Susannah turned serious. "Father, the day is so lovely. I have had no fresh air since we arrived. Will it be possible for me to stroll the promenade after dinner?"

Captain Smith tried to suppress a smile. He remembered well the infatuations of his youth.

"Well, after all the rain and humidity, it is a spectacular day. We could impose on that Morrissey lad again if that meets your approval."

Trying not to appear pleased, Susannah answered, "If I'm not to be trusted alone, then Mr. Morrissey is acceptable, father."

Captain Smith carried his daughter's bags to his stateroom at the Empire, smiled at her, and told her he'd escort her to dinner at seven bells. As the door to the stateroom closed, Susannah threw up her arms and twirled around.

When seven bells sounded, John was in the crew quarters. The rest of the deckhands used the dinnertime opportunity to clean the decks and polish the brass. John had already dressed in a pristine white shirt and collar, pulled on his new trousers, and tied and retied his silk tie. Now he added the double-breasted silk vest. There was a moment of guilt as he pulled on the soft leather boots. His sisters, he knew, had so little.

John headed to the grand salon deck with his new jacket draped over his arm. He peered through a window on the starboard side. A crowd gathered around the captain's table, obstructing any view of the captain or Susannah. When the group parted, John glimpsed Susannah at her father's side, her arm wrapped in his, smiling.

A dinner bell rang, and people took their places at the elegant tables. John had an unobstructed view of Susannah. She sat as servers delivered course after course of food and wine. Susannah's silk bodice and skirt were bright yellows on white. Again, she wore no jewelry. Her composure, and the sophistication of the scene, gave John pause. He did not belong in such company. He never would; *Irish Need Not Apply*.

With dessert served, Susannah became anxious. She had scanned the port exit over the final dinner courses. There was no sign of Morrissey, and she wondered, *did he decline?*

John thought he saw Susannah look toward the port exit, not sure until she did it again. He gathered himself and proceeded to rendezvous. Once there, he kept his attention focused on the captain's table. After a moment, Susannah glanced his way. No reaction. Then she turned again and smiled. Was she happy to see him or mocking him?

As servers removed the dinnerware, Susannah leaned close to her father. Captain Smith smiled, nodded, rose, and held his daughter's chair as she stood. She took her father's arm as they headed toward Morrissey.

"Good evening, Mr. Morrissey. You look well-turned out this evening." Captain Smith smiled and nodded at the transformed deckhand. "I'll see you in our stateroom, Suzie. Enjoy the fresh air." He released her arm and returned to the grand salon, where the band had begun to entertain.

Susannah waited for John to speak, but he could not find words. She took his arm. "Come, my big, handsome warrior. I need to show you off."

The pair walked for quiet minutes as the Empire accelerated up the Hudson and past the Palisades under a full moon and a canopy of stars.

"You look lovely, Susannah." John avoided eye contact.

"It's Suzie. I thought we'd become friends, John. And thank you for the compliment. The dress is my favorite."

"You make it pretty."

"Why, John Morrissey, that's quite a poetic thing to say. But you are Irish, after all."

"I'm Irish, but no poet."

"My father was right; you are well-turned-out this evening. Do you have plans after I am off to bed?"

John blushed.

Susannah squeezed his arm. "Oh, no," she said, "there I go again. While you can't find words, I can barely govern mine."

"No," John said, "I have no plans for later, Suzie. I wanted to look a gentleman if we met tonight."

"You look splendid. I hope you don't mind my being so bold." She led him to the rail and looked up into his eyes. "You are the finest-looking gentleman on this fanciest of ships."

The pressure of Susannah's hand resting on his forearm sent waves of warmth and need through John's body. He desperately needed to pull her near when she stared into his eyes, but his mind raced; *she's too young, too Protestant, and far beyond my station...and she's the captain's daughter.*

Susannah grabbed John's other arm and turned him to face her. She was utterly unconcerned about the passengers strolling by. "You think yourself not good enough. I know that, but you are wrong, John. It is no sin to be poor. To be Irish. Even to be Catholic. You will be more than the best fighter in America. I'll be able to brag that I am friends with the great John Morrissey, and we once walked arm in arm on the greatest steamboat on the Hudson."

John bent to kiss Susannah's forehead. She raised her face and pressed her lips against his.

Eleven

"What about Petrie?" asked Dad Cunningham.

"He'll understand," John answered. "He'd be doing the same if he were young and free as us. They're coming back rich from California every day. We need to get ours, Dad. Besides, Hyer's there. Sullivan's there. The important fight promoters are there. I'll miss my chance if I don't leave."

The SS *Ohio*, part of the United States Mail Steamship Company, would leave for Chagres, Panama, at eight a.m. on March 28. She was preparing at Pier Twenty-Nine at the end of Warren Street. In addition to her twin steam engines, she had acres of sail on her four masts. Tickets to Chagres were seventy dollars for first-class, fifty-five for a lower cabin, or thirty-five for steerage berth. She would carry seven hundred and fifty passengers.

Morrissey and Cunningham strolled past Pier Twenty-Nine before dawn on March 27, where they studied the stevedores loading cargo for the next morning's departure. Morrissey saw deckhands and crew leave and reboard the ship. He was sure they could board without tickets. Between them, the reckless young men had sixteen dollars. At 4:30 a.m. on the twenty-eighth, arms draped around each other, the pair joined crewmembers returning from a night on the town and staggered up the gangway, each carrying a canvas bag.

The *Ohio* built steam and left the pier minutes past eight on Friday morning. She would stop at Charleston, Havana, and New Orleans to transfer mail.

"We're on our way!" John shouted as he pounded Dad's back. They stood among hundreds watching New York City fade away, and soon they were beyond Brooklyn and Staten Island, entering the Lower Bay. Sailors hoisted canvas, and the *Ohio* lurched over the swells into the Atlantic.

John observed that Captain Schenck had his ship well-staffed to deal with the trouble that anxious young men, crowded on a ship for days, guaranteed. John noted the fighting deckhands, sporting red armbands, had the swagger of experienced fighters.

The ship would cross the Gulf of Mexico before continuing down the Atlantic coast. Heat and humidity made time in the staterooms, cabins, and steerage unbearable. A mix of humanity strolled the deck. Panama drew gold-seekers, merchants, bankers, gamblers, and criminals, plus hundreds of rough laborers headed into the jungle to build the Panama Railroad. Women, often with children, braved a long, treacherous journey to join their husbands. Single women, out to make fortunes as dancehall girls or prostitutes, mixed playfully with the young men. Trouble was inevitable, and trouble always found John Morrissey.

Three days before arrival at Chagres, the stowaways' luck ran out. John and Dad were weaving their way through the congestion on deck when they stopped to see a dispute between two men. One was a gentleman with his wife on his arm. The other, Jim Hughes, leader of a gang of roughs onboard, had addressed the man's wife suggestively. When the gentleman took exception, Hughes punched him, knocking him to the deck, and Morrissey stepped in and shoved Hughes.

Not wanting to draw further attention, Morrissey drew close to Hughes and whispered, "I won't fight you here, you coward, but I'll fight you when we land at Chagres."

Hughes's mates had gathered around. He could not refuse the challenge. "Pistols, then, it is. You've traveled a long way to die."

Cunningham tugged at Morrissey's sleeve. Deckhands with red armbands rushed their way, with two quickly positioning themselves between Morrissey and Hughes. The third helped the bleeding gentleman to his feet. Meanwhile, Captain Schenck appeared.

"That man," shouted the wife of the injured gentleman, pointing at Hughes, "addressed me rudely, and my husband objected. He struck my husband. That man," she said, indicating Morrissey, "rushed to help."

Captain Schenck looked from Hughes to Morrissey and addressed Hughes. "Sir, how are you traveling with us?"

Hughes withdrew his second-class ticket and showed it to the captain.

"Take this gentleman," Schenck said to one of his fighting deckhands, "to his cabin, and place a guard outside. Mr. Hughes, you'll stay there until we dock at Chagres."

As the deckhand led Hughes away, the captain turned to Morrissey. He saw friends of Hughes pressed around and wanted no further trouble. "Sir, thank you for coming to the aid of this gentleman and his wife. But, for your safety, I'll have you escorted to your cabin. May I see your ticket, please?"

Morrissey smiled and shrugged. "Name's Morrissey, John. This is Daniel Cunningham. We boarded with no tickets in New York. Trying to get to Panama."

Captain Schenck sighed. There were few voyages during the last year that did not include stowaways. Since Chagres was the next and final stop, he told the pair, "You'll stay on the ship at Chagres and serve in the coal bunker during the run back to New York. If you serve well, I'll set you free there. If not, I'll turn you over to the police. Huntington," the captain addressed a ship's officer, "please escort these men to retrieve their belongings, then secure them in the brig."

The brig included four barred cells. Each had sleeping berths. Surprisingly, only two of the cells were occupied.

John looked around. "We got beds to sleep in! Remind me to thank the good captain."

Dad fell onto one of the thin mattresses. He put his arms behind his head and said, "If I knew the brig was so lush, I'd have surrendered days ago."

They laughed.

"Do you think Mr. Petrie will welcome us back?" Dad was serious.

"Well, if he doesn't, you can just go back to cleaning the church for the archbishop and chasing the nuns."

On their third day in the brig, the engines stopped, and the *Ohio* dropped anchor.

"Have we arrived at Chagres?" John asked when a mate brought breakfast.

"Nearly. The harbor, if you can even call it that, is backed up. We'll wait our turn. Could be days."

Late that afternoon, an officer entered the brig and approached Morrissey and Cunningham's cell. He inserted a key and instructed, "Bring your bags. Follow me."

The pair followed him to the main deck and the ship's pilothouse.

Captain Schenck dismissed the officer and smiled at the stowaways. "I thought you should see Chagres. Look at the chaos. Gold fever has changed this godforsaken swamp. Men you saw on this ship will die trying to build a railroad through that jungle. Young men, women, and children will walk off this ship and perish crossing to the Pacific. You're fortunate you can work your way back to New York. Now, go about your business and cause no trouble."

John and Dad left the pilothouse.

"What do you make of that?" Dad whispered.

"Don't know. Let's walk."

The two carried their canvas bags and joined others along the rails, where crowds cheered as impatient travelers leaped over the side, clutching their meager possessions. Canoes, with two or more natives, rushed to the men. Competition to carry intrepid jumpers the short distance to Chagres was brisk and negotiations swift. Natives dragged men into the canoes, extracted their fee, and raced toward the docks. A canoe of two natives could make more in a day than a normal year. Each time someone jumped, the passengers shouted bravos and laughed along the rails as the men struggled to hold onto their possessions and avoid drowning.

John grinned at his partner and asked, "Would you be trusting me, Dad?"

"Will I have a choice?" Cunningham smiled.

"Let's be off to Panama!"

John seized his bag, climbed onto the rail, and leaped into the water. Dad didn't hesitate. In seconds, he joined his friend in the warm water with encouraging shouts from above.

A canoe was at their side in seconds. John and Dad accepted the hands of the natives, tossed in their bags, and joined them in the canoe. One native, a mere boy, paddled toward shore. The other held up five fingers. "American dollars. Now."

John fumbled in his wet clothing for cash. He watched and delayed as the canoe moved closer to shore.

"Five American, now!" came the demand, louder this time.

Morrissey smiled as he extracted a five-dollar note and offered it. When the native reached to take the money, Morrissey planted a foot in the native's midsection, grabbed him by both arms, and tossed him over his head into the harbor. The younger native dove into the water. Morrissey handed one paddle to Cunningham and took the other.

Canoes turned to give chase, screaming threats in their native tongue, while people on the *Ohio* exploded with laughter and shouts. Morrissey and Cunningham were no match for the experienced natives, but they were close to shore and landed well ahead of the pursuit. In minutes they melted into the crowds at Chagres.

The distance to Panama City on the Pacific coast was less than fifty miles, but the trip wound through and over trails. The dense jungle had overgrown the old Spanish trail, which had once connected the Atlantic and Pacific. It was no longer a possibility. Daily temperatures in April averaged over ninety degrees, with constant humidity or torrential rain punishing travelers.

One could reach Panama City by first hiring a canoe for a three-day trip that would take you to Buena Vista or booking passage on a steamer to Gorgona, which arrived in a matter of hours. Either way left travelers with an arduous hike through the tropical forest and over the coastal mountains.

The urgency of those heading to Panama City was palpable. John watched the crowds pressing forward at ticket offices to book transportation. He thought, *we need to keep moving, or we'll starve before getting to San Francisco.* So, despite their limited funds, they opted for the faster trip via steamer to Gorgona, arriving at first light the next day. That left the pair with seven dollars and thirty-six hot, humid, and dangerous miles to walk. As soon as they stepped onto the dock, John pointed toward a lengthy line of men and mules. "There's the way to Panama City."

The trail was well-traveled and wide enough for the young men to advance past scores of men and mules. Possessing neither food nor drink, reaching Panama City without delay was a matter of life and death.

"How far, Johnny?" asked Dad after hours of arduous hiking.

"It'll be dark soon. After that, the trail should be cooler and less crowded."

"I'll make it, Johnny. I will. But how far?"

"We'll see Panama before the sun sets tomorrow." John hoped his estimate was accurate.

Fellow argonauts continued through the night, pushing on like spirits, heads down and hushed. The fog made it difficult to see the trail ahead. Howler monkeys made the thick canopy of trees their deafening home. Fear of poisonous snakes and jaguars hung over the travelers. Mosquitoes tormented day and night. John stayed close behind Dad, ready to support him if needed.

Dawn arrived by degrees in the heavy growth of trees. It was heartening to see the dim light heralding the day. They were climbing now. Dad had been quiet for a long time, but John watched as his feet scuffed the trail. They walked through an entire day and night with no food and only occasional rest at streams for water. John had no way to know, with certainty, if they'd see Panama by the end of the day. So, they pushed on, often cresting a peak only to see taller summits ahead.

They came upon a narrow stream when the sun was directly overhead. It was the perfect time and place to stop. They peeled off shoes and socks and soaked their aching, blistered feet.

Dad turned to John. "I'm going in!" he shouted. He raised his arms and fell backward, hitting the icy water and exclaiming, "Praise God. I'm saved!"

John roared as he jumped in to join his friend.

Hunger urged them on. They pulled their shoes over dry socks, wrapped their cool, wet shirts around their heads, and fell into the steady procession west. The sun had dropped lower and lower, causing John to worry that another night would pass before they reached Panama City. Dad had slowed on the latest climb. Now he stopped, staring into the distance. John caught up. Spread out below was a glorious city, set against an enormous orange sun setting over the vast Pacific horizon.

John started running down the broad, winding trail to Panama City, with Dad trying to keep up. Both were suffering from extreme thirst, hunger, and sleep deprivation. The site of the bustling walled city shot them with adrenaline.

The pair had to wade through a vast tent encampment on the outskirts of the ancient city. Seven thousand argonauts were already there, awaiting ships to San Francisco. No hotel rooms were available, even if they could afford one.

John and Dad approached a fruit vendor and spent fifty cents on two bananas, two mangoes, and two papayas. Neither had ever seen, let alone tried, these exotic fruits. Nothing could have refreshed their bodies and spirits better.

"I'm needin' sleep." John yawned.

"Not as much as me, Johnny."

John pointed at a nearby grove of trees. A bit of rest in the shade would serve them well. They plodded in that direction, settling under flowered branches.

They slept through the night, awakening soon after dawn with aching thirst and hunger.

Vendors were busy hawking freshly cooked food, including one offering sweet-corn cakes topped with roasted plantains, four for a dollar. They bought and devoured them in seconds. Next, they found a tent with a scrawled saloon sign and spent another precious dollar on four beers. Finally, with food in their bellies and their thirsts quenched, they turned to the difficult challenge of getting to San Francisco.

Steamships with the largest capacity carried only seven hundred passengers. There were far too few in service between Panama and San Francisco. Sailing vessels of all ages and sizes offered options, but they could take months, traveling far out to sea to catch the winds and currents that would take them to their destination. Ticket prices soared. Thoughts of stowing away, as they had in New York, were abandoned. Armed sentries roamed the docks, and tickets were checked and double-checked before boarding. They needed money, plenty, and quickly.

John knew faro was a game that could help. He had experience, and games were everywhere throughout the tent encampment. With knowledge of the game and discipline, John and Dad began to gather winnings. By the end of a month, they had almost three hundred dollars. It was a beginning but far less than the inflated cost of passage to San Francisco, even for one.

They bought food from street vendors, avoided barrooms and brothels, and went from faro table to faro table every afternoon and evening, finally collapsing under mosquito netting beneath their tree.

It was still dark when shouting awakened them. Dad shook John awake.

From nearby, a man shouted, "A steamer has arrived."

Dad and John were up and running, joining hundreds of excited men racing to the waterfront.

The SS *Panama* had arrived and anchored offshore. Authorities in Panama City expected her a week earlier. When his crew deserted at San Francisco, Captain Wickham scrambled to pull together whatever crew he could.

Prolonged delays at Panama City and uncertainty wore on everyone's nerves. There was a severe lack of food and supplies. Confrontations between the San Francisco-bound and locals became more common and violent. Cases of malaria and cholera were on the increase. Ticket prices continued to soar, with people bidding over one thousand dollars for one of the ship's four hundred and twenty places.

John and Dad visited the docks and watched as coal, wood, water, food supplies, and passenger belongings were loaded onto a ship's tender. Crew members, sailors, and officers arrived to visit local restaurants, barbers, brothels, and bathhouses. Passenger boarding would begin at four o'clock that afternoon, with departure scheduled for seven the following morning. Armed sentries were on high alert.

John and Dad were desperate as they strolled along the shore and stared at the ship at anchor less than two hundred yards away. They needed a plan, no matter how remote the odds.

When the fog rolled in late that afternoon, John tapped Dad's shoulder and pointed. Along the waterfront were countless small fishing boats, left unguarded. If they approached the steamer from the port side, the passengers boarding the starboard side would command the attention of the crew and guards. At least, that was John's hope.

"When it's dark, and if this fog stays, we'll take one of them and board the ship."

Dad looked from John to the steamer, then to the small boats.

He shook his head, shrugged, and said, "If I said no, would it change your mind?"

John smiled.

"Thought so."

The fog gathered offshore, a blessing for John's plan. A steady stream of passengers queued along the dock, waiting to board. It would take hours to carry the hundreds of travelers to the steamer. Two armed officers checked tickets as the passengers boarded with sentries standing watch.

John and Dad strode south along the water. They selected a rowboat half in the water, tied to a nearby tree.

"Here we go, Dad. Let's make it quick."

John walked toward the boat, saw the oars sitting on the bottom, tossed his canvas bag, and released the securing rope. "Get in," he whispered.

Dad tossed his bag and settled, while John pushed the boat into the water and jumped in. Dad grabbed the oars, set them in the oarlocks, and pulled away. They struggled in the dark and through the fog as the village's lamplight faded. Fog hovered over the water, obscuring, then revealing the large ship.

They had to approach the sidewheel on the port side. The pair were conscious of the sound of the oars dropping into the water. They lost sight of the ship as the fog rolled over them. They had only one hundred yards to go when it lifted.

"Who goes there?" A shout arose from the deck above. Louder, "Who goes there? Identify yourself, or we'll fire."

Dad dug an oar deep into the water and pulled the rowboat around to distance them from the armed sailors. The air exploded with rifle shots.

John threw himself into the bottom of the boat and shouted, "You hit, Dad?"

"No, but by God, that was close!"

After pulling the rowboat ashore, the discouraged pair headed back along the waterfront. An empty ship's tender had just returned from the steamship. Only a dozen passengers remained on the dock. Wagons of assorted sizes were queuing, waiting for the tender to tie up. The wagons held an assortment of late-arriving food for the trip north. A ship's officer berated the lead driver, who signaled the wagons behind to hurry. Men grabbed crates and sacks and rushed them to the tender.

"Johnny, they need our help, can't you see?"

John saw what his friend had in mind and smiled.

They hurried to the last wagon, hefted their canvas bags and sacks of produce to their shoulders, and followed onto the tender. No one paid attention as they added the produce sacks to the large pile of assorted containers. One of the delivery drivers and four helpers remained aboard. The ship's officer, his work ashore done, moved to the bow of the tender.

John and Dad rose and grabbed produce sacks when the tender tied up alongside the SS *Panama*. At the top of the loading ramp, the officer checking tickets motioned for John and Dad to approach. "They're okay," shouted the officer supervising the late food delivery. John and Dad kept moving toward the hatchway to the galley. As soon as they reached the hatchway, they lowered the food sacks and headed toward steerage. Somehow, they were aboard the SS *Panama*.

Steerage filled, and the air was humid and foul. John and Dad were glad to join those finding a place in the open air on deck. Neither man had much to say as the ship lay at anchor and people roamed the deck, enjoying a slight breeze. After midnight, the activity quieted, and they settled with their backs propped against their canvas bags along the bulkhead. The familiar sound of the ship building steam woke John. The steamer raised anchor, the starboard wheel turned, and the ship's bow oriented toward the Pacific.

It was still over four thousand miles to San Francisco. The SS *Panama* would reprovision fuel and supplies at ports along the way. The foodstuffs available in Panama City were sufficient for only eight days. Captain Wickham would need to begin rationing if arrival at Acapulco, Mexico, was delayed.

The steamer had picked up favorable winds during the first days and had full sails to help speed their way and conserve fuel for the boilers. By day four, however, fortune changed. When a pressure valve indicated a problem with one of the two boilers, the head stoker ordered both engines to shut down and reported to Captain Wickham. The winds, alone, would keep the SS *Panama* on course but at a much slower speed.

Captain Wickham ordered reductions of food rations for everyone except first-class passengers and staff. There was no general communication about the situation. Emotions grew raw. The thought of further delay was too much for the young gold-seekers keen to seize their share of whatever gold remained when they arrived after such a long journey.

John and Dad were grateful there were no ticket checks since departure. Dad spent hours on deck reading Charles Dickens's recent novel, *David Copperfield*, while John circled the ship, exchanging greetings or small talk with deckhands. He saw that an inexperienced, disgruntled crew staffed the ship.

Dad sat on the deck next to a bored John on the fifth day out from Panama City. He asked, "Why don't I teach you to read, Johnny?"

John looked down at the thick book Dad was holding. "I'm afraid you'd be wasting your time," he said.

"We've got time. It'll be good for you to read."

John was about to respond when a young mess boy came crashing at his feet, holding his ear, screaming in pain. A bully had struck the lad, and Morrissey jumped to his feet, standing chest to chest with a burly older man. He spat, "You hadn't ought to strike a boy like that."

"What have you got to say about it?" The man pressed closer to Morrissey, unintimidated by the larger, younger man.

"Well, I say you hadn't ought to strike a boy like that!"

"Mind your business, or I'll have you in irons!" shouted the bully.

Morrissey, in his anger, did not recognize the ship's captain, "You look like a hifalutin cock. Who do you think you are!"

The captain retreated a step, glancing around at the ship's officers and deckhands that had appeared.

"My name is Wickham. I'm the captain of this ship."

Morrissey caught Cunningham's sad look and shrugged. "Name's John Morrissey. I was a fighting deckhand on the *Empire of Troy*. My travel mate's Daniel Cunningham, the handsome red-haired man, seated over there. Boarded without tickets, we did. Had no choice. My San Francisco friends promise to cover us when we get there."

"I have a better idea, Mr. Morrissey," said the captain. "My officers will put you and your friend in irons and set you free at Acapulco. You'll be over two thousand miles from San Francisco. It's hard to escape from there. Seems like the right punishment to me." The captain jeered at Morrissey and turned to leave as his officers placed restraints on the stowaways. Morrissey and Cunningham, again, found themselves in a ship's brig with shattered hopes.

The SS *Panama* limped north under sail power. She should have arrived at Acapulco in eight days, but the boilers' prolonged repair cost precious time. Leaders appeared among the disgruntled, "We're led by an incompetent," they shouted. "He and the swells in first-class eat like kings while we starve."

By day ten out of Panama, demands for more and better rations became louder and more frequent. The captain ignored the requests. Next came threats of mutiny.

The staff could not control a determined mutiny, especially if crew members joined. Captain Wickham would need all the help he could muster. The big Irishman, who claimed he was a fighting deckhand, might serve in exchange for delivery to San Francisco. He sent for Morrissey and Cunningham.

"Remove the irons," Wickham instructed his officer. He looked from Cunningham to Morrissey and back. "I'm sure that you hear talk of mutiny in the brig. I cannot allow that to happen. Mr.

Morrissey, you claimed you served as a fighting deckhand on the *Empire of Troy*. Will you fight?"

John rubbed his wrists and smiled at the captain. "That's something of a trade with me."

Wickham offered, "We'll carry you two to San Francisco if you fight for the ship."

"We can, Captain."

Morrissey and Cunningham were provided cutlasses and loaded pistols, with moments to spare before the mutineers gathered and moved aft to execute their plan. The stowaways found themselves in the center of a line of officers and loyal crew members. Morrissey folded his arms and stared with contempt at the would-be mutineers.

"What do you intend?" shouted one of the mutiny leaders to Morrissey.

Morrissey sneered. "Cold steel and hot lead for them that try to pass this line."

Though they outnumbered the defenders, the mutineers were not ready to die for more food. "Can we huddle with the captain?" they asked. Captain Wickham agreed to consider their grievances and address them as he could, but only if they dispersed. The mob dissolved.

A grateful captain rewarded the stowaways with a second-class cabin for the balance of the trip to San Francisco. As soon as they entered the new accommodations, Dad looked around and said to John, "You're the boldest and luckiest man on God's earth! The Lord must love you, though I can't imagine why."

Twelve

~~~

While Morrissey was chasing his ambition to fight Tom Hyer for America's prizefighting championship, Susannah Smith was completing her studies at primary school. The academic demands would never pose a challenge for Susannah. She excelled in all her studies, but she was frequently disruptive in her boredom. During her third year, Miss Chichester asked her to assist the first and second-year students with reading and basic arithmetic. That helped. By her fifth year, however, Susannah was twelve and prematurely blossoming into womanhood. There was little Miss Chichester could do to hold her focus or that of the older male students.

The concerns and frustration felt by Phebe Chichester mirrored the increasing worries of Susannah's parents, especially her mother. When Miss Chichester and Miss Theodosia Hudson, Vice Principal of Troy Female Seminary, requested a meeting between school years, Susannah's parents quickly accepted.

Hearing her father's voice and her mother's sobbing one evening, Susannah pressed her ear to their bedroom door. Between the sobs, she heard her mother say, "Levi, I worry Suzie will find herself with child, as I did. You've seen how boys and even men look at her. What if she's no longer welcome at school? What will become of her?" Susannah did not wait for her father's response. She retreated to her room, angry and confused.

Over the last year, Susannah grew taller than many adult women, and her figure had matured. Some older boys at school fought over her. When she walked the streets, boys and men turned to watch, often smiling and tipping their hats. In most cases, she didn't object to their attention. Susannah thought *I would never do what Mother did to become pregnant.*

Susannah joined the interview with Miss Chichester and Miss Hudson at her parents' insistence. Her mother's hands were shaking as they took their seats. Miss Chichester's smiled at Aldine and Levi, then nodded at her student.

"Your daughter, Susannah," Miss Chichester announced, "is our top student at the Troy-Lansingburgh Common School."

Aldine reached for Susannah's hand. Hers was sweating.

Miss Chichester continued, "She has exciting potential for advanced learning and a career as a teacher." She gently smiled at Susannah, then turned to Aldine and Levi. "Miss Hudson has a proposal for you to consider."

Theodosia Hudson offered an abbreviated history of Troy Female Seminary, its founder, Emma Willard, and her many accomplishments, profiles of a few graduates, including Elizabeth Cady Stanton, and examples of the fields of study at the seminary. She looked directly at Susannah and said, "If you are interested, we'd be delighted to have you visit, Susannah."

Father appeared crestfallen as he looked first to his wife and then to Miss Hudson, "I'm a steamboat captain," he said." We are blessed, but we have barely enough to support our family. More education for Susannah is something I'm afraid we cannot afford." Susannah's spirits rose at this possible reprieve from her dreaded fate.

Miss Hudson smiled and said, "I apologize, Mr. and Mrs. Smith. I should have been clear. The seminary will cover your daughter's tuition, supplies, room, and board." Aldine released her daughter's hand, raised both of hers to her mouth, and turned to Captain Smith, who smiled broadly. Susannah's fate was sealed.

Should I run? Susannah Smith wondered as the summer of 1849 ended and her dreaded boarding at Troy Female Seminary approached. She'd believed anything would be preferable to living with a group of strangers, particularly wealthy young women who were bound to belittle her. Anxiety caused sleeplessness and weight loss. She pleaded with her parents to reconsider, to no avail. Her final effort was a plea to her father on the *Empire*. It failed. She barely left the room she shared with Addie as summer turned to fall.

On September 16, Levi and Aldine hired a carriage and accompanied Susannah and a trunk of her possessions to the seminary at Ferry and Second Streets. A tall, distinguished gentleman approached their carriage and offered a gloved hand to Aldine. "Welcome to Troy Female Seminary," he said in a polished baritone, "my name is John Willard, and I am honored to serve as seminary's principal." Levi and Aldine climbed down and introduced themselves.

Principal Willard turned to Susannah and said, "We have heard good things about you from your Common School. You should be well-prepared for success here," he added, with an unsettling wink, "with proper commitment and effort."

A staff member had silently appeared, prepared to accept Susannah's trunk, and show her to her room. Aldine embraced her daughter, sobbed deeply, and retreated to the carriage. Captain Smith shook Principal Willard's hand and said, "Thank you, sir, for this opportunity." Levi placed both hands on Susannah's shoulders when the principal turned to leave. His eyes were wet with tears as he squeezed and said, "You have a great future ahead, Suzie. Keep your eyes on the horizon, dear child."

Susannah followed the staff member and her trunk to a room on the fourth floor. A young woman was staring out the window when Susannah entered. She turned, beamed a luminous smile, and rushed to greet Susannah with her hand extended. "Julia," she exclaimed, "So good to meet you. I'm Julia Van Wyck. Just arrived from Mount Holly, New Jersey!"

Accepting her dainty hand, Susannah replied, "Susannah Smith, from a few blocks north of here. Pleased to meet you, Julia." The room had two small beds, two mirrored closets, two worn desks and chairs, and an ornate iron stove.

"Julia," Susannah said to her short, petite, effervescent roommate, "as the first to arrive, please select a bed and closet!"

Julia bombarded her new roommate with information as they attacked their trunks. She'd spent her early years in Nashville, Tennessee, where her father was a family doctor. When Julia was eight, her father inherited a large estate. It included a fourteen-room house at Mount Holly and his father's thriving medical practice. Susannah half-listened until Julia said, "I fear I've hardly made his job as a father very easy."

Susannah laughed aloud, "I'm sure my parents returned home with relief! My mother had her first child when she was fifteen, and we just kept coming. I'm here because she's terrified that fate will befall her oldest daughter."

Now, it was Julia's turn for a good laugh. "There's not much chance of that happening here, now is there?"

That evening they met their fellow first-year students in the library before dinner. Susannah wore one of her best outfits, kept her chin up, and spoke as little as possible as she and Julia mixed with young women from at least fifteen states, twin sisters from Canada, and one stunning beauty from Mexico.

Miss Hudson rang a delicate handbell to capture attention and asked everyone to move to the dining room across the hall and take any available seat. There were two long dinner tables in the most elegant room Susannah had ever seen. One long stone block wall facing south featured a series of narrow stained-glass windows, each celebrating a famous scientist or philosopher. The opposite wall held an enormous fireplace, which promised to warm the coldest winter meals. Above the fireplace was a large portrait of the famous Emma Willard in a gilded frame.

After everyone found a seat, Miss Hudson asked the young women to bow their heads. After grace, she made several announcements and instructed all to check the bulletin board in front of her office before retiring to their rooms. That's where they'd find their personal interview time for the next day. An efficient uniformed staff served a four-course dinner. *Perhaps,* she thought, *this will not be too terrible a fate.*

The next morning, Susannah arrived at Miss Hudson's office at the appointed time. Theodosia Hudson rose, walked from behind her desk, and warmly greeted Susannah. Behind Miss Hudson's desk stood a tiny, severe woman holding a ledger. "Susannah," said Miss Hudson, "allow me to introduce Miss Nancy Hinsdale. She is matron-of-the-household and manages the staff who will care for your needs." Miss Hudson pointed to a chair across from her desk, "Please be comfortable, Miss Smith."

Miss Hudson opened a folder, rested eyeglasses on her nose, and studied for several minutes. When she looked over the glasses at Susannah, she smiled and said, "Based on discussions with your teacher at Troy-Lansingburgh Common School and a review of your school records, we've prepared recommendations for your initial courses. Here is a copy of those with the days, hours, location, and instructor. It's an ambitious course of study, Miss Smith, but we believe you are capable of succeeding."

The vice-principal handed the folder across the desk. "Do you have any questions?"

Susannah held the materials to her chest, considered several questions, but responded, "None at this time, Miss Hudson. Thank you."

"Good," Theodosia Hudson removed her spectacles. She nodded to Miss Hinsdale, "We provide you with two uniforms and a list of rules of the house that keep everyone healthy and safe."

Susannah followed Miss Hinsdale to a long table next to the office door. Wordlessly, the matron-of-the-house assessed Susannah's size and handed her two bundles marked "large" and a list titled *Troy Female Seminary – Rules of the House*.

Susannah smiled at a fellow student who awaited her turn with Miss Hudson, then proceeded to her fourth-floor room with uniforms and rules in hand. After dropping the new uniforms on her bed, she went to her desk to review the initial courses assigned. These included algebra, moral philosophy, universal history, Latin grammar, and rhetoric.

The door burst open while Susannah tried on her pathetically simple and far-too-lengthy uniform. Julia flew in, stopped abruptly, pointed at Susannah, and burst into laughter. "My God, is that what that shriveled old hag gave me?" Julia looked at the bundle under her arm with horror. "I simply cannot!" she shouted, dropped her pair of uniforms to the floor, and renewed her uncontrollable laughter as Susannah lifted the hem of her uniform and danced around their room.

Despite the discomfort of being away from family, the rigor of the studies, and the relationships to navigate, Susannah settled in quickly. Though she missed her local friends, especially her best friend, Rebecca Watkins, it didn't take long to develop a circle of young women with whom she felt comfortable. Helen Lathrop from Vermont, Elizabeth "Becky" Mason from Louisiana, Florida Ferrell from Georgia, and Nancy Hitchcock from across the Hudson in West Troy became permanent members of Julia and Susannah's *seminary sisterhood*. Several members admitted pining for special young men. When Susannah dared to share that she was smitten with a notorious Irish gang leader, her friends were shocked and curious. "How did you meet?" "Is he handsome?" "How old is he?" "Have you kissed?" "Do your parents know?" Susannah took pleasure in embellishing Morrissey's notoriety and their meeting on the glorious *Empire of Troy*.

To some of the sisterhood, especially those from the south, the idea that Susannah would consider a relationship with someone of such low standing was scandalous. Yet, all seemed captivated by the possibility of a romance with such associated danger.

While she enjoyed entertaining her peers with fantasies about a future with the notorious John Morrissey, Susannah was realistic about such a future. John Morrissey lived in a violent world beyond her comprehension. There would be other men and other fantasies, she knew. Susannah's eyes would remain fixed on the horizon as her father had counseled. That horizon for her included wealth and social standing. It always would. Regardless of how handsome and brave, the young Irish pugilist was a poor candidate to help steer a course toward that horizon.

The curriculum demands at the seminary were grueling. Mrs. Willard insisted that requirements were as demanding as those of the nation's leading colleges for men, and the school attracted talented subject matter instructors from around the world. Young women unable or unwilling to meet the academic standards left or were asked to leave. As much as Susannah resented boarding, her pride would not allow her to fail. Those who graduated often went on to teach at or lead other seminaries forming around the country and worldwide. Susannah had no aspirations to follow that path, though she completed her studies and graduated in 1852.

Emma Willard addressed the graduates, commissioning them to "waste not a day of our life, spread our knowledge with joy and passion, and serve as the moral anchor for our families and communities." From the text of Mrs. Willard's speech were printed these words to guide them on their way:

Then, too, I saw your gathering groups, dear girls,
Of maidens best, most loving and belov'd;
And ye, my sisters, elder daughters, too,
Who share my labours, and e'en now with smiles
Double your own, that I may be reliev'd;
Then were before me, too, the groups who, twice
Each annual sun gather from distant states,
To mark with new delight the blossoming of female genius.

Susannah left Troy Female Seminary to return to her humble home on the Hudson with a head crammed with information, her virginity intact, and a burning drive to rise above her humble social status. She longed to escape from tiny, gritty Troy. Art, culture, entertainment, and wealth abounded downriver in New York City. Her ambition was to marry into New York's best social circles and raise brilliant children.

The best part about liberation from the seminary was the freedom to spend time with Rebecca, who had greatly expanded her social network while Susannah received a classic education. Rebecca's current love interest was a senior at Rensselaer Polytechnic Institute.

Russell Price, III, was a brilliant, albeit amoral, a bundle of energy and mischief. He wasted no time matching Rebecca's best friend with college friends. During the summer of 1852, Susannah dated three handsome, arrogant, oversexed young men from successful families. Each promised to satisfy Susannah's ambition to marry into the right social circles and raise brilliant children. Despite good intentions and regular misgivings, she rejected each suitor. She often thought of John Morrissey and wondered; *Will he remember me? Will he return? Will I even see him again?* This obsession made no sense, but it lingered.

Waiting for the Fates to intervene while she sat around her family's home was not in Susannah's make-up, and she needed income. The president of Bank of Troy, Joseph Warren, and his wife, Eugenia, were looking for a tutor for their four children. Mr. Warren approached his neighbor, Emma Willard, for a referral. The Warren family lived within a few miles of the Smiths in Lansingburgh, Mrs. Willard arranged an interview, and Susannah accepted the position.

Thirteen

❦

The SS *Panama* entered San Francisco Bay on June 24, 1850. It was a clear, chilly morning as the ship lowered its sails and steamed forward, flanked on both sides by towering redwood highlands. The long journey was about to end. Morrissey and Cunningham joined the jubilant crowd on the starboard rail as they glimpsed a forest of masts bobbing near the shoreline.

John and Dad pushed through the crowd, looking for Captain Wickham. Finding him stationed above the departure ramp, John said, "We thank you, sir, for the kindness."

"No," answered Wickham, "it's I who is indebted. I might have lost this ship without your help."

John and Dad shook Wickham's hand, exited the *Panama*, and climbed aboard a tender for the final hundred yards of their improbable journey.

Yerba Bueno, or San Francisco, was a place in 1850 with little established government, including laws or law enforcement. It was a place well-suited for John to plant his flag. Men entered and exited raucous saloons, gambling dens, and brothels on all sides of the wet and muddy streets and into the narrow alleys. Men returning from successful digs with pockets full of gold and sailors desperate for an escape from long, harrowing journeys had no trouble finding places to lift their spirits and empty their pockets.

"Almost makes Five Points look dandy?" John grinned at the sights and sounds.

They needed a place to stay and to find work. Pacific Street looked promising. They were two blocks up the steep road when a man came flying out of a saloon. Three men rushed out and kicked the fallen victim, even after the man lay unconscious and bloody.

Morrissey had seen enough.

"That'll do unless you wish to see him dead."

Morrissey edged toward the beaten man while the three administering the beating looked dismayed. Others from a nearby street corner surrounded the activity. Cunningham moved to stand beside Morrissey.

"Well, what do we have here, boyos? Two new arrivals in the wrong place, I'll be thinking." The accent was pure Irish. The speaker was a giant, half a head taller than Morrissey.

"I'm for fighting, not murder," answered Morrissey.

The huge man grinned. "You're Irish, are you not?"

"From New York. Morrissey, John. Born at Templemore and shipped to America as a wee lad. This here's Cunningham, Daniel, also from Ireland and New York. We just stepped off the *Panama*."

"Murray, Ewan." The ruffians' leader introduced himself and indicated the crowd of men gathered around. "My friends here are late of Ireland, all. The British jailed us in Australia, then sent us here when they no longer wanted us there."

Morrissey pointed at the unconscious man at his feet. "And him?"

"He assaulted a whore in the Graystone," explained Murray. "The business is under our protection."

"You a gang, then?" Morrissey asked. The discovery of an Irish gang in this remote place shocked him.

"They call us Sydney Ducks. A lawless place it is here. These businesses," Murray said, with a broad sweep of his huge hand, "need protection, and the Ducks provide it."

"Well, you might know where we'll find the boxing champion, Tom Hyer?"

Murray responded, "Why?"

"I aim to take the belt off him, that's why."

Murray and his fellow Sydney Ducks burst out laughing.

"Well, if that's your aim, young man, you'll be needin' to take the next boat to New York. The so-called champion didn't like our fair city. He left on a clipper two weeks ago."

Ewan Murray and his men turned and walked on, leaving the bloodied man in the street.

The news of Hyer's departure was devastating to John. He and Dad had little money and no friends. The weather, at least, was better than the suffocating heat of Panama. They'd find a spot outdoors to rest for the night and consider their situation the next day.

They were heading toward the waterfront when they heard a man pleading for help. John and Dad rushed toward the voice. Racing down the narrow street, they saw two figures leaning over a fallen man. "Keep your mouth shut," warned one of the assailants, "or I'll put this knife in your heart!"

"Try this heart, you cowardly dog!" Morrissey shouted as he rushed at the men.

Cunningham reached into a pile of loose boards, grabbed one, and moved toward the struggle, tapping the board on the ground as he advanced. The assailants disappeared into the gathering fog.

L. H. Roby was also a recent arrival, having left London four months earlier for Boston, where he boarded a clipper, sailed around Cape Horn, then up to San Francisco. He was bleeding from a cut over his eye and staring at his ruined suit. As he struggled to stand, Cunningham took an arm to steady him.

"My name is Lewis Roby," the slim, middle-aged man offered, "and I am in your debt." Roby pressed a handkerchief to the wound above his eye. "Do you suppose you could escort me to my hotel? That assault has undone me."

Offering further help to an Englishman, even one in distress did not appeal to John. Before he could object, Dad asked, "Where's your hotel?"

"It's on the water. It's called *Niantic*. If you are kind enough to walk with me, I'll point it out."

John looked at Dad and shrugged. Dad kept a grip on Roby's arm as they returned to Pacific Street and headed toward the waterfront.

The *Niantic* was a British sailing vessel abandoned offshore in early 1849. Enterprising arrivals hauled her ashore to use as much-needed accommodations. Because of her location, half in the bay, she'd survived a series of great fires that had leveled the city's waterfront structures.

A consortium of business owners from London converted her into a fine hotel, gambling parlor, and restaurant the previous year. She was among the best the city offered. The consortium was content with every aspect of their investment except one; they were hemorrhaging money. In L.H. Roby, they discovered the man to stem the flow.

"Here she is." Roby pointed at the *Niantic*. "I'm just discovering my way around her, but if you will, it would be my pleasure to offer my rescuers a drink from one of her fine pubs."

John and Dad stared up at the converted ship. Oil lamps glowed from its windows.

"We'd be happy to join you," Dad said. He glanced at John and saw his reluctance. Drinking with an Englishman was one of the last things Morrissey would find pleasurable. Curiosity, however, got the better of him. He said nothing and followed.

Roby, steadier now, started up the wide planking to the enormous carved doorway leading to the converted ship. The *Niantic*'s former grand salon was now an elegant lobby.

"Welcome back, Mr. Roby," a uniformed bellman offered the Englishman.

A man rushed from behind the registration desk, "Were you assaulted, sir? Can I call for help?" The man eyed John and Dad with suspicion.

"I daresay that I have been, Mr. Helmsley, but these Irish gentlemen rushed to my rescue. Had they not, my tenure as your boss would have been very brief."

Helmsley offered a practiced smile and extended his hand. "Lawrence Helmsley, night manager of the *Niantic*."

Dad returned the smile. "Cunningham, Daniel. This is my friend, John Morrissey. We arrived from New York this very day."

John frowned.

Roby turned to Helmsley and instructed, "Please go with these gentlemen to the Neptune. Tell the bartender to provide my saviors with the refreshment of their choice. I'll go to my suite to wash and discard these tattered rags for something decent." Then, turning to John and Dad, he said, "I'll join you, posthaste. We can all use a decent meal, I'm sure."

John and Dad had downed two exceptional whiskies recommended by the bartender when Roby joined them at the Neptune bar. John signaled Dad that he was ready to leave. Coming to the aid of a defenseless man was one thing, but he had no more time for an Englishman.

"Let me show you about this amazing property before we dine." Roby gestured for his guests to join him. He addressed them as he walked away, "I was dumbstruck when I saw this property. The locals have done an extraordinary job converting a beached ship into a fine resort."

Dad followed in Roby's wake. John was ready to bolt but couldn't break away without his partner. Roby kept moving and talking, first showing off an elegant guest suite, then a standard guest room, a formal dining room, a second bar with a table serving fresh oysters, and a deck below was a large, glimmering gambling room.

Dad paused in the entry to the gambling room. The vast space offered option after option for betting men, but most striking was the ladies. Dad asked, "Where do all the women come from? Are they wives?"

Roby smiled. "Most, I assume, young man, are harlots. They

arrive by themselves, or in small groups, from everywhere. The pretty and industrious will earn more tonight, bringing pleasure to a lonely man, than they could earn in a year wherever home might be. For prostitutes, there's gold in the men's pockets." Roby laughed at his cleverness and turned to start back to the *Niantic*'s lobby.

"Please join me in our dining room?" Roby held Dad by his elbow and steered him through the double doors. John held back, having seen more than enough. Roby turned to him and said, "I understand your feelings toward the English, Mr. Morrissey."

"I doubt you do." Morrissey glared at Lewis Roby.

"Right you are, Mr. Morrissey. Forgive me for the presumption. I will leave you and Mr. Cunningham in peace to enjoy a fine dinner, but first, let's share a glass of excellent California wine. Roby gestured to the maître d, who approached Roby and spoke privately with him. The maître d escorted John and Dad to a table overlooking the harbor, and a server arrived with three crystal wine glasses and two bottles of red wine. He opened one bottle, filled the glasses, and left.

Roby lifted his glass and said, "To brave and honorable men."

Dad lifted his glass and shot a look at John, who sighed deeply before lifting his glass to acknowledge the toast.

"I've taken the liberty of ordering dinner for you," Roby said. "I know you arrived today after a long journey. I'll leave you to enjoy it, but before I retire, I have a question: is there anything I can do to help you settle? I value my life far more than a drink and dinner."

Dad saw John's jaw tighten, but he was not about to waste the opportunity. "We'll need work and a temporary roof over our heads," he said, refusing to look at John. "Both of us have run games of chance before."

"Well, then, this will be easy." Roby looked at John. "Mr. Morrissey would prefer not to work for an Englishman, which I respect. So, I would be interested in owning a stake a in new gambling business. Everywhere pubs and gambling halls are full of

Irishmen, but you seldom see any of your race here, for the same reason Mr. Morrissey can't wait to leave. If you're interested in opening a gambling hall for the Irish, I'll loan the funds to get you started. You can pay fifteen percent of the revenues until that loan is satisfied. I'll have no hand in the operations. Regarding a place to stay, Mr. Helmsley will supply a room until you find a more suitable place."

Dad tried to read John but with no luck. "Mr. Roby, I think Mr. Morrissey and I should discuss this. Could we meet again tomorrow?"

"That would be fine, Mr. Cunningham. I hope that you'll consider my offer."

John and Dad turned to leave but stopped at the door when Roby asked, "Mr. Morrissey, if you'd known that the man in distress was English, would you have come to his assistance?"

John turned to face Roby. "I always fly in when I see someone bullied. So, yes."

"I thought as much." Roby smiled. "I'll see Mr. Helmsley and leave you to enjoy dinner."

John was sullen during the wonderful dinner courses and the second bottle of an excellent California red wine. Mr. Hemsley stopped by their table with a room key and told them to stay if they wished and to let him know when they left. John unlocked the door at their room, went inside, walked to the window, pulled aside the rich curtains, and stared out over the bay.

Dad paced the large room. "Johnny, we gotta discuss this. Our own gambling house. We'll be our own boss. Talk to me, will you? It's a miracle we made it this far. Now, along comes Mr. Roby with exactly what we need, can't you see that?"

"I don't trust him," said John without turning from the window. "You know what the English did to the Irish at every turn. Starved us and scattered us to the wind; they did. Partnership with an Englishman! I can't."

Dad knew how hopeless it was to argue with John when he was closed off, but this was a matter of survival. He shouted, "Aren't we as cunning as an Englishman, Johnny? Aren't you strong enough to snap him like a twig if he does us wrong? Let's take the Englishman's money. We'll make enough to go home so you can fight Hyer. That's what you want, isn't it?"

He was right. John knew it. After a mostly sleepless night, he relented.

They made their deal with Lewis Roby, who rented an excellent location on Kearny Street near Broadway, where a newspaper had recently burned to the ground. The Englishman paid for the essential equipment and furnishings, and they were ready for business within a month. The three men watched as a new sign rose over the entrance. It read "Acushla" and featured the four queens from a deck of cards. Every good Irishman knew the term meant "pulse of my heart." It was perfect.

Roby had been right. There were too few gambling houses in the city catering to the Irish, who totaled forty percent of the booming city's population. Acushla always needed two bartenders, two faro dealers, two roulette table managers, and two card dealers for poker and three-card monte. Since the *Niantic* always had more applicants than positions, Roby sent candidates their way.

Word spread, and the Irish quickly discovered Acushla. Ewan Murray made his appearance, with three Ducks, on the first night. He grinned as he looked around, nodding. He squeezed and held John's hand and wished him luck. "I'll be back soon. We'll discuss business." John expected an offer of protection. He knew it would be wise to listen.

At night bar business was so brisk that Acushla needed more bartenders. Dad put a sign in the front window that read, "Bartenders Needed – Only Irish Need Apply." Two former sailors, Robert "Robbie" Byrne and Christopher Doyle saw the sign and stepped inside. They had served together on the *Hornet*, a clipper out of New York. Like thousands of others, they had abandoned that occupation to pan for gold. The duo had luck, returned twice to San Francisco, converted their gold to cash, and spent it all. This time, exhausted and chastened by past indiscretions, they deposited the proceeds from their latest gold-mining efforts in a local bank and looked for work. Dad hired them that day.

John used his newfound cash to buy stylish clothes. He greeted the guests, watched over the staff, and kept an eye out for trouble. In all such places in 1851 San Francisco, violence was frequent. There were few, if any, more suited to the challenge than John Morrissey. Locals soon realized that it was unwise to cause trouble at Acushla. Morrissey, on most occasions, could manage difficulty without help. Byrne and Doyle enjoyed flying in when needed.

Dad had observed Tom Petrie manage a successful saloon and gambling business. It was also an epiphany to see the operation of the *Niantic*. To compete successfully in San Francisco required attractive women to entertain legions of lonely men. Wondering how to manage that aspect of the business, Dad turned again to Roby. The English owners of the *Niantic* would only hire "American" women. By that, they meant white. Women of color were out of the question, so Roby was delighted to send them to Cunningham.

A sixteen-year-old Mexican beauty named Carmelita Fernandez visited Roby and offered her services and those of seven young "cousins." Carmelita was tall and shapely, with long, luxurious black hair and a perfect complexion. She exuded sexuality. One look at Carmelita and Dad abandoned any thoughts of negotiating. The sixteen-year-old Carmelita and her "cousins" brought their considerable charms to Acushla.

The owners of Acushla lacked business experience but were quick studies. After their first month, they opened an account at Mills Bank and made daily deposits. Dad kept a record of all expenses, including their wages.

John was not surprised when Ewan Murray visited and asked for a private meeting. He came alone, just after opening. Murray's height required him to bend as he entered the front door and scanned the barroom.

John took his measure. *He'd be one rough buffer if it came to it.*

As soon as Murray saw John, he nodded and approached.

"It's good to see you're tasting success." John's right hand was swallowed in Murray's handshake. "Acushla's a clever name. Is there a place where we can speak privately?"

This meeting was inevitable. Murray waited until they had more to lose without protection. John's pride made it hard to consider paying the Sydney Ducks; however, he had learned in New York City that a man alone would not survive for long.

John led Murray to a table in the saloon's far corner, close to the window. John took the seat facing the entrance. Murray gave him a knowing smile and sat across. "The reports are that your business is prospering and that you and your Mr. Cunningham have things well in hand. It's good to see Irish money staying in Irish hands."

John leaned across the table, holding eye contact. "We work hard. Cunningham runs square games, so nobody can say we cheat here. We don't get russers; they take their big money to Parker House, Belle of the Union, or El Dorado. Only the pikers drink and gamble here. They enjoy a fun time, good whiskey, and clean games."

Murray put his hand up. "I know all that, John. We want to help you. I'm told that you have enemies here from the great city of New York. They will try to cause you harm." Murray looked around the small place, grinning. He stuck a cigar in his mouth and lit a match, watching it burn down before dropping it to the floor. With another match, he fired his cigar. "You have something to protect here. It would be tragic to see harm befall it."

John held his temper at the veiled threat. "It's all we got. We intend to keep it."

Murray looked out the window, enjoying his cigar. Then, after minutes of silence, he looked at John and said, "I've earned my place as leader of the Sydney Ducks. Not just because I'm the best fighter but because I'm a wise and fair leader. We protect the businesses that keep growing along these hills. It's the only protection there is. We survive on the fair tithings the businesses pay us. We want to offer our protection to Acushla."

It was what John had expected. "What's the cost?"

"Our customers are happy to pay fifty a month; however, we'll ask thirty from two young Irishmen who serve our kind well."

John stared out the window as Ewin waited.

"Before I agree," whispered John, turning to look Murray in the eyes, "I've one request. You've seen the Mexican women here, no doubt. We don't pay them. They live and work in a cheap hotel, where they're sometimes robbed and beaten. I'd like them to be part of my protection. It'll make us more successful."

Murray kept eye contact while he considered. When he offered his hand, he smiled and said, "We have a deal, Morrissey. One of the Ducks will visit you. He'll be your contact. If you need anything, let him know. We'll protect your Mexican girls at no added cost."

Dad Cunningham soon fell in with Maria Morales, one of Carmelita's cousins. They moved into a boarding house on Stockton Street. Most troubles for Carmelita and her extended family stopped when they came under the Sydney Ducks' protection.

It seemed inevitable that John and Carmelita would fall into bed together. Neither, however, formed an emotional bond, nor was the relationship exclusive. Carmelita was too damaged and distrusting for that. John knew better than to give any part of his heart to a prostitute, even one as stunning and enthusiastic as Carmelita. Lust was one thing. It was quickly satisfied and gone. Love put a hook in you and didn't let you go. He suspected he was in love with Suzie Smith. When he returned to New York, he hoped to court her if she'd have him.

Fourteen

∽

obbie Byrne and Christopher Doyle were content and enthusiastic bartenders. Though they'd lost their appetites for seafaring or mining life, they took great interest in the stories of the sailors and miners who frequented Acushla. Recent rumors of gold discovery on the Queen Charlotte Islands intrigued them enough to share with Morrissey. Doyle asked John if he would meet privately after work. He, of course, accepted.

Doyle looked around to be sure nobody would overhear. "John, me, and Robbie hear rumors. Most we ignore." Doyle looked at Byrne, who nodded. "Recently, we've heard reports of gold on the Queen Charlotte Islands. One British sailor, who'd traded there dozens of times, says he walked inland and found a clear stream littered with gold. He's planning to return with fighters to seize as much as possible before word spreads."

John never entertained mining for gold, but picking it out of a stream? He looked from Doyle to Byrne and asked, "Are you proposing to leave your job here?"

"No," answered Doyle, "we're not suggesting anything. We just wanted you to know."

John considered what he'd just heard. "Do you think it's true?"

"The British sailor sure is convincing," responded Byrne. "He showed us a sizeable hunk of gold he claims he plucked from a stream. He offered me and Doyle equal shares if we got a boat and fighters to join him."

John had his back to his bartenders. He asked, "How far to those islands?"

"Almost two thousand miles," Doyle said. "Four weeks to get there and the same to return."

John turned and studied Doyle and Byrne. "Let's talk with your sailor friend."

The sailor, Gustaf Andersson, met with John, Chris, and Robbie.

"I served on two British warships that patrol the coast of Canada," Andersson explained. "We made stops at villages on the islands. We traded for fresh water, fish, and fruit. Sometimes we traded for jewelry made with gold and gems. The native people call themselves "Haida." Britain claims the islands but has no interest in settling them, so there's little trouble with the natives."

Andersson reached into his coat and retrieved a large bracelet that was pure gold. "This is one of the gold pieces I bartered for. The natives put little value on gold, so I think it must be plentiful and easy to find. They use it everywhere, even in utensils."

John leaned across the table and said, "You saw gold in a stream?"

"I did. Me and mates went looking for native girls. You understand, right?"

John nodded.

"We approached a rocky stream running down the nearby hills toward the ocean. Removed our boots and rolled up our trousers. I was the last. Toward the middle, the water was deeper and clear. I could see an abundance of yellow stones. I reached down, pocketed bigger ones, and shut my mouth. When we made port at Fort Victoria, I headed ashore and signed onto the next ship coming here. I had the nuggets assayed right away. They're pure gold."

John had questions for Andersson. Satisfied that a small team of armed men could escape with enough gold to make it worthwhile, that Andersson would fight, and that he had told no one else, John began to set a plan in motion.

Dad tried to talk him out of the adventure. "Johnny, all's fine here. We have a great business, and money's growing in the bank. You'll be risking your life."

As usual, his concerns were ignored. Dad agreed to hire enough staff to help manage while John and the two bartenders were absent.

Byrne borrowed a rowboat and, with Andersson, searched the harbor. They needed an ocean-worthy craft that a small, experienced crew could manage. They spied a schooner with a mast fore and aft. She looked sturdy as they pulled alongside and examined her. Andersson climbed aboard and inspected everywhere. Returning to the rowboat, he reported, "She's fit for the voyage. We can manage her with ease." As they turned the rowboat toward the beach, Robbie Byrne read the faded name across the stern: *Lady Eileen.*

Four days later, with help from the ever-dependable Lewis Roby, Dad had the bartender positions filled and hired another roulette table manager. John had no trouble securing four rifles, four pistols, an ample ammunition supply, and four sabers. He bought fishing gear, a small stove for cooking and heating, two large casks to fill with fresh water, a ten-gallon barrel of rum, and a pile of wool blankets to use and trade for supplies. He sent Byrne to buy food for the first part of the trip. They would resupply at ports along the way. Andersson found a nautical map, a used sextant, and a chronometer. The weather in early spring was very cool, so John bought a wool sweater, cap, and an oilskin coat. But he had one more purchase to make.

The tiny crew agreed to meet at the foot of Broadway at eight a.m. Byrne, Doyle, and Andersson arrived on time. John was all grins as a wagon pulled up half an hour later. He jumped down and yelled, "Help me, boyos!"

John pulled a tarp aside, pointed to a swivel gun, and proclaimed, "A proper decoration for *Lady Eileen*, is she not?" He also brought two cumbersome cases full of grapeshot for the tiny but lethal weapon.

The men loaded an old rowboat and pulled it toward the schooner. They offloaded and stowed their gear and supplies, set the rowboat adrift, raised sail, and were on their way. Winds were favorable, and there was no fog on that bright morning.

Andersson, familiar with the waters along the northwest coast, served as navigator. He set a course west before turning due north. Eureka was two hundred nautical miles away. Under favorable sailing conditions, they arrived at the end of their second day, resupplied, and headed back to sea the next morning. The tiny crew reached Portland three days later. Andersson recommended buying enough supplies to get them to the Queen Charlotte Islands. He did not want the ever-curious British navy to stop them and ask for their papers. They had none.

Morrissey had neither experience nor interest in sailing. While Andersson, Doyle, and Byrne went about operating and maintaining Lady Eileen and preparing meals, John entertained himself using rifles to shoot at anything near the schooner. When he became bored with that, he loaded the small canon with grapeshot and fired at passing pods of whales.

"We should be saving our ammunition, John," Doyle finally counseled. He offered to teach John how to cut bait and fish for the delectable fish that loved the icy waters of the North Atlantic. John was hooking ocean perch, rockfish, and lingcod in no time. Doyle was an outstanding cook, so dinners now featured selections of the fish that Morrissey hauled in each day. *Lady Eileen* was quieter, and everyone worried less about what Morrissey would do next to amuse himself.

Andersson sailed the *Lady Eileen* well off the west coast of Vancouver Island, continuing north until they entered Hecate Strait. Once in the strait, British Canada's coast was on their starboard, often within ten miles and patrolled by the British navy. On occasions, Andersson *maneuvered* into inlets along the islands to evade a British warship.

Their destination was a native village and trade center the British called Skidegate. To the Haida, it was Kiis Gwaay, an ancient and sacred place. Haida ancestors had lived at Kiis Gwaay for over thirteen thousand years. It was near there that Andersson had gone ashore and pocketed the gold.

Andersson stood at the schooner's bow for days, staring through his looking glass. "There it is!" he bellowed when he spotted Skidegate at the entrance to a large bay. The crew lowered sails as they stared at the ancient city, with its majestic totem poles standing guard. Burned and still smoldering remnants of ships lay on the beach and in the shallows.

"What, in the name of God, happened here?" Andersson peered again through the looking glass. There was a rush of activity on the shore as dozens of natives climbed into longboats and pushed off. "Gentlemen, we should raise sail and make way."

"No!" shouted Morrissey. "We didn't come this far to get chased off by naked men with sticks!" He rushed to the bow and prepared their cannon to fire a warning. Meanwhile, Doyle and Byrne loaded the rifles and handguns. As the Haida warriors drew near, they waved their weapons and uttered warning cries. Andersson armed himself and joined Doyle and Byrne along the port rail, facing the approaching warriors.

The Haida did not attack. The longboats kept a distance, but the warriors raised their spears to intimidate. Morrissey thought, *two can play that game,* as he fired a warning from the canon. The rest of the crew lifted their rifles, issued loud oaths, and fired over the natives' heads. The longboats split, allowing one, with a tattooed elder, to advance. The battle cries desisted as their leader moved toward *Lady Eileen*. Two unarmed rowers brought him alongside.

"Lower the ladder," Morrissey instructed Andersson. Then, to

Byrne and Doyle, he whispered, "Stand by the sails. If I signal, we fly outta here."

The old warrior grabbed the rope ladder and climbed to the deck. Andersson offered a hand, but the proud man refused. One of the two rowers followed.

The well-built young warrior stood behind the elder and spoke. "This man is my father and our chief," he said, surprising with a perfect British accent. "The people are Haida. This has been our land beyond all memory. My name is Cumshewa. I have traded furs with the English and others for years. You should address me, but never my father. We give you one opportunity to leave in peace. Refuse, we shall set fire to your ship, and all will die." Cumshewa pointed to the remnants of the boats in the bay. "You can choose. White men are coming for gold. You bring fever and pox. We will not allow you to enter Kiis Gwaay. Leave now."

Morrissey had seen that, while Cumshewa spoke, warriors in their long canoes had fired their torches and encircled the schooner. He turned to Doyle and Byrne, shouting, now! He rushed Cumshewa, lifted him above his head, and threw him into the bay. The elder warrior moved quickly. Though strong, he was no match for Morrissey. He, too, was tossed overboard.

As Morrissey had expected, the chieftain was more critical than the schooner and her crew. All dozen canoes rushed to the aid of their leader and his son. *Lady Eileen*'s sails unfurled and caught wind as Andersson pointed her into the nearby strait. No one pursued.

Morrissey was irate. He rushed at Andersson as soon as their ship was in the strait. "A few fighters are what you said! Did you see the torched ships? Did you see the fortifications? They could turn back a small army."

Andersson backed away while Morrissey pulled a pistol from his waistband and pointed it at his navigator's chest. "Now, I'll give you a choice. Jump, or I shoot you."

Andersson was over the side as Morrissey fired into the air.

Byrne had taken the wheel while Doyle joined Morrissey along the rail. They watched the Swede swim toward shore.

"They'll kill him when he climbs ashore," Doyle said.

Morrissey watched Andersson struggle to shore, then turned to Doyle. "I wish they'd killed him the last time he set foot on their island. Can you or Robbie get us home?"

The dejected adventurers headed south. They dropped anchor twice and wandered ashore. Perhaps, they would discover their stream of gold nuggets. On both occasions, groups of hostile natives swarmed from the woods and drove them back to *Lady Eileen*. It was time to return to San Francisco.

Doyle and Byrne had little experience with a sextant or chronometer. They hugged the coastline of Haida Gwaii, studied Andersson's map, and dropped anchor in various hidden coves to evade British warships and to spend the night.

It was a long trip of more than three weeks back to San Francisco. Byrne and Doyle became more familiar and confident with the instruments and Andersson's map. Supplies of food, water, and rum were running out. They needed to resupply soon. Doyle suggested Fort Victoria, where he had resupplied with the British navy.

They sailed for six long days and nights before coming within sight of Vancouver Island. That night they celebrated. The thought of surviving and returning to San Francisco was reason enough to empty the last of the ten-gallon rum cask. John hooked a decent-sized lingcod. He gutted, deboned, and carved it into steaks he cooked on the grill. They had bananas, which he passed around along with plates loaded with fish. The three voyagers rested against the foresail mast with the wheel secured, handing the rum around as they ate.

Doyle, a natural storyteller, shared his imagined fate of Gustaf Andersson. "Well, Gustaf wanted to meet native girls, did he not? Can you picture them hiding in the woods with their big pot of boiling water nearby? They'd be licking their lips, surely." Doyle raised his eyebrows and opened his mouth in horror. "Andersson, our trusted navigator, thought he'd died and met his Maker when, suddenly, half a dozen bare-breasted maidens came bouncing out to greet him. Why," Doyle paused to effect, "imagine his smile when they giggled and surrounded the lucky Swede. Then, they quickly relieved him of his sodden clothes. There he stood, saluting the island princesses with his stiff shaft. Never was there a happier Swede."

John and Robbie roared with laughter.

"Well, the lovely maidens placed their tiny hands all over our man and lifted him. He didn't struggle. Not a bit. They carried him into the woods as they chanted a sweet melody. Imagine what our navigator thought when he spotted the enormous pot of boiling water and realized he was about to be served rather than serviced?"

All three laughed until tears fell and rib cages ached.

The men dropped anchor that night in shallow water outside of Victoria. John awoke to the sound of someone walking on deck. It was Doyle. He had stopped to gaze toward the harbor city. John stood next to him for quiet minutes, then broke the silence. "You've been there, Doyle. How do we get in and out of Fort Victoria?"

"First, as Andersson said, we have no papers. That can be a problem—nothing we can do about that. We need to avoid causing suspicion and get rid of the cannon, firearms, and ammunition. They'll detain us if they catch us with any of that."

"He's right, John," said Byrne, who had just walked up. "We need to look innocent, and we need a convincing story. They'll demand papers and want to know our business in Canada."

John nodded, walked to the bow, dismantled the small cannon, and tossed it into the Pacific. Doyle collected the rifles and ammunition and threw them overboard. They agreed they could justify three handguns as personal protection.

Lady Eileen was seven hundred and forty miles north of San Francisco. The men were eager to have this misadventure end. The quicker they could resupply, the happier they would be. A dinghy pulled alongside soon after sunrise. A weathered man with a thin graying beard shouted, "I'll take you to the city if you wish."

"How much?" John shouted back.

"Ah, Americans. That would be three US dollars each. Be smart about it. Others are waiting."

"Two of us." John looked at Doyle and nodded. Then, to Byrne, he said, "Mind our ship. We'll return with supplies and be on our way." John dropped the rope ladder over the port rail. He and Doyle climbed down, and the dinghy pulled away.

Doyle paid close attention to two nearby British frigates. The HMS *Plumper* and HMS *Termagant* were both anchored close in. The eight-gun frigates provided coastal surveillance. Under sail and steam power, they could sustain a speed of fourteen kilometers per hour. *Lady Eileen* could not hope to escape if either took an interest. It was urgent to resupply and leave the bay before either ship left the harbor.

Retail locations and open stands lined the principal streets of the city. All were bustling with activity. *Lady Eileen* might need food, water, rum supply, and coal for heat and cooking for two weeks. Everything bought would require hauling to the docks, where a tender or dinghy would return to the schooner. A young man with an adequate-sized wooden cart on King Street said, "Can I help?" He gestured to John and Doyle.

John waved the boy over. "We'll be buying supplies to carry to our schooner. How much to haul them to the docks?"

"One US dollar," said the boy with a smile.

"We shouldn't be long. Stay close."

The cart was soon overflowing with fruit, potatoes, onions, carrots, dried fish, a twenty-liter cask of rum, and a barrel of fresh water. The boy struggled to raise the handles to advance the cart. John smiled, nudged the boy aside, and steered the awkward cart toward the docks.

Doyle moved next to the boy. "Where should we go to rent a dinghy?"

The boy pointed left. "Near the end of the docks, I'll introduce you to my father. He's strong and fair. He likes Americans."

John steered in that direction. He asked the lad, "Are there Americans here?"

"Oh, yes, sir. They just keep coming."

"What brings them?"

"Gold. There's word of it north on the Queen Charlotte Islands. England claims the islands and the gold, so our navy tries to stop the theft but can't catch them all." The boy paused. In a whisper, he asked, "Are you going to find gold?"

"No, we're returning to San Francisco." John had been concocting a story to justify their travel in British waters. He tried it on the boy. "We just returned a dying friend to his family. He'd traveled to San Francisco two years ago to start a lumber mill but couldn't keep any workers. They all went lookin' for gold. Doyle here worked for him and watched him get sick and die. The man paid us well to carry his body home to his family."

"There's my father." The boy, bored with the story, pointed to a clean-shaven man with a ruddy complexion and thick jet-black hair. John pushed the cart toward the man and his dinghy.

Doyle approached the man and said, "I'm Christopher. That man pushing your cart is John. We have a schooner nearby. Would you carry us and our supplies to her?"

The man offered his hand. "Paul Nolan. Yes, it would be a pleasure. What currency will it be?"

"US dollars." Doyle looked at John, who carried the cash.

John nodded and asked, "How much?"

Nolan looked over the supplies. "Ten dollars."

"Five," said John.

Nolan smiled at John, then his son. "Eight, and we can load it and be on our way."

An hour later, all the supplies had made it to the schooner. John paid Nolan and bade him goodbye. Doyle told Byrne about the frigates tied up at the docks and that the British navy focused on ships running off with the queen's gold. He repeated John's story about the dying lumber-mill operator. They all liked it. The men decided they were at negligible risk since *Lady Eileen* had no gold to smuggle. They raised anchor and moved to a less conspicuous cove to spend the night.

The trio sailed due south with fresh supplies and accommodating weather until navigating southeast on a course to San Francisco. After stops at Portland and Eureka, the weary, disappointed adventurers entered San Francisco Bay.

Fifteen

When Morrissey stepped back into Acushla, Cunningham rushed to him and pulled him aside.

"While you were away, John, they had a championship fight up the river at Sacramento. George Thompson, Hyer's trainer, beat a local guy named Willis. So now, Thompson claims he's the California champion. Charlie Duane promoted the fight."

"Dutch Charlie Duane?" John was stunned.

"Yes, the same," Dad answered.

"It should be me!" John shouted, and everyone nearby fell silent and turned his way. "I've gotta see that son of a bitch, Duane."

"Calm down, Johnny. Let's get you settled back in." Dad turned to see Byrne and Doyle. "I suppose you adventurers will want your jobs back or have you returned rich men?"

Doyle said, "If you'll be having us, we'll need our jobs."

Dad looked at the ragged men and advised, "Rest a bit and see me in two days. I'll be needing you both at the bar for nights."

John strained to see Carmelita Fernandez in the gambling room.

Dad smiled. "She's there, Johnny. I've put her in charge of one roulette wheel. She brings good luck to Acushla. But, of course, she's still furious, so be careful, my friend."

John headed into the gambling hall.

Doyle and Byrne were weary, ready for baths, new clothes, proper food, and a soft bed. They would need rooms and cash, so they headed to their bank to withdraw from their dwindling savings. After the bank, they parted. They also needed time away from each other.

Carmelita remained furious during John's absence. She might well have moved her charms and those of her cousins to a competing business, but Dad did what he knew others would not. He offered the Mexican prostitutes hourly compensation.

When she saw John strut into the gambling hall, Carmelita ignored him, focusing her considerable charms on the dozen gamblers at the roulette wheel. Her lustrous, black hair fell to her waist. Her red jacket revealed her breasts whenever she swept up the losing bets and paid the winners. Her tight black skirt was slit to the top of her thigh, where her bone-handled knife was strapped.

Carmelita knew the effect she was having on her lover. Within thirty minutes of this foreplay, Cunningham delivered a replacement dealer to the table. Men moaned and objected, even as they handed generous tips to the erotic dealer.

John watched her approach. She came to him without a welcoming smile. "You stink like an animal," she sneered. "Get a bath and a shave. I'll be at your hotel in two hours." She hustled away. John stared as she walked across the room. So did every other man.

Morrissey's absence had changed the dynamics at Acushla. Cunningham took well to his role as general manager. Competent workers staffed the saloon and gambling hall. Ewan Murray had recommended fearsome Sydney Ducks, who now worked as bouncers. Business continued to grow, as did their bank account. John discovered there was little for him to do at Acushla. That suited him fine. He could think only of convincing Dutch Charlie that Thompson should fight him next.

Dutch Charlie Duane was a true forty-niner, the first of the Rynders crowd to rush to San Francisco. He had no intention of searching for gold. Soon after landing, he opened a saloon and became a leader, as Rynders had, of the rougher element of the nascent Democratic party. Duane was also a savvy and experienced fight promoter. When his friend, Tom Hyer, arrived in San Francisco, Duane expected to promote a fight for the championship. A Hyer fight would have attracted an extraordinary amount of interest and betting. He was outraged when Hyer headed back to New York City.

Duane turned to George Thompson, an experienced British fighter who had trained Hyer for his fight with Yankee Sullivan. Thompson was six foot two and two hundred lean pounds. In exhibition fights, he looked superior to both Hyer and Sullivan. Duane could play on rampant anti-British sentiment to promote the fight against a local "American." The fighters settled on a stake of a thousand a side; winner takes all. They would hold the illegal bare-knuckle fight at a Sacramento racetrack. Duane bragged he had reached an understanding with local authorities to avoid harassment.

The local fighter, Adrian Willis, was no match for the much larger, more experienced Thompson. When thousands of spectators arrived, most were eager to bet on the American, the self-proclaimed California champion. The fight lasted six minutes, and Thompson and Dutch Charley walked away with large winnings. Thompson used his to build a bowling alley.

Dutch Charlie was eager to follow up on Thompson's championship fight with another match. The anti-British sentiment created the emotional betting that always favored the house. As the promoter, he was the house. This time, he needed a quality opponent who could compete with Thompson. Yankee Sullivan was in the city, running a saloon. He, however, had seen enough of the big British fighter. In their last exhibition, Thompson had tossed the five-foot-seven, one-hundred fifty-pound bantam twenty feet outside the ring. Plus, Sullivan didn't like and never trusted Duane.

Duane was aware that Morrissey had visited his saloon. He had heard that the arrogant Irish youth had just returned, empty-handed, from a futile search for gold and was begging to fight Thompson. Duane knew that Morrissey was one tough kid but wondered why he should help that arrogant Irish bastard make a name?

Frustrated that Dutch Charlie kept avoiding him and worried he would lose the opportunity, John invited Ewan Murray to dine with him. He complained that the promoter would not meet with him. He deserved a chance to fight the new California champion. Murray stood with arms folded and a tolerant smile until John had exhausted his plea.

Still smiling, Murray shook his head. "I saw the fight at Sacramento, boyo. That Englishman is one big scrapper. He outweighs you by two or three stones and has a big reach advantage. So, what makes you think you can take his measure?"

"I've battled men of all sizes and never lost. I'll fight anyone and never stop until there's no life in me."

"What can I do, Johnny?" asked Murray.

"Convince Dutch Charlie to put me in the ring with his champ."

"If I can do that, John, assure me you'll win or die trying. We Irish lads will wager heavily to see an Irishman beat the English fighter."

"I promise!" John growled.

Murray smiled. "I'll see what I can do. Let's drink to this and enjoy a nice dinner."

Dutch Charlie Duane's saloon enjoyed Sydney Ducks' protection. Duane was a practical and flexible businessman for all his pride and aggressiveness. If it required a gang of Irish criminals to protect his investment, so be it.

When Murray arrived to ask Duane to sign Morrissey to a

fight with Thompson, he ran into little resistance. Duane was struggling to find a suitable match for Thompson. Murray believed Morrissey could prevail, or maybe he had another angle. Either way, Dutch Charlie knew he could earn a fortune taking bets while watching the arrogant Morrissey get humbled. Both fighters agreed to a winner-takes-all match. They posted one thousand dollars each. The fight would be on August 12, on Mare Island, ideally located in the Bay, at the mouth of the Sacramento River. It was a flat, sandy, three-mile-long strip of land next to the designated state capital of Vallejo. Mare Island promised to attract a large crowd.

Duane took on the role of fight promoter and as Thompson's trainer and stakes holder. His idea of "training" included sending him the best wines and liquors from his bar. Thompson needed little encouragement or support. He always took training seriously and was still in condition from his recent Willis fight.

As arrogant as ever, John did little to prepare for the battle. He did not stay away from Carmelita, although it was common to believe sex weakened a fighter. He had lost considerable weight during the two-month travel to Queen Charlotte Islands and back. No amount of food added weight. He approached the August date at one hundred and seventy pounds. Thompson was thirty pounds heavier and had inches of height on Morrissey.

On fight day, John woke early. He slid out of bed, trying not to rouse Carmelita. He dressed and was about to leave their room at the Union Hotel when she sat up and said, "Not without a kiss, *mi amor*." He went to her, bent, and met her lush lips. She tried to pull him back to bed.

"No. That won't do," John said, "I need my strength." He touched her face and left.

Ewan Murray, Dad Cunningham, Robbie Byrne, and Duck lieutenants were waiting in the Union Hotel's lobby when Morrissey came downstairs. The men were excited. Murray threw his arm around the twenty-one-year-old fighter as they headed out the front door. "We have two steamboats to carry your Irish supporters, John. We'll be coming from near and far to watch you beat the Englishman."

Outside, a crowd of men burst into cheer. A parade started toward the waterfront, collecting men along the way. Then, in a perfect tenor, someone began the familiar lines from "Ned of the Hill." It was the perfect song as John Morrissey set out to punish an Englishman.

Two steamers stood at the piers. Smoke rose from their stacks. As Murray led his fighter toward the SS *Carolina*, she and the SS *Franklin* blew their whistles. Crew members unfurled enormous banners to hang over the railing. They proclaimed, "Irish Only!" The crowd let out a lusty cheer. Morrissey and Cunningham led a group that included Murray and his Sydney Ducks lieutenants onto the ships. Chaos ensued as men rushed to grab a place on board one of the two reserved ships. Tickets cost ten dollars. None remained by August 10. On the morning of the fight, they fetched five times that amount. Murray had already made his first killing of the day.

Another steamboat waited to load. The SS *Bennington* would carry Duane, local press members, Thompson, his entourage, and supporters. Also, New York's pugilist community members were on the ship. Most were anti-immigrant, anti-Irish, and anti-Catholic. Though they despised the British, they hated the Irish more. Today, they would put their money behind Thompson. The *Bennington* left one hour after the *Carolina* and the *Franklin*.

As soon as the *Carolina* unloaded her passengers at Mare Island's single dock, she backed away and anchored at a distance. The *Franklin* followed. Other vessels, large and small, waited their turn to offload passengers arriving from various points along the local bays and rivers. Smaller boats dropped anchor, and their passengers jumped into the waist-deep water and waded ashore.

Morrissey, Cunningham, Byrne, Murray, and the Ducks lost no time finding a suitable place to wage the battle. Murray directed two of the Ducks to pace off a twenty-four-foot square. They drove eight stakes at the corners and midway along each side.

Ropes secured the stakes at two and four feet above the ground. They then created an outer ring to keep spectators ten feet away from the combatants. That finished, Morrissey joined Murray, loosened soil in the center of the ring, and set a rectangle of wood level with the surface, which would serve as the scratch line.

Noisy crowds continued to pour into the area. Most muscled in as close as they could. There was a slight elevation from which to see at a distance. Soon, the few trees nearby were full of men. Morrissey watched all of this, excitement coursing through him.

A roar arose from the dock area when the champion arrived. The crowd around the ring turned to watch the arrival of Thompson and his followers. Dutch Charlie, the referee, and the famous fighter, Yankee Sullivan, appeared. Sullivan would serve as Thompson's second. A buzz occurred when the crowd recognized Sullivan. Thompson was yet to appear.

Duane approached Murray for a conference. Sullivan walked around the ring as they spoke, inspecting the stakes and ropes and assessing the ground. As he passed close to Morrissey, he looked him up and down and smirked. With the delay, the crowd continued to await the champion, growing more unruly. Finally, Murray broke free of Duane and stood along the ropes on the dockside of the enclosure. He signaled for his armed lieutenants to approach.

"Men," he boomed, as his fierce gang members flanked him, "everyone on this side," he swept his arm from the stake to his right to the one on his left, shouting, "clear out."

A groan from the crowd.

"If you don't, this fight won't be happening."

Murray shouted over the rising complaints. "If you need help, we're happy to oblige."

The Sydney Ducks lieutenants entered the hesitant crowd with coats thrown open to reveal firearms. Within ten minutes, they'd cleared one side of the enclosure.

"There he is!" Everyone strained to see the champion. He approached with his California championship belt held aloft. The crowd behind him broke free and rushed ahead to secure a place as close to the battleground as possible. Morrissey had wrapped his colors, a green flag, around one corner and stood inside the ropes with his back to the oncoming champion. Cunningham and Byrne stood on the other side of the ropes.

"Today, your journey to the American championship begins, Johnny. It's your dream. You can't fail." Cunningham knew what this meant to his friend.

"I'm ready, Dad. Listen to the Irish lads. This is for them, for my parents, and Ireland."

Before Thompson stepped inside the ropes, one could hear men everywhere shouting bets. When the boats had left in the morning, the champion was a three-to-one favorite to beat the untested Morrissey. It was five to one that Thompson would draw first blood. The crowd saw the size difference when the recently crowned California champion entered the ropes. The odds against Morrissey jumped to five to one. Days before the fight, Morrissey gave Murray one thousand dollars. "Wait 'til they offer five to one." Murray, the stakeholder for the challenger, recorded his bet.

The referee for the fight was Nelson Bigler, the younger brother of California Governor John Bigler. The younger Bigler guaranteed Dutch Charlie that authorities would not interrupt a fight on Mare Island. Bigler was well-compensated to serve as the referee. Murray and Duane selected four umpires. They assumed positions, two on one side, two on the other, within the ten feet of mandatory space between the ropes and the crowd. The referee could confer with them to decide if a foul had occurred. They could also watch the crowd to ensure they did not interfere. In all cases, Bigler's decisions would be final.

Bigler stood only five foot six and was slight of build. When he called the time, both fighters stripped off their shirts and approached scratch. The contrast between the tall and muscular men and the referee set the crowd buzzing. Both fighters looked fit and confident as they faced each other for the first time. Yankee Sullivan, Thompson's second, stood beside him. At five foot seven and one hundred fifty pounds, Sullivan looked like a child next to the six-foot-two, two-hundred-pound Englishman. Betting became frenzied. The more the odds favored Thompson, the more the hostile Irish rushed to back their fighter.

Morrissey was an outstanding street and barroom brawler. He had fought more times than he could remember. He was about to face a seasoned professional prizefighter for the first time. Aleck Hamilton had seen his weaknesses years earlier, but Morrissey had refused to take either counsel or instructions. As a result, he was about to discover how ill-prepared he was to fight at the highest level.

The referee called the fighters and their seconds to scratch. He read the London Prizefighting Rules. He warned them against fouls and promised he would end a fight if one of the fighters ignored his orders. After receiving the referee's instructions, the seconds returned to their corners.

"Get inside fast and punish him, Johnny," Cunningham shouted. He worried about Thompson's reach advantage. Morrissey shifted from foot to foot, glaring at his hated English opponent.

As soon as Bigler signaled the start of the first round, Morrissey rushed Thompson and threw a powerful right toward his head. The experienced champion easily stepped aside, forcing Morrissey to miss. Then, as Morrissey turned to press his attack, he received a volley of rapid punches to his upper body and head. Before ten seconds had passed, the champion had split Morrissey's upper lip. The crowd screamed, "First blood!"

Morrissey's clumsy efforts to counter the Englishman's punches fell on the larger man's arms. Thompson wrapped Morrissey in a powerful hug, threw him to the ground, and landed on him. Thompson's supporters went wild with excitement. Irish supporters were stunned into silence.

Seconds and bottle holders rushed to help their fighters to their corners. There were thirty seconds between rounds for the corner to deal with them. Each fighter had eight seconds to meet within a yard of the scratch line. John's left eye was already swelling. Blood flowed from cuts around his mouth. Cunningham pressed a wet sponge against Morrissey's left eye, then washed the blood from around his mouth and chin. Morrissey rested on Byrne's knee and took a long pull on the water bottle.

"Johnny, he's a big fellow, gotta get inside and stay there. Hurt his body, then chop him down." Cunningham had seen his friend in enough battles to know that he often fell behind but never quit. "Deep breaths, my friend. For Ireland!"

Rounds two through four proceeded very much like the first round. Morrissey tried to rush inside. He knew Cunningham was right. Thompson, however, hit him at will from a distance while moving swiftly from side to side. Whenever he got into Thompson's chest and landed one or two solid blows to the body, the champion wrapped him up and wrestled him to the ground.

Morrissey's face was already a horrifying mass of cuts and welts. Between rounds, Cunningham did what he could to wipe away the blood, sweat, and dirt. Byrne held the water bottle to Morrissey's lips, then emptied the rest over his head. Both hoped for a quick end.

At the start of the fifth round, Morrissey saw Thompson pause on his way to scratch to take a deep breath. *He's blowing*, thought the battered challenger. Morrissey smiled a hideous smile through his damaged mouth and rushed anew. This time, he caught Thompson around the waist, carried him against the ropes, got a leg behind the champion, and threw him to the ground. When he landed on the stunned Thompson, Morrissey placed his mouth to the champion's ear and said, "You're mine now, ya British bastard."

The Irish crowd sprung to life. They urged their fighter to "kill the Englishman!" Across the enclosure, Thompson's backers, including nativists, southern gamblers, and a smattering of Englishmen and other foreigners, sent insults and threats across to the Irish.

The Southerners had their favorite insult for the Irish. They shouted to Thompson, "Kill that inside-out nigger." Fights erupted along the edges of the crowd. The situation inside the ropes and outside bristled with bloodlust. Morrissey stood in his corner, refusing to sit, a ghastly sight covered in blood and dirt. He brushed aside Cunningham and Byrne, wanting to finish this. The big Englishman stood in his way of everything he had dreamed of and worked to accomplish.

Thompson was wary, realizing this was no easy payday as it had been with Willis. Morrissey was unpolished, for sure, but he was dangerous. Dutch Charlie and Sullivan kept screaming, "Keep away. Make him chase you. He's almost done." Thompson used his legs and long arms from rounds six through eight to avoid Morrissey's enraged charges. He punished the challenger with powerful jabs and occasional hooks, targeting the body to save his hands from damage. When Morrissey got inside, the champion slid from his grasp to take a knee on the ground. He hoped Morrissey would strike him while he was down. A foul would end the travesty, but Morrissey held back.

Morrissey landed a dozen heavy blows to Thompson's ribs early in the ninth round. Both heard something crack. Thompson took a reassuring breath and hit Morrissey with a return volley of heavy blows. He didn't see a wild right hook from Morrissey that caught him behind the left ear. All was black for a moment, and the champion held on. Morrissey managed to half carry, half push Thompson into the ropes, where he dropped to the dirt to end the round.

Thompson had hit his opponent so hard, so many times that he thought he should have killed him. Yet this Morrissey was smiling from twenty-four feet away, eager to continue. And the Irish crowd; their hostility was terrifying. The champion wanted to finish this and return to his new bowling alley. *How* he wondered, *do I end this thing?*

The fighters advanced at the start of round ten. Thompson's left hand continued to wreck Morrissey's face, but his punches lacked the power of earlier rounds. Morrissey could barely see with the swelling and blood flowing into his eyes. Thompson saw an opportunity and let loose with a powerful right cross. Morrissey sensed more than saw it. He ducked as the fist whistled past and dug a right uppercut into Thompson's ribs, lifting him off his feet. The champion leaned on Morrissey and held. They crumbled to the ground to end the round. Both fighters struggled to their feet and needed support to make it to their corners.

The uproar from supporters of both fighters was deafening. As Thompson rested on Sullivan's knee, he paid no attention to the veteran fighter or Dutch Charlie. Instead, he saw the crowd surging closer. He knew Morrissey's supporters far outnumbered his. The umpires were struggling to keep the crowd the required ten feet away. A dozen or more Irish supporters brandished handguns when he looked in their direction. Thompson thought, *If I win, that bloody mob will kill me.*

The fighters came to scratch to start round eleven. While Thompson was unmarked, Morrissey was unrecognizable. Bigler signaled the start of the round. Once again, Morrissey lowered his head and charged. Thompson slid to his left in Morrissey's corner, shifted his weight to his right leg, and threw an uppercut that landed well below Morrissey's waist.

"Foul!" shouted Cunningham. Bigler was out of position and unsure. He looked at the umpires for help. They shrugged as Morrissey bent over in anguish. Instead of attacking, Thompson backpedaled. His corner was irate. Sullivan leaned over the rope and screamed for his fighter to "finish him!"

Morrissey recovered enough to continue. Thompson waited, hands raised and ready at the center of the ring. Morrissey tried to tackle the bigger man. Thompson appeared to slip and fall, seizing Morrissey's trousers around the thighs. This time Bigler had a perfect view. "Foul," he called. "Fight over. Morrissey, the winner."

Cunningham and Byrne rushed to Morrissey, helping him to his feet. Murray, with one of his lieutenants, ran to Thompson's corner, stripped his colors from the corner stake, and carried them to the new champion. Morrissey's crew lifted him to their shoulders. More than two thousand Irishmen were delirious with joy. To them, it was more than a victory for John Morrissey. It was a victory for their beloved Ireland.

Word spread in San Francisco that John Morrissey had won the championship. Celebrations started in the city. Few, even among the Irish, expected him to win. In the resulting uproar, an enormous crowd gathered around Acushla. There they sang and danced while waiting for their California champion to arrive.

Ewan Murray had had the foresight to pay a doctor to sail on the *Carolina*. Doctor Meriwether Long refused to attend a brutal fight. He waited in a stateroom, reading, relaxing, and enjoying more than a few brandies. He expected to see a variety of cuts and bruises, even fractures. Instead, the appearance shocked him.

"Get an abundance of towels and a large basin of clean water. Hurry!" Doctor Long helped Murray settle Morrissey on the large bed. The doctor poured six ounces of brandy into a glass and helped the victorious fighter to drink. He took his time cleaning the minor wounds on his face. Then, satisfied that the brandy had taken effect, he threaded his surgical needle with suturing hemp and closed the cut over John's left eye. The cuts on John's mouth and elsewhere would heal independently, as would the welts and bruises on his upper body.

When the SS *Carolina* tied up at San Francisco, John had slept for over two hours, unaware of the uproar on the ship. When he awoke, he was aching but alert and eager to arrive at Acushla. Cunningham had brought a fresh outfit for his friend. It included a felt, cream-colored hat. The soft, loose sides helped hide John's face when he swaggered down the ship's ramp, waving to the cheering crowd. Murray raced ahead and stood at a carriage to carry John, Byrne, and Dad to Acushla.

Acushla has already enjoyed considerable success. Now, it was the must-visit headquarters of a true Irish hero, the California prizefighting champion. In the days after the fight, crowds gathered and waited for hours for a chance to see John Morrissey and shake his hand. On most nights, John joined a packed poker table, where he won more often than lost.

No one was more delighted by John's victory than Carmelita. The notoriety of the girlfriend of the champion soared. Carmelita could now demand a price for her time and attention only the most popular Anglo prostitutes enjoyed.

The Thompson camp protested. Their man had been far ahead, they accurately claimed. They believed he would have kept the title if Irish criminals had not threatened his life. Dutch Charlie, at first, refused to award the two-thousand-dollar stake money and championship belt, relenting only after a visit from Murray. Both men were interested in pitting the new champion in a rematch against Thompson. John said he'd fight Thompson for ten thousand dollars. "We'll get a schooner and sail to any part of the world, and I'll whip him when we land," he pledged. Thompson, however, was done with prizefighting. He settled into his life as a bowling-alley owner and remained there.

As fate would have it, three young sailors walked in asking for "John Morrissey."

He was near the bar when he heard his name. "I'm Morrissey."

One of the sailors was all smiles as he approached. He thrust out a hand. "Smith. Levi, Jr. You worked for my father on the *Empire*."

John looked at the handsome young man with dismay. It seemed impossible for Susannah's older brother to be standing before him. He extended his hand and shook Smith's vigorously. "Welcome to Acushla. Let me buy you and your friends a drink. You can tell me how you found me and how things at Troy are holding up."

Smith had arrived within the last week and signed on as an officer on the SS *Georgiana*, a small side-wheeler that made runs along the Sacramento River. He was about to set off the following day on his first trip, but first, he wanted to find the famous John Morrissey, his father's "favorite deckhand." John bought lunch and drinks for Levi, Jr., and his crewmates. John and Levi, Jr. laughed when they discussed characters they knew from Troy. They talked about the cholera epidemic that was hitting the East Coast hard.

The Smith family, according to Levi, Jr., had been spared. John wondered about his own family, but Levi, Jr. would have no way to know.

"I met your sister on the *Empire*. She was about to go off to school the last time I saw her. How's she fared?" John felt his face turn red.

"Oh, she'll complete her studies in a year. She hates boarding and always lets our parents know about it when she's home. Our mother hopes for a placement as a teacher. Suzie wants no part of it. That girl is the most stubborn person in our family, which says a lot!"

Levi, Jr., and his shipmates finished their third round of drinks, shook John's hand, and left. A rare sense of loneliness fell over John. There was so much about Levi, Jr. that reminded him of Susannah. So much time had passed since he had last seen her. He wondered; *does she still think of me? Will I ever see her again?*

With two thousand dollars from the fight and another five thousand from his side bet, John was a wealthy twenty-one-year-old ready to return to New York.

Sixteen

၄ၜၜ

Morrissey made inquiries about departures to Panama. He was interested in traveling with Captain Wickham, who planned to leave San Francisco on the SS *Panama* on October 2. This time he booked staterooms for himself and Dad Cunningham.

Dad made more money at Acushla than he had ever dreamed of and enjoyed being his own boss; however, he had a three-year-old child in Cohoes whom he had never met and could now well support. Dad began attending mass at the Cathedral of St. Mary soon after arriving in San Francisco. He resolved to address his past transgressions and accept his responsibilities as a son and father.

John did not share his departure plans with Carmelita. His passion for the erotic young woman had cooled with his plans to return to New York and the hope of renewing his relationship with Susannah Smith; however, the Mexican beauty was not about to surrender her status as the champion's favorite girl.

For Ewan Murray and the Sydney Ducks, the recent championship bout was cause for sustained celebration. National pride played a considerable role, but Murray and his Ducks understood their intimidation contributed to Thompson's defeat.

Despite efforts to set up a citizens' policing force in San Francisco, the Ducks in 1852 were the de facto law enforcement. The price for protection was inflating.

Murray made a point of escorting John around the city's most popular eating, drinking, and gambling establishments. The massive Irish gang leader enjoyed notoriety everywhere in the city. Now the curious got a glimpse of the new champion. Morrissey, short of six feet, and lean muscled, looked like an adolescent next to his patron. Murray had found yet another way to reaffirm his dominance in the city.

By early September, talk of the fight had faded as people learned of a proposed horse race between thoroughbreds Alameda and Carmencita. The wealthy Treat brothers from Oakland, George and John, owned Alameda. Juan Sepulveda, a wealthy rancher and political leader in Los Angeles, owned Carmencita. The ten-mile contest was scheduled near Santa Barbara, three hundred miles south of San Francisco. The owners wagered fifty thousand dollars each, an enormous sum, even by the standards of gold rush-crazed California. This race was about reputation and pride.

Dad Cunningham had learned a bit of Spanish from his lover, Maria Morales. She learned a bit of English from him. Sometimes, with comical efforts and results, they shared gossip from her close-knit Mexican community. Maria bragged about the prowess of the great Carmencita. The five-year-old mare, she shared, was never defeated in races against the best thoroughbreds in Mexico. Carmencita was *"famosa,"* according to Maria. The Californians, she whispered, are *"ignorante."* She promised they would lose "muy dinero" if they bet on Alameda.

Ewan Murray was managing local bets on the upcoming race. Most of the action was on Alameda to beat Carmencita. Still, two days before the race, John found Murray and presented him with one thousand dollars of his money and an equal amount from Dad to place on Carmencita to win. The San Francisco odds were three to one against Carmencita.

Murray looked at Morrissey, cocking his colossal head. "You worked hard to earn that money, boyo. Are you sure you wanna' bet on the Mexican mare?"

"We are. It'll be Carmencita." John handed over two thousand dollars. Neither John nor Dad would leave Acushla for the lengthy trip to Santa Barbara.

News of the great race arrived at San Francisco via the SS *Oregon*, making the nonstop trip from Santa Barbara to San Francisco in twenty hours carrying over six hundred gamblers.

The *San Francisco Daily Herald* had sent a reporter and artist to cover the race. It printed a special edition, including a woodcut illustrating the action the day the SS *Oregon* arrived. The Treat brothers' horse, Alameda, began the ten-mile race with a significant lead that increased through the first six miles. Carmencita's jockey glanced toward Juan Sepulveda at the six-mile mark and saw him raise his right arm. The jockey unwrapped the reins around his wrists, touched the spurs to Carmencita's glossy black flanks, and settled into his saddle. The distance separating the horses decreased. Alameda's jockey spurred his horse on with all he had, but it was hopeless. The last four miles were not a contest.

"You're lucky Irishmen, indeed." Ewan Murray smiled as he counted three thousand dollars for John and Dad.

"No luck needed, Ewan. My friend here prayed, and an angel spoke to him." John shook Murray's massive hand. "I owe you much. I'll not forget your kindness."

When Dad returned to Maria Morales that night, he carried a copy of the *Daily Herald* and read the race's entire report. When he finished, he handed Maria one thousand dollars and kissed her. "*Muchisimas gracias, amiga,*" he said as she grasped the money to her chest and cried.

Leaving Acushla was difficult for the men. It was their first business. With the help of Lewis Roby, they made it a success. They wanted to leave Acushla in capable hands. They requested a meeting with Roby and presented a suggestion.

"We'll be leaving California on October second," John said. "We owe you gratitude and more."

"You owe me nothing, young men. We made a fair deal, and I recovered my investment. I am saddened that you gentlemen are leaving."

"We have something to propose, sir." Dad leaned across the table. "We have two employees, Robert Byrne, and Christopher Doyle. They tend bar for Acushla. Former sailors and prospectors. Good, smart men. We'll leave Acushla in their hands if you continue as a silent partner."

"That's very generous of you." Roby turned to the young men. "That business is now worth thousands. Can they raise any money to pay you?"

Dad glanced at John, then Roby. "We've got enough in our bank account to set up the new owners and split what's left. We arrived without money. We'll get home with a wee fortune. Make any agreement you wish with Byrne and Doyle."

Roby offered terms that surprised and delighted Byrne and Doyle. They would pay Mr. Roby 10 percent of revenues, and he would serve as an advisor and source of employees.

Ewan Murray agreed to supply continued protection for Acushla but asked for seven percent of the revenue. "Without you there, Morrissey," he explained, "revenues will decline."

John asked Murray to meet with Carmelita Fernandez to discuss ongoing protection for her and her growing number of Mexican cousins.

Carmelita showed little emotion when John shared his plans for the forthcoming departure. She had items in his hotel suite. She gathered those and turned, smiling, to John. "My heart was dead to you when you ran away looking for gold. Don't worry about Carmelita. I am now the best girlfriend of the great Tom Maguire, more rich and powerful than John Morrissey." She strode toward the door as John watched. She never looked back.

Two days before John's scheduled departure, Levi Smith, Jr. visited Acushla and asked John to carry a communication to his family. John was, of course, delighted to accommodate. When Smith returned that evening with a sealed letter, John packed it away in his travel trunk. It could be the perfect way to reconnect with Suzie.

John and Dad were able to travel in comfort for their return trip to New York. Except for a night in an Acapulco jail for joining a fight between passengers heading south and Mexican gold seekers heading north, the trip was without incident. Dad read to pass the time. John socialized with the crew and found a group of travelers with an appetite for poker games. With the last hand, John was richer by six hundred and thirty dollars.

On November 17, 1852, the SS *Empire City* passed Castle Garden and entered Pier Two. Morrissey and Cunningham stood on deck. Clouds hung low over the city. The afternoon temperatures were seasonal at forty-four degrees, but it felt frigid after California's far more salubrious climate. They immediately booked a night steamer to Troy.

John and Dad shared a stateroom on the *Isaac Newton* the night they returned from California. They slept little and spoke less. Both had much on their minds. When the ship docked at Troy, they disembarked, retrieved their travel trunks, and shook hands. They promised to reconnect "soon" at the Gem Saloon in New York City.

Dad continued the short distance to the train station, where he took the next train to Cohoes. John hired a carriage. "Five-Eighty-Three River Street," he told the driver. "I'll pay you to wait. I won't be long."

The carriage pulled up in front of an attractive two-story residence. "This is Five-Eighty-Three. I'll wait right here, young man."

John reached inside his coat and touched the envelope from Levi Smith, Jr. He stepped from the carriage, made his way to the Smith's front door, and knocked. A young girl pulled back a lace curtain in the bay window and waved enthusiastically. He was waving back when the door opened.

A tall boy, a younger version of Levi Smith, Jr., smiled. "Can I help you?"

"I just returned from California. Got a letter from Levi for Captain and Mrs. Smith."

"I'm David. Come in, sir."

"Morrissey. John. I was a deckhand on the Empire."

The young man smiled and offered his hand.

"Father has spoken of you, Mr. Morrissey. He's not here, but I'll let Mother know you have a message from Levi." David left John standing inside the door while he raced upstairs.

The young girl from the bay window walked out of the living room. She looked to be seven or eight years of age. She stared at Morrissey, bouncing from one foot to the other.

"Are you here to see my sister, Suzie?"

John blushed.

"Addie!" came a voice from the top of the stairs, "please do not annoy our visitor."

John watched as Mrs. Smith came down the stairs, with David following. Addie continued staring at John before dashing away when her mother reached the vestibule.

"It is good of you to come, Mr. Morrissey. I'm Aldine Smith." She approached with a warm smile. "Please come in," she pointed to the living room, "Can I offer tea?"

"I'd like that," John answered.

"Wonderful, I'll prepare it and be right back. I'm so excited to hear about Levi. Please, have a seat, but don't make California sound too exotic for our David."

"When did you return?" David leaned forward on the chair across from John.

"Yesterday afternoon. Me and a friend took a night steamer here. Your brother asked me to deliver this."

Morrissey held the sealed envelope for David to see.

"Is it true you're the California champion? Father showed me a newspaper report that said so. He said you were his fighting

154

deckhand until you left for California. He'll be surprised you were here in our house."

Mrs. Smith walked in with a tray and tea.

"Here, Mrs. Smith." John presented the sealed envelope with two hands as she placed the tray on a small table. "I came straight away to deliver this."

"He arrived in New York yesterday and took the night boat." David was excited to be near a famous fighter, especially one from Troy.

Mrs. Smith held the sealed envelope to her bosom. A single tear appeared. She tented her hands in front of her mouth and said, "Thank you, Mr. Morrissey. Will you be in town for a while? I'm certain it will delight my husband to see you and thank you."

"I'll be here for a day or two, Mrs. Smith. My family's here. Haven't seen them for two years."

"Well, I'm sure you're anxious for that reunion, Mr. Morrissey. My son entrusted this correspondence to a kind man. Would it be possible for you to join us for dinner tonight? I understand that you have a family to visit. If tonight's not possible, two nights hence?"

John took a sip of tea while he considered the possibility. Of all the scenarios he'd conjured during his return to New York, the possibility of an immediate dinner with the Smith family was not one. He'd begun to sweat. After another sip of tea, he responded, "It'd be a pleasure to join you tonight, Mrs. Smith."

"Seven o'clock, then," she said, "Captain Smith will be very pleased."

Aldine and David saw John out. Young Addie was again at the bay window, waving and smiling.

John climbed into the carriage. "Eastern Hotel," he told the driver. John ignored the saloon door and entered via the adjacent hotel door. He left his trunk with the registration clerk and went ahead to Hamilton's second-floor office.

"Well, if it isn't the California champion himself?" Hamilton sat at his desk, the ever-present cigar dangling from his lips. He pushed his chair back, placed the cigar in an ashtray, and rushed around the desk to hug John.

"Have a drink. You can tell me about the great fight. It's all anyone wants to talk about since the news reached us."

John noticed that his old boss had lost a great deal of hair and what remained was mostly grey. He realized he'd missed this man, "I'll tell you all the details, Aleck, but first, I gotta find my family. Does my father visit? Do you know how I can get to him?"

Hamilton sat back down, opened a desk drawer, and searched before pulling out a scrap of paper. "Tim thought you might ask for your family if you contacted me. He left an address. It's One-Thirteen Canal. That's between First and Second." Hamilton stood and handed the paper across the desk. "Will you be staying with us for a while, Johnny? We have a room if you'd like."

"I'd like to stay, Aleck, but only one or two nights. I'll visit my family, then get to New York. Hyer's there. I chased him out west, but he left before I arrived. He'll look like a coward if he refuses to fight the champion of California."

Aleck Hamilton recognized an opportunity when it stood in front of him.

"While you're here, can we schedule an exhibition? I could line up decent fighters. It would give the locals a chance to see their hero. We could make easy money."

"Maybe," was all Morrissey said.

John unlocked his room on the fourth floor and looked at the tawdry room through fresh eyes. He had stayed at a luxurious suite at the Union Hotel in San Francisco, then on staterooms on the steamers arriving and returning from San Francisco and Chagres. This tiny, dark room with battered furnishings reminded him of the deprivation of his former life. *I'll never return to that condition*, he promised himself.

John opened his travel trunk and removed a fresh change of clothes and his toiletries. After washing, shaving, and attending to his unruly hair, he put on clean clothes, returned to the trunk, and removed two heavy cigar boxes. After locking his trunk, he put on his coat and hat, took the cigar boxes, and exited and locked his room.

It was a short walk from the Eastern to Canal Avenue. John kept a brisk pace on First Street, clutching the cigar boxes inside his wool coat. Once he crossed the Poesten Kill, he turned left on Canal. One-Thirteen was a two-story residence. On either side were empty lots with charred remains of foundations. Somehow One-Thirteen had survived the ravages of neighborhood fires, but not those of time and neglect. The stairs leading to a covered entryway were rotting, and the railings were long gone. The door on the left entered the first-floor apartment. The door on the right led upstairs to the second floor. As John tried to decide which might lead to his family, the door on the right flew open, and two young women came charging out.

"Hello," giggled the older of the two. "Sorry, we almost ran you over. Late for school!"

"Are you Morrissey girls?" He looked at them, trying to remember their faces.

"I'm Mary Anne," said the older of the two, "and this is Hannah."

"I'm your brother, John."

They exchanged looks of confusion.

"You were in California? Is that true?" Mary Anne looked up at John. Hannah pulled on her coat sleeve.

"We have to be off to school," announced Mary Anne. Will we see you later?"

"I hope so," John said to their backs as they jumped off the porch and flew up the street.

Reaching the top of the stairs, John knocked three times. He was about to give up when a voice inside asked who was calling.

"It's me, Johnny."

There was no reply. John was about to knock again when the door opened. Judith Morrissey took awkward steps back into the apartment, staring. "Come," she ordered, turning her back on her son and walking toward the rear of the apartment.

John's mother was much thinner than he remembered and stooped.

"Would you be joining me?" she asked, "I'm having tea, and it's getting cold."

Everywhere the apartment was filthy and in disarray. The kitchen was the worst. Judith pointed John to a chair. He sat and placed the cigar boxes on the table.

"Your da won't be home for some time, if at all."

"Ma, I saw Mary Anne and Hannah while they were heading off to school. Are my other sisters about?"

"At school, except for Mary and Bridget. They're grown and gone, you should know."

Judith placed the cup of tea in front of John, spilling a bit. She retreated across the table and slumped into her chair to sip tea.

"I've thought of you and Da and my sisters every day; I have."

No response.

Judith set down her tea. Her jaw clenched, and her bloodshot eyes narrowed.

"You're no better than your da. We needed you here. Look at you in those fancy clothes. I hear men talk about my famous son, the fighter. All the time you're away, not a word. I imagine you dead. Your sisters ask, 'Where's our brother?' What can I tell them?"

John had no excuses. His mother's anger and disappointment were just. As she spoke, he noticed the streaks of gray in her thinning hair, her fingers disfigured by decades of hard use, the deep creases in her forehead and lining her eyes. Though not forty-seven, Judith Morrissey was now old in the body and spirit, worn out by her labors, disappointment, and chronic alcohol and opium abuse.

John pushed the two sealed cigar boxes toward his mother.

"I had luck in California, Ma. I'll be able to help more now."

Judith stared out the window. John stood, grabbed his coat and hat, and glanced at his mother.

"Please tell Da I'm at the Eastern. I'd like to see my sisters too."

The walk back to the Eastern was under heavy clouds and the threat of a storm. His mood, a blend of sadness and irritation, matched the weather. He tried to picture his mother prying open the boxes of gold dollars. He knew it was more money than she had ever seen or imagined having. She might, he hoped, realize what this gift could mean for her family—a safer, larger place to live, enough food and fuel to comfort them through the winter, and new clothes for the girls. *Was she thanking God?* He wondered. *Would she ever forgive him?* He doubted that. *I must do more for them.*

John Morrissey had barely noted the passage of streets when he arrived at the Eastern and started up the saloon's familiar steps. His reverie ended as soon as he opened the door. An excited crowd pressed inside, straining to see the local hero. Hamilton stood on the bar and shouted, "Three cheers for our California champion: hip, hip, hurrah!" The fans joined in, hoisting free beer from the proprietor.

John spotted Marcel Archambeault's head above the rest, shoving his way toward him. Nathan Parker was one of the first to throw an arm around his old friend while his two young sons stood by anxiously to meet Morrissey. Downtown Gang friends were there. Veronica, decked out in her best red wig, smiled from a distance. At least four of her girls mixed with the celebrants. John got caught up in the excitement.

Someone started playing dance tunes on the battered old piano, and Veronica and her girls spun from partner to partner. John, no dancer himself, joined in with Veronica. "I'm still angry, Johnny." She spoke so anyone near could hear, feigning a severe frown. "But I'm proud of you." She planted a bright red kiss on his cheek. The crowd roared its approval.

Everyone wanted a chance to shake the hand of the California champion. John tried to accommodate young and old. Soon, Hamilton pushed through with a drink in hand, raised it, and shouted, "Brandy for our hero!"

159

He offered the glass to the young fighter. With a start, John remembered his seven o'clock engagement. He knew that Hamilton always carried his prized pocket watch.

"What's the time?"

Still holding the brandy, Hamilton checked the timepiece. "Ten minutes before six. Is there a problem?"

John did a quick calculation. If he left at once, he could rush to his room, dress for dinner at the Smith's, and hire a carriage to take him there. He turned to Hamilton and whispered, "I gotta leave. I've dinner and can't be late. Can you get me a carriage?"

"Of course, Johnny. Say something, then go. I'll buy another round. They won't even miss you."

John elbowed his way to the bar and sprung up.

"Thank you. Well, I'm no good at talking, but I wanna say I'm proud to be of Troy. Mr. Hamilton gave me a good beginning here, and now, I'm champion of California because of him."

The crowd roared a loud cheer for their host.

"I promise," Morrissey shouted, "I'll come back soon as the champion of America."

Another burst of cheers.

"I must go. A beautiful young lady awaits."

Cheers and hoots arose from the crowd as John jumped down.

Hamilton shouted, "Another round for everyone."

In his room, John removed his collar and shirt and washed his face and upper body. He laughed as he scrubbed the big red smear of Veronica's lipstick from his cheek. He powdered under his arms with baking soda, a trick his father had shared with him years earlier. John hurried to dress and headed downstairs where a carriage was waiting.

It was dark on River Street as the carriage pulled in front of the Smith family home. John stepped down, paid the driver, and stared for a moment at the welcoming glow from the house. Then, as the carriage pulled away, he realized the day had been too busy to worry about dinner. The thought of making small talk with Susannah's family was frightening. His limited education was an embarrassment, and while he was proud of his Irish heritage, he knew others held all Irish and Catholics, particularly, in disdain.

Forcing himself to approach the home, he recalled how decent the captain had always been and how friendly Mrs. Smith and David were earlier that day. But, most assuring, he had not forgotten Susannah's words the last night he had seen her, moments before a lingering kiss he could still feel. *You think yourself not good enough. You are wrong. It is no sin to be poor, to be Irish, or even to be Catholic.* He took a deep breath.

John knocked on the door and waited. David answered. From inside, he heard a voice admonishing politeness as Addie peeked around the corner.

"Hello, Mr. Morrissey, can I take your coat and hat?" David's smile was as broad as at the morning introduction. "The captain is in the living room. He'd be pleased if you'd joined him."

John removed his coat and handed it and his top hat to David.

Captain Smith didn't stand as his former deckhand entered the room. He did, however, smile and gesture toward a nearby chair. "It's good to see you, Morrissey. You look surprisingly well if I might say. I read about your triumph in California. I read you suffered injuries in the battle.

John responded., "Thompson's a good fighter. He grew tired of thumping me and fouled me. The referee gave me the belt."

"From what I read, Mr. Morrissey, you were gaining a significant advantage and would have prevailed if Thompson had continued. We are all proud of you here at Troy and on the Empire. No less so in New York City, from what I read and hear."

"Thank you, Captain, for having me to dinner."

"No need to thank us, young man. We are indebted to you for delivering an overdue correspondence from our son. It brings us joy to know he's well."

Before John could reply, Mrs. Smith appeared at the door, smiling.

"Good evening, Mr. Morrissey. It's good of you to join us."

Then, to her husband, she said, "Dinner is ready if you'll join us."

Captain Smith rose and motioned for John to follow.

Captain Smith took a seat at the head of the table and pointed John to a chair on his right. David sat opposite John. Addie's chair was next to her mother's. A place was set on Addie's right. Mrs. Smith addressed their guest. "You've met our David." Then she smiled at Addie and said, "This is our youngest, Addie."

"I met him already this morning, Mother!"

A voice came from the doorway, "We know you did, Addie. That's all you've talked about this afternoon."

Captain Smith said, "You remember our daughter, Susannah, of course."

"I do," said John, pushing back his chair and rising as Susannah circled the table to take her seat. He wanted to say more, but words wouldn't come. He'd missed her, even longed for her. The girl that mystified him in her budding adolescence had transformed into an elegant woman. For the balance of his years, he would never forget how she looked when she entered the dining room that evening.

As soon as she settled into her chair, John sat again, trying not to stare. Susannah, however, did the opposite. She pierced John with the all-knowing stare and faint smile that had gripped his young heart. He was aware of how red his face must have looked. Captain Smith proposed grace. He asked his family and guest to bow their heads as he thanked the Lord for their food and good fortune.

After grace, Captain Smith introduced his guest. "Mr. Morrissey, as you know, has served as a valued deckhand on my ship. Like your brother, Levi, he has been off to California to seek adventure and fortune. Mr. Morrissey returns to us with a letter from your brother. He also returns as the boxing champion of California. I want to thank Mr. Morrissey and wish him good health and new opportunities," Levi Smith smiled at their nervous

162

guest and added, "including work upon my ship, if he's so inclined."

A woman arrived from the kitchen carrying a large platter of meat and vegetables, which she placed near Captain Smith. Aldine Smith offered an introduction. "Morrissey, this is Bernadette Kelly. She helps with our home, children, and even our rare entertaining." The Irish woman averted her eyes and returned to the kitchen. There was an awkward moment before David launched into a barrage of questions about California and their older brother. John did his best to respond to each question, even as Mrs. Smith interrupted with the admonishment to "allow Mr. Morrissey to enjoy his meal."

Susannah spoke little through the meal, though she often looked up and smiled at the young man across the table. Addie was atypically quiet. From her seat near her mother, she looked back and forth from her older sister to their guest.

"They're in love!" she exclaimed.

"Addie, I warned you!" Mrs. Smith glared. Then, to John, she explained, "Our daughter is prone to saying such things. Please accept our apologies."

"They are, Mother! Can't you see?"

Captain Smith laughed, breaking the tension. "Addie, go with your mother and help clean up. David, would you bring Mr. Morrissey's coat and hat? I'll visit with him in the parlor." He rose and motioned for John to join him. Susannah had gathered dishes at the table. She offered John a parting smile.

John remained red-faced after Addie's outburst, wondering what Captain Smith and his wife thought. He entered the parlor and sat across from his host.

"I hope you enjoyed your dinner, Morrissey."

"I did, sir. It was my most enjoyable meal in years."

David appeared with John's hat and coat. Once his son left, Captain Smith stood, and John followed him to the foyer.

"Addie is quite special, Morrissey. She's prone to curious sayings and behaviors but is a great treasure as the last of our children."

John realized he was crushing his hat and struggling to speak. Finding his voice he whispered, "She's just a child, sir. I hope Susannah's not too embarrassed."

Captain Smith laughed.

"Addie knows very well that her darling older sister is an attractive woman and that men easily fall in love with her. I'm sure that the idea both thrills and terrifies her. It terrifies her parents, for certain!"

"I'm sure it does, Captain."

"There's a place on the Empire for a worker and fighter like you whenever you like. Thank you for bringing the letter, Morrissey.

"Please thank Mrs. Smith for dinner, sir, and tell Susannah it was good to see her again."

It was not a great distance to the Eastern. The chilly air and breeze off the Hudson felt good. A near-full moon kept sliding in and out of the clouds as he started south on River Street. He had only gone ahead half a block when he heard soft footfalls rushing his way. Morrissey spun around and was shocked to see Susannah.

"Are you leaving without a proper goodbye?"

This stunning new adult version of the young woman who'd captured his heart was upon him before he could respond. She stood close, staring into his eyes, clutching her coat, and shivering.

"Didn't we say our last goodbye with a delightful kiss?"

John bent to place a kiss on her forehead, but Suzie had a different idea. She raised her mouth to his. The kiss erased John's lingering doubts.

"I must rush now, John. My parents will be upset if they discover I've left the house. Meet me tomorrow afternoon, if you can, at Peale's Museum. I'll be there at two."

She turned and rushed north on River Street before disappearing around the side of her home.

Susannah could not sleep that night. She had rehearsed reunion scenarios with John since his departure for California. At Troy Female Seminary, Susannah had bragged about her affection for the Irish fighter with members of her sisterhood. Though she had dated handsome, promising young men, the thrill she felt with John was never there with the others. Now, he was back, more handsome than ever, with the same awkwardness she found endearing.

When John arrived at the Eastern, it was far too early to retire. He entered the saloon. There were few customers. The crowd that had greeted him earlier had cleared out. Archambeault spotted him and nodded from the bar. A couple of middle-aged patrons seated near the end turned, spotted John, and whispered.

"Can we buy you a drink, Mr. Morrissey?" It was the closest of the two patrons.

"Thank you." John moved toward the men and took a seat. "Whiskey," he said to Archambeault.

Archambeault delivered the drink and leaned toward John.

"Your father was here asking for you. Wanted me to tell you he'd come by after dinner tomorrow."

John nodded, finished his drink, and thanked the men next to him. He said "good night" to Archambeault and headed upstairs.

Sleep also eluded John. During the long voyage back to New York, he had questioned whether young Susannah would be pleased to see him. She obviously was. She was taller than the first time she had raised her face to meet his kiss. Her wavy black hair was longer. The smell of her perfume lingered, as did the softness of her lips on his. When she'd wrapped her arms around his neck, her body pressed close. Despite the chilly night air, the feel of her breasts and thighs ignited his passion.

There had been no way to predict how she would react to him after so long an absence. During the long travel home, John had convinced himself that she would no longer share an attraction equal to his. But, tonight, that fear lifted. The next day he would be waiting at Peale's Museum before two o'clock.

Seventeen

◦~◦

When John woke on Tuesday morning, he was ravenous. He pulled on his wool coat and stepped out into a wintry morning. The Savoy Hotel on Third Avenue was a popular destination for breakfast. He ordered boiled mutton chops and rice and consumed three cups of strong Brazilian coffee. After breakfast, he enjoyed a brisk walk around downtown Troy before heading to Francis Conway's barbershop.

Rusty LeBeau spotted the fighter before he even opened the door. "Look who's here, will you? It's the California champion himself." Conway and the other three men in the shop turned as John walked in, doffing his hat.

"Your hair's the same as everyone else, Morrissey. Grab a seat. We'll get to you when we can." Conway turned back to his customer and continued to clip away. He could not pretend any longer. He placed his scissors on the counter and rushed over to put a bear hug on the young fighter. "You make us proud; you do, young man. At least now you're paid for beating people."

John struggled free from the barber and smiled. "I'm lookin' for your luscious daughter, Francis. My heart ached for her when I was gone."

Conway put up his fists. "Those are fighting words. Shall we step outside?"

John slapped the barber's hands and returned a hug. The teasing from Conway and LeBeau continued during John's haircut and shave and even on his way out.

At the Eastern, John chose the same long jacket from the previous evening but opted for a silver double-breasted checked vest, a silver necktie, and checked gray trousers. It was a more youthful look. He would have his black leather shoes shined on the way to the museum.

Peale's Troy Museum sat on the corner of Elbow and River Streets. It was more than a mile from the Eastern, north along the Hudson toward Lansingburgh. John wanted to be there when Susannah arrived.

Susannah avoided her mother as much as possible during the morning before her rendezvous with John. Her father had left before dawn to prepare the *Empire* for its day trip to New York City. Though her parents had greeted him with warmth the previous evening, she knew they would never approve of her seeing an Irishman, especially one five years older with a criminal record.

Rebecca Walter was Susannah's best friend since they had started public school. She lived nearby on Fifth Avenue. Susannah would inform her mother that she and Rebecca were going to Peale's to see the latest exhibits. Susannah selected a day dress that always brought compliments. After struggling to arrange her thick, wavy hair, Susannah decided she looked attractive but not enough to raise her mother's suspicions. She headed downstairs and enjoyed a light lunch with her mother and Addie.

"You look so pretty!" exclaimed Addie when Susannah came down the stairs.

"You do, indeed," remarked Mrs. Smith.

"Rebecca insisted we dress up today. She's fascinated with a manager at the museum. She wanted to wear a new dress she had recently completed. So," Susannah said, as she spun around, "here

I am, just as requested. Thank you, Addie. You look lovely yourself."

Talk over lunch included Addie's progress with piano lessons and Mrs. Smith's plans for their church's holiday charity event. She'd agreed to serve as chair again. Susannah was helping clear the table when Rebecca knocked at the door. As planned, she had dressed in a lovely new outfit. Susannah rushed upstairs, tied her hat, and fastened her winter shawl around her shoulders. On the way out, she shouted a cheerful goodbye.

As Susannah and Rebecca approached Peale's, they saw a man pacing back and forth in front of the building. As they drew closer, Susannah said, "That's John."

John recognized Susannah and waved.

"My, he is handsome!" whispered Rebecca.

"You look rather dashing, sir," said Susannah when John reached the pair. She smiled and bowed. "This is my best friend, Rebecca. She agreed to serve as my chaperone."

Surprised, John looked from one of the attractive young women to the other. "Let's go inside where it's warm. I'll get another ticket."

"You still don't know what to make of me, do you, John Morrissey?" Susannah reached out and took his arm. "Rebecca's my coconspirator for the afternoon. She helped me plan my escape. She'll meet us here at five, and I'll walk home with her."

Rebecca offered a conspiratorial smile, then walked away.

The museum included four floors of natural and archeological wonders and a host of what the owners liked to call "curiosities." On a Tuesday afternoon, it had very few patrons, as Susannah had expected. The pair checked their outerwear and started along the exhibits on the first floor. Susannah took John's hand. Neither was keen to discover the wonders on exhibit.

The couple strolled the first floor, speaking softly. The wondrous and curious collections went unnoticed. Susannah ran her fingers over John's swollen, outsized knuckles. "Do they hurt?"

"A bit after fights." He wanted to pull his hand away but resisted.

"Will you fight Hyer soon?" She turned to look at his face.

John looked away. "I will. I got to."

"I've missed you, John," Susannah admitted. "You have never been far from my thoughts. "

Susannah paused. She'd rehearsed her words at least a dozen times, but rejection, she knew, was quite possible. Nonetheless, she forged ahead, "Since that silly girl met you on the deck of the *Empire*, you have occupied her mind and heart, John Morrissey. I've spent time with attractive boys and promising young men who show an interest in me, but you were always in my mind and heart, so I waited."

Susannah tried to read John's response. He'd gripped her hand tighter as she spoke but kept his head bowed and avoided eye contact. The silence was unbearable.

John finally raised his head, faced Susannah, and sighed. "You once told me there's no sin in being poor, Irish, or Catholic. You meant it. I know you did. But others don't feel that way." John allowed two women to pass, conscious of their disapproving glances, then continued when the women were out of earshot. "You got a fine family, Suzie. An education. Doors will always open for you. Me, I'll always be Irish and any children too. Doors will slam in our faces, and people will hate us. I don't want that for you."

Susannah glowered at John. "Well, if you remember that conversation so well, you should also remember that I said you'd be more than a famous fighter in New York City. If you think that it's this," she grabbed and lifted his right hand, "that makes you special, you're wrong." Poking her free hand into his chest, Susannah said, "It's there. Your courage. Your will. Your rage. That, John Morrissey, is what makes you special." Susannah let go of his hand, shaking with anger.

John reached for her hand, but she pulled away. She was not done. "I know that you will be the American fighting champion.

What then? Have you ever thought about that? Have you considered where that courage, will, and rage might take you?"

"I have. Every day." He tried to take Susannah's hand again, but she crossed her arms. "Let's walk, Suzie." They walked through the empty exhibition hall. John could feel her anger.

John knew he needed to say more to explain his concerns, but, when he turned to speak, Susannah interrupted. "Has it occurred to you, John, that my drive and courage are as fierce as yours? Of course, it hasn't! Men frown on drive and courage in a woman. I refuse to let others fail to see or respect me. Do you think I'm afraid or unable to stand by your side, fight at your side, or protect our children? If that's what you think, then you don't know me and don't deserve my affection." She shook with anger.

The most important conversation of their life together had begun.

Eighteen

~~~

Tim Morrissey was enjoying another free drink at the Eastern when his now-famous son entered. A cheer exploded from the patrons. Tim rushed to embrace his boy. "Would you be lookin' at the size of yourself?" Tim had his hands wrapped around his son's biceps and smiled up at John's beaming face. "Your ma told me you were here; she did." John wrapped his father in a massive hug, lifting him off his feet to the delight of everyone watching.

When John released his father, he was thrilled to see that, though he'd turned fifty while John was away, his appearance was unchanged. There was no hint of gray in his thick wavy hair, and still that sparkle of mischief in his eyes. Tim said, "Come to dinner tonight, Johnny. Tell your sisters about California. After dinner, your da will take you about. I'll be showing my champion off."

John agreed to join his family for dinner. Then he bought a fresh drink for his father and went up to his room to change. It would not do for his mother to see him in another fine outfit, nor could he join his father's circle of friends dressed like a dandy.

The Morrissey apartment was a riot of noise. The five school-age girls vied for their brother's attention. When Judith called, eight people squeezed around the table. Tim had stopped at the butcher and bought a mutton loin for the reunion. Judith filled plates with small chops layered with boiled cabbage, onions, and potatoes. After setting the last dish on the table, she asked sixteen-year-old Catherine to offer grace.

John tried hearing and responding to his sisters' questions while enjoying the meal his mother prepared. He had glimpsed Hannah and Mary Anne the previous day. Now he looked around at Catherine, Ellen, and Margaret. They had all grown and changed so much. That they were still alive gave him great relief. Levi Smith, Jr. had told him of Troy's hundreds of cholera deaths, mainly among poor Irish. He didn't know his family's fate while he was away.

Judith had remained quiet and distant throughout the meal. Tim tried, from time to time, to admonish his daughters to speak one at a time. Finally, after digging into the stew, Tim sat back and smiled with paternal pride before announcing an end to dinner. "Help your ma with the table and be off to your homework now, lasses." The Morrissey girls groaned, pushed back from the table, then took turns hugging their big brother.

"Let's be on our way, son." Tim retrieved their coats.

"Good night, Ma," John offered to his mother's back as she scrubbed the kettle of what little remained of the stew. She did not respond.

Tim was rushing John off to cockfights at Spencer's barn in West Troy. He had rented space there for years. Tim couldn't wait to show off his latest champion fowl. "Da," asked John as they rushed along, "where are Mary and Bridget?"

Tim kept his quick pace. Then, without turning, he said, "Gone, Johnny."

"Where?"

"Don't know. Left one day and never came back. I pray they entered a convent. In my prayers, they're cloistered and praying for our souls each day."

During the last weeks of 1852, John joined his father as often as possible. He was a hero to Tim's community of Irish refugees. Tim had been raising and fighting cocks since childhood and had proved himself as one of the best breeders and trainers in the area. Now he could claim to have raised not only the toughest fighting birds but also a champion fighting son.

John had watched his father raise, train, and send fighting cocks into deadly battle all his life. He had also watched his father win and lose money that his family desperately needed to climb out of poverty. Emotions drove betting, as did alcohol consumption. Thus, John never handed money to his father.

When he arrived at Troy from California, John had expected to remain for two days. Getting to New York City to start a business and challenge Hyer was his priority. John had not known what to expect when, or if, he saw Susannah Smith after so long. To his surprise and delight, her feelings were as strong as his. They needed time to explore these feelings; distance would make that impossible. John's illiteracy was now more than an occasional embarrassment. It impeded his happiness.

Susannah continued to manufacture opportunities to meet John. She recruited her brother, David, to carry messages. The two, close in age, had been confidants for as long as they could remember. Susannah knew her mother would eventually discover she was spending time with the notorious Irish fighter and criminal, but she accepted the risk. She would announce her love and intentions soon enough. For now, she and John had more to share and learn. Theirs would not be a simple life to navigate. She needed reassurance that he was ready. She knew she was.

With the holidays over, Susannah resumed tutoring, which restricted time together to evenings and weekends. She and John enjoyed carriage rides, strolls in parks when the weather allowed, and precious Saturday nights at the Imperial before John would return to New York. They found conversations easier and more revealing, their intimacy urgent and satisfying, their laughter more frequent, and their ambitions equally bold.

Nineteen

⚮

When Morrissey could no longer delay returning to New York, he and Susannah said a painful goodbye. John promised to visit monthly. He had exchanged his remaining gold coins at Troy National Bank for banknotes, securing the substantial fortune from California in a new money belt. After bidding his father, Hamilton, and friends at the Eastern goodbye, John was ready to return to New York City. He had enough money to invest in a business and carried the California boxing championship belt, which should put him in the top tier of challengers for the American championship.

Arriving at the railroad depot, John bought a ticket on the eight-thirty express train. After settling in a seat in the second of three passenger cars, he fell asleep, only to be jolted awake when the cars lurched forward. Today, John would arrive at Chambers Street in four hours, much faster than the great steamboats, and even during winter. John could not get there fast enough. He needed to share his plans with Dad Cunningham and meet with Tom Petrie.

The Irving House was a six-story building with residences on the top floors. A one-bedroom on the fifth floor was available. John paid a month in advance before heading to the Gem Saloon.

When Dad Cunningham saw his friend walk in, he waved him over to the roulette wheel, shouting to the patrons, "The California champion, gentlemen!"

Everyone turned to see John approaching and cheered as Dad walked around and embraced him. "It's great to see you, Johnny. It took you a bit to visit your old travel mate."

John held his fellow argonaut at arm's length and looked him over. "We have important things to discuss, Dad. Dinner?"

Dad asked, "Would you want to see Petrie? He's in his office."

"Not yet. After we've talked."

The Delmonico family ran a restaurant next door to Irving House. John and Dad agreed to meet there that evening to celebrate their reunion. They leaned over their plates, heaped with abundance, knife in one hand, fork in the other, catching up between mouthfuls of delicious food and a couple of bottles of red wine. Dad told John about his tepid reunion with family at Cohoes. Dad had discovered, upon arrival, that his child had been adopted at birth. The whereabouts of the boy or girl were unknown. He didn't linger in his hometown. He was back at the Gem within two weeks.

When John told him that Susannah had agreed to marry the following summer, Dad leaped out of his chair, raced around the table, and slapped John's back, exclaiming, "Congratulations, Johnny. You're the luckiest man I'll ever know."

Anxious to share a plan, John leaned in and whispered, "I wanna buy into the Gem or open a new place. I've two thousand to invest, and my name's got value. Would you care to join on?"

Dad said, "There's nothing I'd like more, Johnny. I was going to use my money to support my child, but that's impossible. So, count me in for two thousand."

The friends ordered a bottle of wine, toasted their plan, and agreed to meet with Tom Petrie the next day.

Petrie was delighted that John had returned with the California championship belt. Nevertheless, he resisted the proposal to sell an interest in the Gem. "If we're going to be partners, it will have to be a new location, not in this neighborhood. What'd you have in mind?"

Tom Petrie heard the young men out. Cunningham showed a great deal of promise as a manager. Despite being brash and a magnet for trouble, Morrissey was hardworking and loyal and would draw a large sporting crowd. Petrie wanted to expand. Four thousand dollars would seed a decent second location. He agreed, assuming he would serve as the managing partner.

Next, John visited Captain Rynders.

"Ah, Morrissey, my lad." Rynders rose behind his desk and threw his arms around the Irish fighter. "You've returned at last! Let's have lunch." Rynders took hold of John's elbow and rushed him down the stairs and onto Park Row.

As they hurried to a nearby oyster bar, Rynders never stopped talking. "You might have heard; Tammany credits me with helping to get 'Fainting Frank' Pierce elected president." He turned toward his young companion, looking for a response. Lacking one, he shrugged and kept up his excited chatter. "Tammany's stronger than ever. They've cast their lot with the Democrats and you Irish. It's a numbers game, you see. Yours keep growing, here more than anywhere. You can't fight that now, can you? Here we are."

Rynders continued his monologue throughout lunch. He described fierce battles over ballots during the recent campaign. "Not long ago, I could hire any volunteer firehouse or gang to round up votes for Tammany. Cash and free drinks were all it took. Not anymore. The American Party has aligned with the Whigs. They hate immigrants, Blacks, and Jews, but you Irish Catholics top the list. So now I only use the Irish gangs for elections. Work with me, John, and we can dominate the lower wards. Beyond even."

"What can I do?" John pushed forward, leaning on his elbows.

"You're a big hero with your Irish already. The papers have been full of news of your victory against Thompson. 'Irish fighter from New York beats English giant in California.' That's what the *Sun* said. See Shane Allen. Help him lead the Dead Rabbits. They're strong, but the Plug Uglies, Bowery Bhoys, and their allies are getting bolder. Allen needs you. Go. Be the Irish champion. Help me get them naturalized. Get their votes recorded. As I said, if you do that, we can dominate elections and enjoy all the power that comes with it."

"One thing," John responded. "I came back to fight Hyer. It ain't enough to be California champion. I aim to be America's champion. Then, I'll be more valuable to both of us."

Rynders remained silent for minutes before responding. "Hyer's a leader in the Whig Party and their hero. We're now enemies. He's lost interest in prizefighting, but perhaps if he recognizes you as the hero of all the hated Irish Catholics, it might be enough to call him out."

Rynders rose to leave, and John joined him. The men parted, Rynders back to his club, John up Broadway.

As John walked past Pétale de Rose, he considered how much had occurred since he'd stumbled in that door, frozen and starving, during his first winter in New York. Kate Ridgely gave a young man a way out of Five Points. She was his rescuer, stern taskmaster, temporary lover, and inspiration. One day, when her fancy carriage rolls by, he thought, *she'll wave and nod at one of the most powerful men in the city.*

The following day, John headed to Belson's Livery, where Shang Allen worked. His back was to John as Shang hammered a shoe onto the front-right hoof of a massive Cleveland Bay. John watched until he released the horse's foot.

Morrissey shouted over the din, "How might that leg of yours be?"

Allen turned to see John watching.

"It only hurts when I run, so I choose not to!" Allen stepped toward the young man who had saved his life and embraced John.

"It's good you've returned. We've much to discuss. Dinner tonight?"

"I'm at the Gem every night but Sundays," John replied. "I'll be at Troy on Sunday this week. Do you break for lunch?"

"Every day at noon. At my place tomorrow. You can congratulate my bonnie wife. She's with child again; she is."

John grasped the blacksmith's strong hand and shook it. "Congratulations, Shang. Tomorrow, then."

John worked his poker table at the Gem six nights a week while renovations were underway for the new saloon and gambling hall at 12 Ann Street. They named it Belle of the Union. The chairs at John's poker table were filled by eight o'clock, with games often going until sunrise. Faro had been a great entry into gambling for John, but his first love was poker, and he excelled.

On the first weekend of every month, John took the Sunday-morning express to Troy and checked into a suite at the Imperial Hotel. Only Susannah knew he was there. Their time together was too precious to share with others. Susannah's friend, Rebecca, supplied Sunday sleepovers as the ideal excuse for Susannah to escape to her lover's arms. A fireplace warmed their suite, where they took dinner on Sunday nights. Between soft linens on a massive poster bed, Susannah gradually abandoned her insecurities and surrendered to her passion and the patient and gentle love of her older and far more experienced fiancé. Later, they spoke of events of the week and ambitions for their future. Monday morning always arrived too quickly.

Shang Allen insisted John join him for lunch as often as possible. Over lunch, he told John about growing attacks on Irish in the city. It was not only men who suffered. Women and children faced regular harassment as they walked the streets or rode omnibuses and horsecars. In addition, Irish domestics were experiencing increased physical and sexual abuse.

"It's the American Party and the Whigs fueling this hate," Shane insisted. "They don't want us here and don't want us voting. Archbishop Hughes and the parishes do what they can to help, but the troubles grow worse, John. The Church has no way to answer the threats and violence, but we can. It's good to have you back."

Shang, and local Irish gangs, started compiling lists of those known to abuse the Irish. Morrissey led teams of two or more Dead Rabbits searching for the predators. When they found them, they exacted retribution. It was Morrissey who took the greatest joy in that effort. To the Irish, he became an avenging angel. To the anti-Irish zealots, he became enemy number one. The Dead Rabbits posted guards around Morrissey whenever they could.

Rynders kept his word. He used his contacts to figure out Hyer's interest in a prizefight against the Irish hero, John Morrissey. Hyer made it clear that he had no interest in training again for a prizefight. The champion's saloon had enjoyed enormous success. He was rising in the local Whig organization with national ambitions. According to the New York newspapers, he was a more recognizable figure than President Pierce.

Morrissey had chased Hyer for years. He was not about to give up. On April 14, after returning from a Sunday visit with Susannah, he walked into Hyer's saloon and saw him standing at the bar, regaling a group of guests. Morrissey approached the champion and shouted for all to hear, "I'm here to call you a lowly coward, Hyer. I beat your trainer in California. Now, it's your turn. I'll beat you anywhere, anytime. You choose."

Hyer stiffened at the insult in front of his friends. Everyone stopped talking and glared at the young Irishman. Hyer stood to his full six foot three. "So, you must be that impudent John Morrissey. I know what happened in California. Your Irish thugs threatened to shoot and kill Thompson. You couldn't last five minutes inside the ropes with me." He turned his back to Morrissey, and the crowd laughed.

"Put up the money and name the time and place," John shouted. "If you won't, you're the cowardly cur they say you are!"

Hyer tore off his jacket and tie, threw his hat on the bar, and screamed into Morrissey's face, "Now! Out to the street. I'll show you who's a coward!"

Morrissey removed his coat, folding and placing it with his hat on the bar. The crowd picked up a lusty cheer and followed Hyer onto Hester Street. They stepped aside as Morrissey strode out to face the champion. Others nearby heard and saw the developing situation, and rushed to catch a glimpse.

Two police officers had just exited a nearby grocer and spotted the activity. They withdrew their nightsticks and waded through the crowd until they stood between Hyer and Morrissey. The officers carted Morrissey away to be charged with inciting a riot. A patron rushed to retrieve and hand him his coat and hat.

The House of Detention, known as *the Tombs*, occupied an entire block in Five Points. The officers deposited John in a holding cell with thirteen others. His seat at the Belle of the Union poker table would remain empty that night.

When Chief of Police George Washington Matsell reviewed the day's court appointments, he saw John Morrissey's name. He wondered if it was the notorious Irish fighter. If his impressive memory was correct, there was an old warrant for his arrest related to the Astor Place Riot. Upon his request, an officer delivered John to Matsell's office.

"Have a seat, young man," Matsell said, pointing at one of two straight-back chairs anchored to the floor opposite his massive desk. Behind Matsell was a library that extended the room's width and stood ten feet high. Matsell sat on a throne-like chair. He stood six feet and weighed more than three hundred pounds. Anyone entering that room felt dwarfed.

Matsell ran a finger down the pages of a gigantic ledger. He ignored the officer and John while he scanned. Then, looking over his reading glasses, Matsell addressed the man across the desk. "Take a seat, Mr. Morrissey. Trying to incite a riot, were you?"

"No, sir. It's personal between Hyer and me."

"You've participated in riots in this city before, have you not?"

John shook his head.

"Young man, you were indicted in this city in June of forty-nine for rioting, but you weren't seized and tried. Isn't that true?"

John nodded. "I was in the crowd that night, sir, but never in the troubles. I was serving as a deckhand on the *Empire* that summer."

Matsell turned to his officer. "Leave us, Sergeant." When they were alone, Matsell said, "I was not in this office then, Morrissey. I've studied the records from that night. There's enough blame to go around. This office has no interest in pursuing that with you. I'm aware, however, of everything that happens in my jurisdiction. I know that you befriended Captain Rynders. I know you've run immigrants for Tammany, and I also know you fight with the Dead Rabbits. A deckhand, indeed, young man." Matsell watched John slump into his chair and avoid eye contact.

Matsell pulled a folder in front of him, picked up a pen, and started writing. Without looking up, he said, "Morrissey, you and your gangs can kill each other off. The quicker, the better, as far as it concerns me. However, I will exercise this office's powers if your activities involve innocent citizens or destroy public or private property. You're free to leave, Mr. Morrissey. The next time justice may not be so blind." Matsell called for Sergeant Rivers, who processed John's release.

After his close brush with a jail sentence, John went to see Captain Rynders. He was as close to forcing Hyer into a championship fight as he would ever be. Rynders suggested that a good-faith deposit of one hundred dollars and a post in the *National Police Gazette* might force a positive response.

Tom Hyer and his representatives agreed to meet at the Gem to negotiate terms. As soon as he arrived, he stared at Petrie, refusing to acknowledge Morrissey. "I'm retired from prizefighting, as I've repeatedly made clear; however, if you can put up ten thousand dollars, I'll agree to one more fight."

Tom Petrie looked at John, who shrugged.

"We don't have access to that amount, sir. We're prepared to put up three thousand."

Hyer smirked. "You've got twenty-four hours to agree to the ten thousand." With that, he placed his hat on and walked out. Hyer was thirty-four. Health issues were an increasing concern. He despised the rigors of training and had no intention of fighting again. The ten-thousand-dollar demand saved face. He knew that neither Morrissey nor any other fighter would have access to that much for a fight they were almost certain to lose.

When told of Hyer's demand, Rynders said, "We'll declare Hyer's vacated his claim to the title." Rynders submitted that John's path to the championship had to be through a victory over someone the public would accept as the natural heir to Hyer's vacated title. "We need to match you against Sullivan."

John answered, "He's in California."

"Sully's been back here for a month, John. Got into trouble with the law out there's what I heard. He's tending bar on Delancey. I'm sure we can arrange a fight. He always needs money. I'll talk to Fox at the *Police Gazette*. He can declare that Sullivan is the American champion by default. Then we'll issue a challenge."

As publisher at the *National Police Gazette*, Richard Fox was riding the rapid growth of interest in sports in America. Though illegal, prizefighting drew greater interest and betting than any other sport. There had not been a championship fight in four years. Fox was anxious to drive interest in a Sullivan-Morrissey battle.

Protocol required an exchange of insults. As the now-recognized American champion, Sullivan waited for Morrissey to make his move. Rynders suggested John recruit his old partner, Orville "Awful" Gardner, to go with him to Prescott's Saloon on Delancey. The two wandered into the saloon and spotted Sullivan behind the bar.

"Why, if it ain't the boy Thompson beat up. I'd have tossed the towel if I'd been in your corner." Sullivan sneered at the young challenger as Morrissey stepped close. At five-eleven, he looked down on the five-eight anointed champion and sneered, "The world knows Hyer mauled you at Baltimore. Sent you to the hospital; he did. Like Hyer, I'm too big, too strong, and too fast for an old man like you."

Neither Morrissey nor Sullivan felt any serious animosity toward the other. To Sullivan, Morrissey was just the most recent in a prizefighting career that spanned decades and continents. For young Morrissey, it marked the fulfillment of his great ambition.

They met two days later and signed articles spelling out the terms of their fight. The contest would be a "fight to the finish" under London Prize Ring Rules. Each fighter would deposit one thousand dollars. They would fight on October 12 at a location within one hundred miles of New York City.

The Police Gazette published details of the agreement the next day. Word of the deal spread via telegraph and newspapers throughout the country. During the balance of spring and summer, speculation dominated discussions and arguments wherever sporting men gathered. At least among the sporting fraternity, John Morrissey was now a celebrity and symbolic hero in New York City, where he had already proven himself as a protector of the Irish Catholic population.

Morrissey needed to train rigorously for the October fight with Yankee Sullivan. His deficit of skills was plain in the Thompson fight, even to him. But circumstances made it difficult for him to train properly.

He discussed his situation with Petrie and Cunningham. They agreed it would be better to prepare for the championship away from New York City. If he could secure a deckhand position on a night boat, he could stay aboard when the ship docked in New

York City during the day. When at Troy, he could train and enjoy more time with Susannah.

John met with Rynders and Shang Allen to explain why he would avoid New York City until after the championship fight. Though disappointed, each understood. John offered his old immigrant runner partner, Orville "Awful" Gardner, a chance to manage his training. Gardner accepted, agreeing to move into the Eastern Hotel in July to begin formal training.

All that remained was to meet with Captain Smith. John checked out of Irving Place on the morning of June 21. He left a large trunk of possessions with Dad Cunningham, then shouldered a new canvas bag to the pier at the end of Barclay Street. There stood the beautiful *Empire of Troy*. Stevedores were busy unloading the last supplies and belongings from the overnight trip from Troy. Passengers gathered nearby to retrieve their belongings. John took a deep breath and started climbing. Before he reached the deck, a familiar gravelly voice called, "If it's not the great dandy, John Morrissey, himself!"

Bosun Maloney, scowling, as usual, approached John. He offered his hand and grinned at his former deckhand. "Champion of California, and soon of this great country. To what do we owe this honor?"

John answered, "I'll be training at Troy. There's no peace for me in this place, Bosun. Maybe the captain will take me on 'til October. I'm needin' a job."

The bosun nodded. "He's in his stateroom. Catch him before he's asleep.

John eased forward to Captain Smith's stateroom, stood at the door for a moment, then steeled himself and rapped. Hearing no response, he rapped again, louder. Still no answer. He was about to leave when the door opened. Captain Smith, hatless, shoeless, and with his crisp white shirt hanging over his trousers, did not recognize his guest for seconds.

"Morrissey," Smith said, as he tucked his shirt and pulled his suspenders over his shoulders, "come in, lad. I didn't expect to see you."

John followed the captain into his stateroom. "Have a seat, young man. I was about to have a bit of rum before sleeping. I'll pour one for you." The captain went ahead to his liquor cabinet, withdrew two glasses, and poured half a glass for each. "To your health, Morrissey!" offered Captain Smith, handing John his drink.

John lifted his glass. "Thanks, Captain. My da always says, 'May your troubles be less, and your blessings be more, and nothing but happiness come through your door.'" John swallowed half his rum. The captain smiled and downed all his.

"To what do we owe this honor, lad?"

John chewed on his lower lip, a nervous habit. "Well, sir, I seek employment, but a more important matter, if you might." He was not about to ask Levi Smith for a position on his ship until he requested permission to marry Susannah.

Captain Smith, a man of the world, had observed his daughter and this young Irish fighter. Their mutual attraction was obvious. Unbeknown to her, Captain Smith had followed Susannah when she left the house after the dinner with Morrissey. That affectionate embrace confirmed what he had already suspected. He neither confronted her nor informed his wife. Instead, he waited for John to reveal the "more important matter." He could well imagine how nervous the lad was.

"It's about Susannah, sir." John had not made eye contact. "I'm in love, Captain. I'd ask your permission for her hand, sir."

Captain Smith rose, retreated to the liquor cabinet, and refilled his glass. Then, with his back to John, he asked, "And she has expressed a desire to marry you?"

"Aye, sir."

Smith returned and sat facing John. "Even if I find my way to agree to this, I can't imagine Mrs. Smith will. How, by God, would you propose to provide a stable life for our daughter, lad?"

"On October 12, sir, I'll win the American championship. Of that, I'm sure. After I win, I'll open the finest gaming parlor and restaurant in New York. I'll run fair games and let no youth or women in the gaming area, sir."

From the beginning, Captain Smith liked the fearless, hardworking Morrissey and didn't doubt his ambition or potential. But Irish and Catholic? He thought *Aldine would not take this well*.

Mrs. Smith had insisted that their strong-willed daughter complete her education at Emma Willard's Troy Female Seminary. Marriage to a professional of standing, and a career as a teacher, was her dream for Susannah. For Mrs. Smith to accept their daughter's wedding to an Irish Catholic ruffian with a criminal record was unimaginable. The captain could only sigh.

"I will discuss this situation with my daughter. For the moment, I will not discuss it with Mrs. Smith. We have an opening on the *Empire*, and you're welcome to join our crew. See Bosun Maloney if you wish. For now, I suggest you prepare to win that fight in October and keep your relationship with my daughter discrete. For God's sake, stay out of trouble at Troy. We can discuss your request again in October."

Smith rose, offered John his hand, and escorted him to the stateroom door. Smith shook his head as he saw John out. *Susannah's bound to be the death of my wife.*

Twenty

T he Eastern Hotel, once more, became home to John when the *Empire* docked at Troy. Aleck Hamilton, thrilled that his protégé would fight for the American championship, offered rooms at no charge to John and his trainer. Gardner hoped to move into his room in June; however, before joining John at Troy, he needed to serve a sentence at the Tombs for assault. So, it wasn't until July 7 that Gardner arrived at Troy. It was not a promising start to John's training.

With fewer men traveling to California in 1853, trouble aboard the *Empire* was less frequent. Having the famous prizefighter on the ship was itself a deterrent to violence. Captain Smith insisted John dress and join him at his table at dinner, where he'd introduce the California champion to passengers. They invariably offered lusty cheers for the handsome young champion. John remained on board when docked at New York, with rare exceptions.

With Gardner's arrival at Troy, John could begin serious training. Not forgetting how Thompson had easily exploited his lack of ring skills, he vowed to work hard over the months ahead. He could not lose. Too much was at stake. On July 9, after docking at Troy, John rushed to the Eastern and changed into his exercise clothes and shoes. Gardner was sober and ready. He knew Yankee

Sullivan exceptionally well, having trained Hyer and serving in his corner for their fight in forty-nine. He knew the veteran Sullivan would cut Morrissey to shreds if he did not train properly.

It displeased Gardner to manage an every-other-day training schedule, but John insisted there was no alternative. To Gardner, there were three critical elements - endurance, speed, and discipline. First, Gardner had to see what deficits his student had. He had seen Morrissey beat all comers on the docks of New York. Contests in the twenty-four-foot square against experienced professionals were entirely different. Sullivan had never lost in scores of prizefights before the Hyer clash. The veteran knew and used every trick in the business.

Gardner saw three of Sullivan's earlier fights. The loss to Hyer he would never forget. Nor the Billy Bell fight. Sullivan was having an easy go with Bell until he got careless. Bell got Sullivan against the ropes and pressed a forearm across his throat. Gardner was close enough to hear Sullivan. "I can't stand this anymore. Let me go, Billy. I'll give in to you." Bell let him off the ropes. Sullivan backed off and struck an unexpected and decisive blow, knocking Bell unconscious.

As soon as John came out of the hotel entrance, Gardner was there to meet him. "Let's go," he said as he started jogging toward the river. Wrapped around Gardner's neck were two pairs of padded leather gloves. John had no trouble keeping up, although he wondered where they were heading. When they reached the river, Gardner led them to an aging rowboat. "Row. Upriver," Gardner instructed as he climbed into the back while his fighter settled in the middle and took hold of the oars.

The river traffic was heavy as John hung close to the Troy shoreline, heading toward Lansingburgh. "Where to?" he asked., "I just got off this damn river."

"Not far. Pull harder on the oars."

John dug the oars into the Hudson. He was sweating heavily when thirty minutes later, Gardner said, "Cross here," pointing at the Van Schaick mansion on the large island on the west bank. "Head north, past that fancy old house, and pull ashore." Once the rowboat struck bottom, Gardner jumped out and dragged the boat ashore. He wrapped the leather gloves around his neck and plowed ahead through the thick brush. He weaved along an ancient path, past a family cemetery plot filled with violets and up a slight incline until they arrived at a stretch of flat land with little vegetation. Gardner looked around. They were alone.

"Here, put these on." Gardner tossed one of the two sets of leather gloves at John. "We're going to come here to start your training every day. I know Sullivan. I'm about his size." Gardner had picked up a fallen branch and dragged lines in a square of approximately twenty-four feet per side. "Before you step into the ring with him, I want you to be familiar with all his tricks. I want you to know the rules inside out so you can use them to your advantage. You're much younger, taller, heavier, and stronger, but that won't help if you let him fight his fight. He's the most experienced fighter, and he's only lost once. He believes the championship belongs to him. Taking it won't be easy. Let's see what you've got."

For two hours, Gardner spent his time dodging John's charges, blocking punches with his arms and hands, taking a knee, and slipping out of wrestling grasps. Gardner flicked rapid left jabs at John's eyes whenever he charged and combined hooks and crosses with both hands whenever John was off balance. All the time, he chattered, "This is what Sullivan will do, but he'll do it faster and better. He'll do this for hours if you fight his fight."

When Gardner felt his fighter had nothing left, he said, "Take off those gloves and follow me." Gardner then ran north over the shale rises until they reached the island's tip. There Gardner turned south, following the island's western edge along the Mohawk River. When he saw a large rock, he picked it up and handed it to John to carry. Finally, they turned around the island's southern edge and ran north along the Hudson, past the Van Schaick family mansion.

When they climbed back into the rowboat, John was filthy, breathless, and discouraged. Gardner let him stew as John rowed them back to Troy. He knew John needed to appreciate the challenge ahead and the work it would take to prepare. John Morrissey was no Tom Hyer. He was at least three inches shorter, lighter by twenty pounds, and lacked the former champion's easy athleticism and steady demeanor.

Gardner knew that his young fighter felt invincible. Why not? He had fought hosts of tough men for years and always prevailed. In his mind, he'd won the battle against Thompson, so the much older and smaller Sullivan would be no problem. That made it hard for Gardner to instill proper respect in Morrissey.

The every-other-day rowboat trip to Van Schaick Island continued. Before strapping on the gloves, Gardner would describe the fight plan John needed to practice and follow. "Keep hands up to protect the face. Keep balance, strike in combinations, and wrap up the smaller man. Toss him and land on him. Get him against the ropes and choke the son of a bitch."

Gardner did his best to play the part of Sullivan. Their size and fighting styles were similar. *I'm no Sully, but I could beat this kid.* When John did not follow the proposed fight plan, Gardner would call for time and explain what would happen.

"If you don't keep those paws up, he'll close your peepers within the first rounds. Every time you get a clean shot, he'll drop. Follow up with quick combinations before he goes down. When it looks like he's going to drop, follow him down and land on top, hard. Get him on the ropes with those brawny arms around him and squeeze. Break his ribs or choke him to death. Trust nothing, he says. If he promises to quit, don't believe him."

Gardner's doubts grew. Morrissey was a strong enough lad. He was full of youthful confidence and swagger. He had the heart of a lion and would die before quitting; however, Yankee Sullivan was likely to cut the young man to pieces.

John's next training session with Gardner was the sixteenth, after his return from New York. The *Empire of Troy* pushed out of Pier Four in New York at 7:06 p.m. on the fifteenth. Captain Smith was in the wheelhouse with the ship's pilot, Nathaniel Lewis. It was a warm and humid evening. Passengers remained on deck to watch the city pass by and enjoy whatever breeze blew over the bow. Dinner in the grand salon was at nine.

The crew quarters were empty at this hour. All hands went about their various duties. John enjoyed this quiet time early in the trips up and down the Hudson. He dressed for dinner as eight bells sounded. Then, he joined the captain at his table, taking his bows when he introduced "the California prizefighting champion and soon-to-be champion of America." After the dinners, John changed into work clothes and joined Bosun Maloney and the deckhands.

After midnight, passengers, with few exceptions, abandoned the deck and went below to sleep. Deckhands used this time to scrub and secure the deck. After examining their efforts at around 2:30 a.m., Maloney released the deckhands. They retreated to their quarters for sleep or to play cards. John joined the bosun at the bow for a cigar before turning in.

"Are you allowed to smoke while training?"

"So far, my training is rowing an old boat and scuffling in a filthy field." John took a deep drag on his cigar. "Hamilton tells me I should eat this and that, no alcohol, no smoking, even no sex. Thank God, he's not my trainer."

Both men laughed.

"Look there!" Maloney pointed the glowing tip of his cigar at a large sloop tacking hard to cut across their bow. "She's cutting it mighty close."

Maloney had just spoken those words when their pilot, Nathaniel Lewis, reacted and threw the *Empire*'s wheel to avoid the sloop's sail. This action positioned the *Empire* broadside to the fast-moving ship. Unable to escape the *Empire*'s wake, the *General Livingston* was out of control. Maloney and John rushed to the port rail, glancing up at the wheelhouse, waiting for the pilot to sound a warning. As the *General Livingston* slammed into the *Empire*, Maloney and John fell to the deck.

Captain Smith was in his stateroom when the *Empire* had made the sudden turn. He rushed to the wheelhouse just in time to get jolted by the impact. He ordered the ship's bell to ring and keep ringing. Within a minute of the collision, there was a gigantic explosion. The boiler had dislodged, and super-heated water flooded the lower cabins.

It was terrifying how rapidly the *Empire* filled with water and listed to port. Captain Smith had rushed to the deck to assess the situation. To Maloney, he screamed, "Go below and get the passengers on deck, now!" To John, he shouted, "Get the deckhands up here!"

Within minutes, two ships came alongside; a sloop named *First Effort* and a towboat named *Wyoming*. Maloney and other officers and staff ushered terrified passengers onto the deck. John encouraged the ship's crewmembers to hurry above.

"There's someone in the water," shouted a voice from the towboat. Maloney, who was at the port rail, saw a woman thrashing in the water. He dove into the blackness and disappeared. Moments later, reappearing with his arm tucked under a woman's neck, Maloney struggled toward the towboat. The woman was a young chambermaid who had leaped into the river to escape the deadly steam. Unfortunately, she was dead before they pulled her out of the water.

Captain Smith displayed professional calm as his great ship sank, and he supervised the transfer of passengers to the *First*

Effort, then the crew to the *Wyoming*. The *Empire* continued to take on water. She was lost. Captain Smith turned to John, "What are you waiting for?"

"Why, you, Captain. I'll not be leaving without you."

"We must check below for any injured we missed, Morrissey, then we need to get this ship pushed toward shore."

John struggled up the tilted deck and headed below. Captain Smith was right behind. "Morrissey, go aft and start there. Don't miss the boiler room. Shout if you need help."

The men slogged through the water, calling out at each doorway. Between them, they found the bodies of eight victims. They had no choice except to leave them. "Here," came a shout from fore. "Morrissey, we need help here."

The captain heard feeble voices calling from inside a stateroom. When John arrived, they forced open the door and helped an elderly couple through the water. John carried the woman on his back. Captain Smith followed with the elderly gentleman. They made it up the ladder, onto the slanting deck, and then across to the *First Effort*. With these final survivors on board, the steamer left for New Hamburg. The passengers, including fourteen with severe burns, were transferred to the Van Rensselaer family's nearby home, receiving generous aid and comfort until transportation would bring them to their respective homes.

The *Wyoming* attached towlines to the *Empire* and pulled her into shallow water. At that point, Captain Levi Smith and John Morrissey abandoned the ship. The captain remained near the accident scene to meet the owners and testify to authorities. The *Wyoming* carried the crew of the *Empire* back to Troy. News of the collision would travel quickly. John volunteered to deliver that news to the Smith family home. "

"This is the third such accident my husband has survived." Mrs. Smith wept at the news. David wrapped a consoling arm around her. John nodded at David and left. Upon returning from work, Susannah would hear that her father and lover were safe.

No job meant there was no way to pay for his meals, help his family, compensate Gardner, or secure any room at the Imperial. In addition, John had another installment of stake money due on August 1. The money would be lost, and the fight forfeited if he did not make the deposit. His mind raced as he hurried to the Eastern. There was only one man near at hand to whom he could turn.

When John arrived at the Eastern, Aleck Hamilton was neither in his office nor the saloon. "At the bank, Johnny," was all Marcel Archambeault could tell him. John needed a bath and a change of clothes. He took time for both, then returned to Hamilton's second-floor office.

"We heard about the *Empire*, Johnny. It's all anyone is discussing. Glad you're okay." Hamilton pointed to a chair. "Sit."

John lowered himself into the chair. He sat, head down, not knowing what to say.

Finally, Hamilton said, "Leaves you in a tough spot, no doubt."

"It does, sir."

"Aleck. Please call me, Aleck."

"Not sure what to do. The fight's in less than three months. The stake money's due on August first. Gardner must be paid. My family needs my help."

"I want you to observe what I do, Johnny." Hamilton had removed a ledger book and pen from his desk. He looked across at the young fighter. "How much is due on the stake money?"

John looked at Hamilton, pen poised over the ledger. "Three hundred."

"What have you agreed to pay Gardner?"

"Thirty a month. He got paid for July."

"Are you still giving your mother and sisters ten a month?"

"Yes."

Hamilton sat, adding numbers while John watched.

"Okay, Johnny, here's what I see. You'll need four hundred for your bills until the fight. You also need personal money. I wouldn't do this for anyone else, but I will loan you five hundred. One condition; you work five nights behind the bar. From six until midnight. Until October 11. I'll pay you five a day. Archie will be there too. Plus, we've got another young fighter now. He's good. Irish too. It would be best if you didn't have to fight. Save those fists for Sullivan. You'll be great for my business."

John stumbled for a response. "I don't know what to say."

"Well, try 'thanks,' and 'when do I start?'"

Hamilton wasted no time advertising that the challenger for the American boxing championship was tending bar at the Eastern. The bar crowded every night with the curious and well-wishers. The men who thought to earn a reputation by taking on Morrissey never got past Archie and the new kid, another immigrant from Canada, named Al Fredette.

Gardner now had Morrissey five days per week. He added sprints after lessons and practices on Van Schaick Island. He timed the rowboat trips back and forth to Troy, pushing for faster and faster transit. John's fitness, never in question, was improving; however, his lack of boxing skills, notably hand speed and footwork, continued to worry his trainer.

John delivered money to his mother and sweets for his sisters each Sunday. Tim was faithful to Sundays with his family. With his beautiful baritone, he would entertain with old Irish ballads. Judith would occupy herself in the kitchen preparing the Sunday dinner. She refused to invite her son to dine with the family.

On Saturdays, John would visit Conway's barbershop before walking to Peale's. Susannah would arrive there with Rebecca Walter. John would flag a carriage, and the lovers would check into the Imperial. John would tease that a fighter in training could not engage in sexual activity. Neither took that counsel seriously. They longed for the day when they would never have to part.

Twenty-One

The illegal championship fight between John Morrissey and Yankee Sullivan would be on a farm at Boston Four Corners, one hundred miles north of New York City, near the Harlem Railroad line. The selected farm was not only isolated, but legal authority was in question. New York State and Massachusetts claimed the area, but neither cared enough to prosecute their claim. It was unlikely that authorities would try to prevent or disrupt the fight. As a result, the fight was well-publicized.

When Wednesday, October 12, arrived, extra railroad cars filled for both northbound and southbound trains. The atmosphere was that of a spirited holiday. It was four and a half years since the last fight for the American championship, and much had changed in young America.

Railways enabled thousands of spectators to travel long distances in hours to see this fight. News of this event would travel faster than any prior event, with telegraph lines speeding the news of the fight throughout the country in hours. Newspaper presses would deliver the blow-by-blow accounts within a day. The winner was certain to be among the most famous people in America.

Passion drove the men who packed trains and walked miles to a broad field at the remote farmstead. Parties and factions now dominated America's politics, and this fight was a proxy for one of the country's frothiest divisions. To the Irish fans, John Morrissey embodied their resistance to repression. His victory would be theirs. Those who despised the new Irish and Catholic immigrants traveled to see him destroyed. Though Irish-born, Yankee Sullivan was accepted as a worthy American champion because of his association with Tom Hyer, other nativist, and American Party leaders.

John rode the southbound train that morning with a large following from Troy and the surrounding area. A crowd gathered at the Troy station to send their champion off to battle as he stood on the steps of the car, soaking up the adulation.

Awful Gardner never left his fighter's side. He had done all he could to prepare John for the day. He hoped that lessons and practice would help. Experience taught Gardner that everything changes when the fight begins. *Just keep the boy calm* was all he could think now.

Sullivan had served in Thompson's corner and watched the ease with which he'd outfought Morrissey at Mare Island. The most he could credit the brash young Irishman with courage. For his part, Sully had taken the much larger Hyer too lightly four years earlier, losing the American championship. He would not make that mistake this time.

On the fight day, John, age twenty-two, stood at five-eleven and weighed one hundred seventy-five pounds. Sullivan, age forty-one, stood five-nine and weighed one hundred fifty-four pounds. Sully was old enough to be Morrissey's father and looked it. Betting favored the younger, larger man.

Choosing a referee for the fight was difficult. There was no selection process in advance. Someone in attendance had to be willing and acceptable to both parties. The excited crowd grew restless while the parties agreed on Charles Allaire. It was Allaire's first and only experience as a fight referee.

Someone presented Allaire a well-worn copy of the London Prize Ring Rules, which he opened to a section supplying instructions to the fighter. He called both corners to the scratch line and read the instructions. The fighters glared at each other. It was one-twenty when Sam McLaughlin, the designated timekeeper, called Morrissey and Sullivan to scratch, and the crowd surged forward.

Both fighters started with caution. Sullivan attacked first with a left that caught Morrissey on the nose, drawing first blood. Sullivan supporters sent up a wild cheer. The fight was on. Morrissey rushed his foe, swinging with wild rights and lefts, none connecting. The experienced Sullivan slashed at the young man's face. When Morrissey landed a blow, Sullivan slipped and fell, ending the round.

Gardner was seeing what he had feared during training. Morrissey was paying a terrific price for his lack of patience and skill. Sullivan, of course, saw the same. He sprinted to scratch with a smile to begin round two. Morrissey charged the smaller fighter, letting a roundhouse fly. Sullivan avoided the punch, countering with a solid right to Morrissey's left eye. The fighters stood toe to toe, exchanging blows to the crowd's delight. Morrissey landed solid punches, but Sullivan remained in control, pecking away at Morrissey's face, working at the eyes.

As round two ended, the betting odds had shifted from Morrissey to Sullivan. The Irish hero's supporters had grown quiet. Aleck Hamilton, Marcel Archambeault, Dad Cunningham, Nate Parker, and Shang Allen were there. They had seen Morrissey in similar peril and watched him prevail. They stood by their wagers and waited.

Morrissey performed better in rounds three through fourteen. He still absorbed three blows to each one he landed, but those had an impact. He staggered Sullivan with blows to the head in the fourth, sixth, and tenth. In round eleven, Morrissey connected with a blow to the ribs that "sounded like the crack of a whip."

"Go on, Johnny," screamed his corner, "more like that will finish him."

However, it was clear that Morrissey lacked the hand speed and experience to follow up on opportunities. Sullivan continued to slash and hammer at will. Morrissey's appearance was now repulsive. His nose was crushed. Blood flowed from both nostrils, staining his shoulders and chest. A deep cut above his left eye and swelling around both made it impossible for him to see. Somehow, he kept advancing, throwing wild punches, and trying to tackle Sullivan.

Morrissey sat, exhausted, on Tom O'Donnell's knee between rounds while Gardner sponged blood from the fighter's face and body. He lanced Morrissey's left eye to keep it open enough to see and urged his fighter to wrap Sullivan in his arms, drop on him, or bully him to the ropes and strangle him. It was desperation time.

In Sullivan's corner, Bill Poole assessed his fighter's condition. The left eye had swelled to a slit. Blood flowed from a gash on his left cheek. Worse, he had lacerated two of the knuckles on his right hand on Morrissey's teeth. Poole looked Sullivan in the eyes. "Take your time, Sully. Keep moving. Dart in. Quick jabs, then go to the grass." Sullivan nodded.

Morrissey, thereafter, never laid a glove on the cagey fighter who dropped to the turf before Morrissey could strike. Aleck Hamilton kept screaming at Allaire to disqualify Sullivan for falling without being hit. At the start of round twenty-seven, Sullivan came out laughing. "Now, do you think yourself the champion of America?" he taunted.

In round thirty-two, Allaire responded to Hamilton's constant demands to disqualify Sullivan for dropping. He paused the fight and asked for the rule book. Somehow, he did not read or ignored rule twelve, which states, "If either man willfully throws himself down without receiving a blow, he shall be deemed to have lost the fight." Instead, he allowed the fight to go forward and Sullivan to continue violating the rule.

Morrissey was very unsteady in rounds thirty-three through thirty-five, unable to mount an attack or defend himself. Sullivan was blowing hard from the exertion. He would take a step back, take a deep breath, and resume his assault on a now helpless opponent. Gardner picked up the sponge and was ready to end the fight. Hamilton screamed, "Not yet!"

Round thirty-seven began like recent rounds. With the damaged right hand, Sullivan's punches lacked impact, but Morrissey could not capitalize. Sullivan stepped back to catch his breath, and as he did, Morrissey rushed forward, wrapped his right arm around Sullivan's neck, and backed him into the ropes. He picked the smaller man off the ground and prepared to choke him into unconsciousness—or death. This was legal under London Prize Ring Rules. Allaire did not intervene.

Bill Poole rushed in and slammed into Morrissey, breaking his grasp on the suffocating Sullivan. Suddenly free from the vice grip, Sullivan attacked Morrissey while still on his knee. Awful Gardner and Tom O'Donnell rushed in, and a melee was on. Allaire should have cleared the ring and passed judgment on the fouls. Instead, he shouted into the melee for the fighters to approach the scratch line to start round thirty-eight. Too absorbed in a battle with Awful Gardner, Sullivan ignored Allaire's repeated demands. Morrissey stood, wobbling, at scratch. After a three-minute effort to resume the fight, Allaire raised John Morrissey's right arm, declaring him the American champion.

Even as Sullivan's supporters howled in protest, Morrissey accepted the championship belt and rushed from the scene. Morrissey had realized his great ambition. He was twenty-two and the champion of America.

Twenty-Two

"S he can't see me like this." The new champion struggled to speak through his swollen, bleeding lips. He sat between Marcel Archambeault and Nathan Parker in a carriage Hamilton hired to carry them back to Troy. Hamilton sat across from the unrecognizable youth and leaned close. "What did you say, Johnny?"

"Suzie can't see me like this." John leaned forward, covered his devastated face with his hands, and wept.

"I'll have a doctor see you at the Eastern. That nose is bad, but the swelling, cuts, and bruises will heal. You know that."

Within minutes, John was asleep. He remained that way until the carriage pulled up in front of the Eastern. A large and boisterous crowd had gathered at the hotel, awaiting news of the fight. Madam Veronica and her girls waited on the porch, straining to see. When Hamilton climbed out, they shouted for news of the outcome.

Hamilton lifted his hand, smiling at the excited gathering. "John Morrissey is the new champion of the United States!"

An enormous cheer went up. More men and boys came running.

"Give us space now, please. The champion will see you later. A free drink for every man. Inside now, all of you!"

Archambeault climbed down and helped Hamilton herd the curious crowd inside. Parker placed a cloth over John's head and guided his unsteady friend into the hotel and up to the fourth floor.

Veronica was already in John's room. She and Parker helped him onto the bed, pulled off his shoes, removed his blood-stained clothes, and covered him with a blanket.

John turned to Parker, trying to lift his head. "Go to the Smith house? Tell them I won. Now, Nathan. Please."

Fetching a bucket of water and towels, Veronica worked to clear the blood and grime. Tears streamed down her face as she dabbed the wrecked face of the recently handsome boy. *What have you done, Johnny? By God, what have you done?*

Parker found the Smith home and knocked on the door. Addie peered out the bay window and shouted, "It's a Black man! It's a Black man!"

David opened the door. "Can I help you?"

Parker removed his hat and said, "John Morrissey asked me to inform you, sir, that he's prevailed."

Addie stood behind her older brother, and Susannah rushed down the stairs.

"How is he?" asked David.

"He's suffered injuries, sir, but will recover."

Susannah now stood next to David. She asked Parker, "Where is he?"

Parker looked from Susannah to David and back again. "At the Eastern Hotel, miss, but it's not yet time to visit."

Susannah was pulling a shawl on when David grabbed her shoulder and said, "I'll go. He retrieved a light jacket and hat from a nearby coat rack and rushed away with Parker.

Hamilton sent for Doctor Whetstone before addressing the packed crowd in the saloon. "Your champion stood a heroic test for thirty-seven brutal rounds and is resting." The proprietor accepted a brandy offered by Archambeault. "A toast, fellow Trojans, to John Morrissey, champion of America!"

Dozens raised a glass and sustained loud cheers for their local hero.

Then, a voice rose urgently from the crowd. "Aside, step aside; where's my son?" It was Tim Morrissey, struggling to reach Hamilton.

The proprietor went to him and took him by the arm. "This way, Tim." He led him through the saloon and up the stairs to the fourth floor.

Doctor Whetstone was tending John when Hamilton and the fighter's father rushed in. Veronica remained by the bed, ready to help. The prostitutes waited in the hallway, crying, and comforting each other. Doctor Whetstone turned to Veronica and asked her to close the door.

"This is the boy's father," Veronica said to the doctor.

Without turning, he said, "The superficial damage will heal quickly. I'll stitch the cut above his eye and that nasty one on his cheek. The nose, as you can see, took a smashing. I did my best to reset it, but it will never be as it was. He has damage to his knuckles, but no other broken bones that I can tell. Some loose teeth, but I think they'll stay put.

"It looks worse than it is." Dr. Whetstone withdrew a needle and catgut and sutured the cut above the eye, then the cheek. John flinched but uttered no complaint.

The doctor closed his large leather bag and turned to Veronica. "Would you see to those bandages tomorrow morning and evening? Must prevent infection, you know. Boil your water, mind you. I'll return tomorrow to check on him." The doctor instructed Hamilton, "Get the boy six ounces of whiskey every few hours and keep things quiet around here. He needs rest. No visitors." To Tim Morrissey: "Don't worry. He'll be fine. Not pretty for a while, but he'll be presentable in a couple of weeks."

David Smith walked briskly to the Eastern with Nathan Parker. Along the way, Parker recapped the terrible struggle at Boston Four Corners. Still, Smith was ill-prepared when he walked into John's room and saw the wrecked face of his sister's lover. Parker took him by the sleeve and walked him to the hallway, where Veronica joined them.

"Who might this be?" she asked.

"Name's David Smith. Morrissey's been a deckhand on my father's steamer. He's a family friend."

Veronica nodded and whispered, "The doctor just left. He sewed a couple of nasty cuts. The rest, he said, will heal. The boy's just gone to sleep, bless his heart."

Smith thanked the madam and Parker, climbed down the hotel stairs, sat on the hotel's steps with his head between his legs, vomited, and headed back home.

Susannah was waiting by the bay window for David to return. She met him at the door. "Please tell me the truth, David. How did you find him?"

"He would not want you to see him now, Suzie. He's severely beaten, but the doctor insists he'll heal completely."

"I have to go to him!"

David stood between her and the door.

"For your sake and his, Suzie, I can't let you do that."

"But I must!" Tears streamed down Susannah's face. She sobbed, trying to shove her brother aside. David wrapped his arms around her. The sobbing brought Mrs. Smith and Addie running.

"What's wrong?" The scene of David trying to comfort her sobbing daughter terrified her. "What's happened?" She could only think that harm had come to her husband.

"I'm afraid I've delivered news that's distressed Suzie. John Morrissey won the American boxing championship today. I went to see him arrive back at the Eastern Hotel. I described his appearance in a way that was too graphic. That's all, Mother."

"Is Mr. Morrissey severely injured?" Mrs. Smith asked.

"Yes, but he'll recover fine. I'll take Suzie for a walk. I owe her an apology." He opened the front door and led his sister down the stairs and onto River Street.

"David, I must go to him. I'm going mad with worry."

"I understand, Suzie, but think. John's not in danger. He's sleeping, which is what he needs most. I'll check on him tomorrow and Friday after the doctor sees him. I'll describe your concern. Let's give him a say about when you see him." Susannah pulled away and stopped walking. The sobbing had ceased.

"I don't care how he looks! I don't care what Mother or Father thinks. We're to marry, and I belong by his side!"

David knew his sister well. There was no redirecting her once she had set a course. He sighed. "I'll go with you after breakfast tomorrow. You can tell Mother we're visiting one of your Troy Seminary friends at the hospital."

"Thank you, David," she said as she turned back toward their home.

Demands to see and interview the new champion began on Thursday morning. Local newspapers were first. Afternoon trains delivered writers from New York City and Boston. They were all directed to Aleck Hamilton. Hamilton had posted guards at the entrance to the hotel and in the saloon. "The champion, John Morrissey," he told everyone, "Is fine." Rumors ran wild. Hamilton did his best to protect the new champion. "No, he's not near death," he insisted over and over. "No, he does not have permanent damage." "No, he is not in a hospital." "Yes, of course, he beat Sullivan." "I don't know if they'll fight again." The questions kept coming, and the longer John remained out of the public eye, the more life the rumors took on.

Tim delivered the news of his son's victory to Judith and John's sisters on Wednesday night. He did not describe his son's physical condition. Instead, he told them it was a tough contest, and Johnny was resting in his room at the Eastern.

"Can we see him?" asked Catherine.

Judith replied, "No daughter of mine will ever go near such a vile place!"

Tim promised to visit his son daily and to report to the family. Tim looked from daughter to daughter, threw back his shoulders, and said, "He's a famous man now. The name, John Morrissey, is spoken today throughout the land."

Fifteen thousand miles of telegraph lines crisscrossed the United States on the day of the championship fight. For the first time in the sport's history, people throughout the country discovered the fight details within a day. Tim Morrissey was correct. Throughout America and beyond, John Morrissey was instantly famous. His life would never be the same.

On Thursday, October 13, Susannah left her River Street home with her brother. They said little as they walked to the Eastern Hotel. Aleck Hamilton had posted a guard in the hotel's small lobby to keep reporters and other visitors from disturbing John. Except for monthly renters, he closed off the fourth floor. When Susannah and David arrived, the hotel manager informed them that Mr. Morrissey was not having visitors.

David stood close to the manager and spoke softly. "Would you kindly tell Mr. Hamilton that Susannah Smith is here to see Mr. Morrissey?"

"Is she family?" The manager looked toward the young woman, then at the posted guard, who scowled at them.

David knew it would take authorization from Hamilton for his sister to visit. "May we speak with Mr. Hamilton, please? Both he and Mr. Morrissey will want to see my sister."

The guard said, "We got orders. Nobody can disturb Morrissey. You gotta leave."

David turned to Susannah, took her by the arm, and whispered, "Let's find Mr. Hamilton." He led her out the hotel entrance and to the saloon. It was too early for patrons to begin their drinking. David peeked inside, then motioned for Susannah to join him. The man who had brought news of the fight and went with David to the Eastern was busy cleaning off the long bar. He wiped his hands and went to the pair.

"David, right?" Nathan Parker smiled as he looked at the young man and young woman.

"Yes, I'm David, and this is my sister, Susannah. We've come to see John."

Parker frowned. "Nobody's allowed to see him. Boss's orders."

Susannah insisted, "We need to speak with Mr. Hamilton."

Parker saw her agitation. He guessed that this was his friend's secret lover. "I'll be right back," he said and went through the door and upstairs.

Within minutes, David and Susannah heard footsteps coming down. Aleck Hamilton looked tired and concerned as he approached. "David, it's good to see you. This must be Susannah. Good to meet you, though the circumstances are not good."

She took his hand and looked him in the eyes. "I'm here to see Mr. Morrissey, sir." Susannah's jaw was set. She did not release Hamilton's hand nor break eye contact.

"His doctor insists that he rest and receive no visitors," Hamilton spoke the truth, but his heart already wavered.

"I must insist. I am not just a visitor. I am betrothed to Mr. Morrissey and belong at his side."

Hamilton turned to David. "I'll escort your sister to Mr. Morrissey's room and provide a carriage when she wishes to return home."

As he walked up to the fourth floor, Hamilton tried to prepare Susannah. "You'll be upset when you see him, Miss Smith. Remember, what you see will heal. He's had stitches over his eye and cheek, so there are bandages. He got his nose busted. There're purple bruises over his face. Lips are cut and swollen, but his teeth are okay. He slept yesterday and was awake for a while last night. I give him whiskey regularly. The doctor will be back sometime today to check on him."

When they reached the fourth floor, Hamilton grabbed Susannah's arm. "Try not to react too strongly when you see him. He didn't want you to see him like this."

She pulled away and ran to John's room. She knew, of course, where it was.

Veronica saw the lovely young lady reach the door and stop. Morrissey was sleeping soundly, and the madam had just put fresh bandages over his left eye and cheek. There was no sign of infection and no fever that she could detect. Veronica went to the corner of the room, moved a chair next to the bed, and turned to Susannah, "I'll be leaving you alone now," she whispered, then walked out the door and pulled it closed behind her.

Susannah sat beside her lover, leaned over, and kissed his matted hair. She found his right hand under the wool blanket and caressed the injured knuckles. *It only hurts after a fight.* That's what he had said at Peale's. The damage to his face was frightful. *What you see will heal.* That's what Mr. Hamilton had just said. Susannah steeled herself, removed her shawl with her free hand, and waited.

At midday, Veronica returned with a plate of food for Susannah. She placed it on the small nightstand next to the bed. "I have to get some water into him," she said as she poured a glass of water from a pitcher. Veronica walked to the opposite side and elevated John's head. She touched the glass to his mouth, coaxing him to sip. Instead, he coughed up the small amount that passed his lips. As she tried again, his right eye opened.

"Here you go, Johnny. You gotta be drinking this." Veronica put the glass to his mouth. He held his head up enough to drink a couple of ounces before letting his head fall back. He moaned as he drifted to sleep.

Susannah had no appetite. Her plate of food remained untouched. When alone again, she leaned close, whispered words of love, recited favorite poems, and spoke of a world of shared happiness and success that awaited them. It was her declaration of devotion to her chosen partner and her new self. He would no longer need to fight in the life she imagined. He would become a great man, and she would be his muse. She released his hand and rested hers over his heart. She closed her eyes and felt the steady beat. "Forever," she whispered.

Twenty-Three

J ohn Morrissey left his suite of rooms on the fifth floor at Irving House, pulled his wool coat around his neck, and stepped into the cold and a blowing snowfall. He looked left and right, a prudent habit whenever he was in New York City, before heading to One-Seventy Nassau Street.

Isaiah Rynders chose ten o'clock for the meeting. The Nassau Street address was the home of the Society of Tammany, a social and political organization where Rynders was a leader, or "chieftain." Rynders was eager to introduce the new Irish Catholic boxing champion to the other chieftains. He had big plans for Morrissey.

When John arrived, he knocked on the door and waited until a smartly dressed man standing a shade over six feet and weighing at least two hundred and eighty pounds opened the door. His right eye was milky white, causing him to favor his left as he appraised the young man before him. "Can I help you, sir?" The voice was deep, the tone suspicious.

"I'm John Morrissey. Got a meeting with Captain Rynders."

A smile spread across the huge man's face. "Ah, the Irish champion. You look better than expected. Read about your battle with Sullivan. Good for you, young man. Please follow me." The doorman turned and started up the stairs with John on his heels. They turned to enter a large room on the left on the second floor. A group of gentlemen sat around a gigantic fireplace. Above the fireplace was an enormous painting of Tamanend, the Lenape tribal leader from whom the organization derived its name.

Isaiah Rynders was among the group who stood when John entered. He said, "Gentlemen, I'm proud to introduce my friend and the new boxing champion of our great nation, Mr. John Morrissey. Please join us, John."

Rynders gestured to a chair as he and the other gentlemen took their seats. The doorman accepted John's overcoat and hat and retreated from the room, closing the massive door.

John recognized two of the men as regular visitors at Pétale de Rose. There was no sign that they recognized him. Rynders did not try to introduce the men.

After an uncomfortable silence, a familiar-looking older man spoke to the champion. "John, I wish to share private things with you. I must ask you to swear an oath of secrecy. You cannot share what you hear today with anyone outside this room. If you so swear, we can continue. If not, you can leave with our congratulations on your championship and good wishes for future success. Do you understand?"

"Yes, sir. I'd swear that oath." John sat forward in his seat and scanned the men's faces.

The current mayor, Jacob Aaron Westervelt, continued. "You may not know all the men here, but you know who I am. Rynders invited you here because my term as mayor ends this year. We're determined to elect a new mayor who'll continue my work and the work of the Democratic Party. We have the right candidate. You'll meet him shortly. He will face a strong American Party candidate in Jim Barker, plus a Whig candidate, and others."

Mayor Westervelt paused, allowing John the opportunity to ask questions. He continued when there were none. "It's Barker and the American Party that worries us. We know that the Temperance League plans to support him. We also have word that the former champion, Tom Hyer, plans to campaign for him instead of his Whig Party's candidate. It won't be easy for us. The Irish vote will decide it. Your people have much to lose if Barker becomes mayor. We need to get every Irish voter registered and at the polls this fall. We think you can help us."

John glanced at Rynders, who was smoking a cigar. Rynders nodded yes to Morrissey. John turned back to Mayor Westervelt, then looked around the room at the others. They were waiting for a response.

"I'm no politician, Mayor," John said, "I fight for the Irish whenever I must. Captain Rynders knows. Are you needing me to fight?"

Westervelt stifled a laugh. "Well, Mr. Morrissey, on election day, you might have to use those famous fists, but between now and then, we would like you to use your influence instead. Rynders will explain more. In the meantime, we can help your new gambling business. We have influential friends."

The mayor stood, and the others joined him. They departed, leaving John and Rynders.

"What's that about, Captain?" John whispered to Rynders.

Rynders motioned John to retake his seat. "The Democrats are afraid they'll lose the mayor's office come November. That's why they come pleading to Tammany. The other parties are stirring up fear of immigrants, especially Irish Catholics, and the papers are mostly with them. The only way Democrats can hold the mayor's office is to get hundreds of Irishmen to the polls. I told them you could help."

"I don't know." John stood shaking his head. "I can't see me standing on corners doing speeches. I got a business to run. So why should I get tangled in this?"

"You heard the mayor, John. The Democrats have powerful friends. So does Tammany. It'll be good for you and your business. But, if the American Party gets control, things will be far worse for you and all Irish in this city. That's enough reason for you to step in."

"I still don't know how I can help. I fight with Allen and the Dead Rabbits, as you suggested. We'd kill all those Irish haters if we could. Ain't that enough?"

"Not for you, John. You're the American boxing champion. You were born in Ireland and arrived as poor as any of them. You're a glorious hero to the Irish. Who you associate with and what you say have an influence when it's voting time. Democrats need to run this city, and your Irish need the Democrats. Remember what I said to you when you met Shang, *Power equals opportunity, and opportunity equals money.* As the champion, you have power. As a friend of Tammany, you'll have more power and money. Trust me on both counts."

John knew he needed friends in the city government to protect and grow his gambling business; however, what Rynders, Tammany, or the Democrats expected from him remained unclear. "I'll help, Captain. Just tell me how."

Before Rynders could respond, a dapper man of approximately forty entered the room. He wore his glossy black hair combed carefully across his head, hiding his balding forehead. He was immaculately attired. He moved gracefully toward Rynders and Morrissey.

"Why, what an immense pleasure it is to meet the great American champion." He extended his hand. "Welcome to Tammany Hall, Mr. Morrissey. May I offer you brandy?"

Rynders jumped in with an introduction. "John, this is the grand sachem of our Tammany Society, Fernando Wood. He has agreed to represent the Democratic Party as their candidate for mayor."

Wood smiled. "Thank you, Isaiah. Yes, I would be honored, Mr. Morrissey, to enjoy the right to lead this great city. Unfortunately, my candidacy is not yet public knowledge. Can I count on you to keep that confidential?"

John could feel the charismatic energy of the man still pumping his hand. "Yes, of course. You can count on it."

Wood dropped John's hand. "Good then. What about that

brandy, young man? I know it's early, but men should always seal understandings with a toast, should they not?"

"Sure, but what understandings?"

Wood looked at Rynders, then back to John. "I expected that my friend, Isaiah, already told you we hoped for your support for the upcoming election."

"I did," said Rynders.

"He's working on it," said John.

"Good. An Irish champion, and one so young and handsome. Our opponents can have Hyer, that swaggering oaf. We have the champion of the people. I won't forget your support, John Morrissey. We take care of our own."

A server arrived with three crystal brandy snifters on a silver tray. Each man lifted one and waited for Wood's toast, "To the greatest city in the world, the Democratic Party, The Society of St. Tammany, our great country, and America's boxing champion, our John Morrissey."

They lifted their glasses and downed the expensive brandy.

Fernando Wood shook John's hand again as he prepared to leave. He studied the young champion and placed his left hand on his right bicep, squeezing. "I look forward to a long and rewarding friendship, Mr. Morrissey." He nodded to Rynders and left.

John and Rynders retrieved their overcoats and hats and exited Tammany Hall. The snow and wind had ceased, but it was colder than when John had arrived. The smoke from the chimneys along Nassau Street appeared suspended in frozen white columns. The usual cacophony of street traffic was eerily muted by the snowdrifts covering everything.

John pulled up his collar and turned to Rynders. "Should I trust that man?"

Rynders saw his carriage pulling up and started down the steps. Without turning, he answered, "As much as you can trust any politician, young man."

Rather than hail a hansom cab, John decided to walk to the Belle of the Union. He needed to consider the meeting with the

Tammany chieftains and Fernando Wood. They wished to use his influence with Irishmen to help gain and control the city government. What were they willing to do for the Irish Catholic immigrants with that control? None of the men he had met were Irish. Oath aside, he needed to discuss his concerns with trusted people.

Dad was thriving as manager of the Belle of the Union. With the initial investments that he, John, and Tom Petrie made, he had opened an operation that was degrees superior to those in the lower wards. Though not large, the Belle of the Union used massive mirrors to create an illusion of size and splendor, a trick Dad borrowed from the *Niantic*. A tall ceiling helped to soften the noise and disperse cigar smoke. A series of chandeliers kept the interior brilliantly illuminated, day and night.

The principals in Belle of the Union agreed that all games would be square, that any employee caught cheating a guest would be terminated, and that minors and women would not be allowed. With antigambling sentiment on the rise, it was prudent to cut the most morally objectionable aspects of the business. Petrie wanted to close on Sundays, but John had insisted they remain open, saying, "Men get one day off. Even if they go to church, they have the rest of the day to relax and spend hard-earned cash!"

After John's victory at Boston Corner, Dad repainted the sign above the door. It now read, "John Morrissey's Belle of the Union." Business doubled in the weeks after the championship fight and continued to grow after the beginning of the new year. When the new champion returned to Belle of the Union, he was surprised by the crush of men who wanted to congratulate and shake his hand. Before taking his nightly seat at an eight-person poker table, he stood inside the entry and greeted guests for two hours. Most, naturally, were Irishmen who looked upon the young champion with adulation. Some brought their sons, who could not enter. John would often go outside to shake their hands.

The Belle of the Union locked its doors at two in the morning, but John's poker table sometimes continued through the night.

Dad would wait until everyone left. John would deliver his table's cash to be added to the rest of the day's receipts. While Dad secured the last of the day's currency and the ledger in the safe, John poured drinks. Afterward, Dad joined his partner for a celebratory drink.

John said, "Can we spend a while? I'll be needing your advice."

Dad smiled. "Of course, Johnny."

John went over the morning events at Tammany, including the request to support a chieftain named Fernando Wood, who planned to run for mayor later in the year. John recounted the Tammany men promising, "it'd be good for the city's Irish and our business interests. They swore me to keep it secret before they'd speak a word, so this stays between us."

Dad downed his whiskey and refilled his glass. "I know the same as the next guy about the mysterious Tammany Hall, which isn't much. Wood's a real estate investor. I hear he's the big boss at Tammany. Makes sense they want him as mayor with Westervelt leaving the job."

"What if Wood loses in November?" John asked. "And we backed him? Would the new mayor and backers come after Belle of the Union?"

"I suppose they would," Dad replied.

"That's what I think too. Don't discuss this with anyone, even Petrie. I'll speak with a couple of others. I'll be back before six, Dad."

John decided to hail a carriage for the ride to Grand Street. The wind had picked up, and snow was falling again. The driver turned onto Broadway and cursed at the snarled traffic and pedestrians trying to cross through the snow piles. John climbed out at Belson's Livery, just west on Grand, more than an hour after boarding the carriage.

No one was inclined to walk on such a day, so a line of returning carriages ran half a block in both directions. Livery workers rushed to prepare horses and carriages for departures.

Others managed those returning, including Shang, who spotted John and waved.

"Johnny," he shouted to be heard over the livery's noise, "I've been thinking about you. Mary Louise wants you to be joining us for dinner." Shang continued to bridle a pair of Morgans as he grinned at his friend. "Thursday night?"

John waited for snow- and ice-caked Brougham carriage to be led past, then hollered, "Yes, six work? Gotta be at Belle of the Union by eight."

Shang shouted, "Yes," and returned his attention to the Morgans.

On Thursday afternoon, John went to the ticket office on Chambers Street and bought a round-trip ticket for the express train to Troy for Sunday morning with a return on Monday. Susannah would be the final person with whom he would discuss the Tammany opportunity.

After securing the rail tickets, he walked to Broadway and the St. Nicolas Hotel. The new six-story hotel occupied the entire block between Spring and Broome Streets. He headed to Phelan's barbershop for a haircut at one of their twelve chairs. Since he could not yet read newspapers, the chatter at Phelan's was a terrific source of rumor and news. Today, he also intended to stop by the hotel's confectioner to buy a box of sugar plums for the Allen children.

Father Finnegan, once again, was a guest of the Allen family when John arrived just before six o'clock. Shang greeted his friend at the door. John handed over the candies, whispering, "Best be giving these to Mrs. Allen." John joined Father Finnegan on the couch where he was regaling the children with a story of ancient giants who roamed Ireland's rugged northern coast, fighting off invaders. The twin boys sat raptly at his feet while their toddler brother rushed to John as soon as he sat, extending his arms.

Mary Louise shouted a greeting from the kitchen. "Welcome, John. Ann Marie is putting dinner on the table this very moment."

Shang appeared in the doorway, shaking his head at the sight of his children with his oddly matched friends, then announced, "Let's be gathering around the table now."

Father Finnegan offered a blessing, the family dug into the rich stew and fresh bread, and the twins insisted that the priest continue the story of the Irish giants. Mary Louise sat next to John, leaning close, as everyone listened to the heroic tale of the ancient giants, and she whispered, "You are quite the famous man, John. We are all proud of you. The children and I would be honored if you'd join us at church on Sunday."

John turned and answered, "I'll be at Troy this Sunday, but I'd be honored to join you next week."

Shang carried a bottle of whiskey and three glasses to the living room. He handed a glass to Father Finnegan, who sat in the corner of the well-used couch, and one to John, who pulled a chair in close. The young Jesuit reached inside his jacket and withdrew a folded newspaper page. "I'd like to read part of a recent editorial if you don't mind."

John and Shang drew closer.

"I'm sure I don't need to tell you about the growing violence against Irish Catholics, but these newspapers fuel this hatred daily. Here is part of an editorial from the *New York Express*." Father Finnegan read in a quiet voice so the children wouldn't hear: *We live to see the day when more than the balance of power is in the hands of those who are neither bone of our bone nor flesh of our flesh—of men who have no love for the country in which they live, no sympathy for what America is. The stripes upon our flag are emblems of the scourges America is to receive from the banded aliens in our midst, who proclaim aloud, Americans shall not rule us!*

The young Jesuit paused to let that sink in, then continued, "So many editorials in our leading papers inflame the hatred and violence we see more of each day. *Americans,* the editorial shouts, *must protect themselves. At present, Americans have fewer privileges than foreigners. If necessary, we are compelled to use bullets to defend our country.*

The priest refolded the newspaper page and returned it to his pocket.

Shang leaned closer and snarled, "Let them bring their bullets. We'll bring plenty of our own, we will."

John nodded.

Father Finnegan leaned forward and said, "Archbishop Hughes asked me to counsel patience. Escalation of violence, according to His Excellency, only makes things worse for us. The Church recently bought an influential newspaper in the city to counter the attacks, and our archbishop travels the world raising money for schools, churches, hospitals, and orphanages. He insists the children's education and welfare must come first. In the meantime, our neighborhoods must have less violence, not more."

Shang stood and walked to the bay window, staring at the procession of people heading home from work. "What's to become of the wee ones if their fathers are dead and mothers abused on the streets and in other people's homes where they work for pennies? Will they all be huddled on these cold streets or raised in orphanages? How would your archbishop answer?"

John walked to the pocket doors between the living and dining rooms and pulled them shut. Father Finnegan waited until he returned to his seat before answering Shang. "The Church teaches it's sinful to respond to hatred and violence in kind, Shang. I would imagine that our archbishop would leave it at that." The priest joined Shang at the window and looked down the busy street. He placed his hand on Shang's shoulder and said, "Those women returning from their jobs can walk this street with little fear. Your efforts, Johnny's, and those of other faithful Irishmen protect this neighborhood and others like it. Your beautiful children and wife enjoy a measure of safety because of you. The archbishop suggests patience and prayer, even as he fights with the Church's pocketbook for a better future."

The three men sat again. Shang poured another few ounces of whiskey into their glasses.

After an awkward silence, John asked, "Can we be trusting Captain Rynders and Tammany to help us Irish?"

Father Finnegan and Shang Allen stared at each other for a moment. Shang said, "Rynders is with Tammany now because it lines his pockets. He's loyal only to himself. Not a man to be trusted, Johnny, but a man that can be useful."

The priest considered his words carefully. "The Society of Saint Tammany is as old as this country. Prominent citizens of this city and beyond are members. The Church has no affiliation with the secret society; however, their alignment with the Democratic Party is good for the Irish currently. Our votes are the margin by which they can control the city government. The aldermen have the power to appoint police, including precinct officers. They grant and suspend saloon licenses within their district, which I know, Johnny, matters to you. Each alderman serves as a judge in criminal courts, deciding who sits for juries and which cases come to trial." Father Finnegan kept his eyes on John. "So, yes, we can trust Tammany, for now, to support the Irish. It's in their interest to do so, and that won't change if they can count on our votes."

John nodded as he looked from the priest to Shang. "Rynders wanted me to meet the mayor and the other swells at Tammany. Wood, the man they want for mayor, needs my help with the Irish vote. He said it'd be good for my business, and it'd be bad for all Irish if he lost. Should I help him?"

Shang said, "You're champion of America, Johnny. To our Irish, you're a great hero. If you ask Irishmen to vote, they will. I know something about Fernando Wood and his brother; they own property here and treat the Irish fairly. If he's the Democrat candidate, you should help him."

John stared at Father Finnegan. The priest had his eyes on the dark whiskey swirling in his glass. After finishing the drink, he met John's gaze. "What Wood said about Democrats losing their grip on power is true. The American Party candidate could be elected this fall. That would give the Irish-hating nativists control of the highest office in the city. They would make it hard for Irishmen to get naturalized, secure decent jobs, and vote. So, yes, I believe you can and should help Tammany and Fernando Wood."

A glistening new steam locomotive sat on the tracks outside the Chambers Street ticket office. It was named the Nathaniel McKay, after one of the McKay and Aldus Iron Works owners. The engineer was doing a walk-around before departure. He spotted John Morrissey as he was boarding the sole passenger car. "Hey, Champ!" he shouted. John paused on the first iron step and saw the engineer smiling and gesturing for him to join him.

"Care to ride up here with me, Mr. Morrissey?" The engineer pointed to the cab at the rear of the brand-new locomotive.

"Long as I don't gotta be the fireman!" John quipped.

"It would be an honor to tell my boys that I rode with the champion. My name is Hogan, Patrick. Family is from County Tipperary, like yours." Hogan removed a work glove and offered his hand to John. "Fireman's already up there, warming the engines. He's a German named Bauer, quiet type, but he's the best fireman on the line."

John looked over the gleaming engine, with its wheels every bit as tall as him. "Can I sound the bell?"

The engineer later signaled John to ring the engine's bell as he eased the train forward. Though the space was cramped, hot, and noisy, the view from that unobstructed perch and the impossible-to-imagine power as they pulled away from the confines of the city was awe-inspiring. Hogan kept a running monologue about the new engine as he pointed at an indicator registering their increasing speed every few minutes. "The tracks are good in sections, not in others. There's a stretch where I can show you what this modern wonder can do."

John stared out the front windshield and saw a curve ahead that followed the Hudson River's contour. He knew the stretch of water very well. The engineer pushed the throttle forward before the train was out of the curve, and the train rapidly increased speed. Twenty-five miles per hour had seemed reckless earlier. The gauge moved steadily to thirty, thirty-five, and finally, more than forty miles per hour before the engineer slightly pulled the throttle back and turned to his special guest. "She can do more, but I dare not get too far ahead of schedule. The bosses will know I was racing her."

When the train stopped at Union Station in Troy, John grabbed his small canvas bag, shook hands with Hogan, bade goodbye to the fireman, and descended on wobbly legs.

While John was in transit from New York City, Susannah and the Smith family attended church services at the Methodist Episcopal Church on North Second Street. Since graduation, Susannah would often, though unenthusiastically, join the family for Sunday-morning services. This Sunday, Susannah informed her mother that she would be going to lunch and the theater after church with her best friend, Rebecca, and would spend the night with her. Susannah had yet to discuss her marriage plans with her mother, and, so far, her father and brother had kept the knowledge to themselves.

After the services, Susannah walked home with her family, changed, kissed both parents on the cheek, and left. The weather had turned pleasant after days of wind and snow. Susannah's mood brightened when a block away from home, and all her thoughts turned to her fiancée. She knew he'd be standing in the lobby, watching the street for her arrival.

All the awkwardness that marked her first hours with John had passed. Susannah never assumed John lacked experience with women. After unsatisfying experiments with schoolboys and youthful suitors, she looked forward to her experiences with a confident, knowledgeable lover. Her fiancée was both, as well as gentle and patient. As soon as they entered their suite, the lovers quickly cast off their clothes and dove into the massive bed.

It was dark when John sat up and lit the lamp on the nightstand. "I don't know about you, but I'm hungry."

Susannah pulled the sheet to her chin and batted her eyes. "I thought you'd never get around to feeding me."

John slipped into his shirt, pulled on his slacks and boots, put two small logs on the fireplace, and promised to return as soon as he had placed their standard order at the Dalton Room Restaurant on the hotel's first floor. While he was gone, Susannah freshened up and slipped into a satin robe she'd packed for the evening.

When dinner was delivered, the pair devoured rare steaks, mashed potatoes with cheese, turnips, and an entire loaf of freshly baked bread in less than an hour. The first of the two bottles of Tennessee-grown red wine disappeared with the meal. They shared the second bottle while sitting by the fireplace catching up.

Susannah told her lover about a visit by Theodosia Hudson two weeks earlier. Miss Hudson was the vice principal at Troy Female Seminary. She had arrived to inform the Smith women that Susannah was the leading candidate for an extraordinary opportunity in Charleston, South Carolina. The Episcopal church of that great city intended to open a female academy based on Mrs. Emma Willard's model. It would be the first school of higher education for women in the state.

Theodosia addressed her recent graduate, "Would you be interested in accepting the honor of such a critical position, Susannah?"

Susannah told John how her mother clasped her hands as if in prayer, expectantly staring at her. "I am honored," Suzie told Theodosia, "That you'd consider one of such modest talent for such a significant role. Other graduates, she said, would be far better suited."

Susannah paused to sip her wine, then added, "Mother has never seemed so crestfallen, John. For me, to have such an opportunity has been her dream. It's time for us to discuss our plans. She'll need time to adjust to our getting married this summer."

"I'm ready whenever you say, Suzie."

"Father, of course, needs to be there. He's leaving in the morning for New York. A house is rented for him while modification of the *Francis Skiddy* is underway. It will be Friday night before he returns. Could you return for Sunday dinner?"

"Yes, send a telegram to Dad at Belle of the Union with the time."

The couple edged closer, and John put his arm around his bride-to-be. They watched the flames dance, lost in thought until Susannah sighed and changed the subject. "Your turn, John. What's new in New York City?"

John described his meeting at Tammany Hall with Isaiah Rynders and four Tammany bosses, including the current mayor, and Fernando Wood, the Tammany leader and Democratic candidate for mayor. "They swore me to secrecy, but I had to ask people I trust for their thoughts. I talked with Dad and Shang. I'm worried, I am, about what happens if the guy I'm backing loses. We'll be married this summer, and Belle of the Union ought to support us."

Susannah continued to sip her wine and watch the fire. "What did Shang have to say?"

"I went to his place for dinner. Father Finnegan joined us, a family friend. After dinner, I asked if they thought I should trust them guys. Shang says Rynders can't be trusted but might be useful. The priest said I need to back Tammany and Wood. If Wood loses, the Irish-hating nativists will get all that power, and things will go bad for us Irish and our businesses. So, it'll matter to us if I decide to help Wood. I need to know what you think."

Susannah turned away and looked at John. "I have questions. Do you mind?"

"No, please."

"Why do you think the bosses at this Tammany Hall want your help?"

"Don't know if they want it or just think they need it 'cause I'm the champion and a hero to the Irish."

"Do you believe that's true?"

"I do."

"And the priest, do you think what he says about Wood losing is true?"

"I fear he's right, sure."

Susannah slid closer to John, took his hand in hers, and stared into the flames. John didn't interrupt her thoughts, sipping the rest of his wine and waiting.

"John," she spoke while watching the flames dance, "in one of our earliest conversations when I was so young and naive, I said you'd be famous in New York City. Now you are, but that fame won't last. If these men at Tammany Hall and the Democratic Party are convinced that they can't hold onto power without your support, then you should demand a fair reward for your services."

"Do you have something in mind, Suzie?"

"That depends, John, on your ambitions. What comes next for you? What comes next for us? How far do we want to go?"

John nodded as he stared into the middle distance. A smile gradually spread across his face. He took Suzie's hand, lifted it to his lips, and kissed it. "I guess I've been worried about what we could lose, 'stead of thinking what we can win. When gamblers start thinkin' that way they're bound to lose."

John put his arms around his muse, hugged her close, and said, "You're right, Suzie, what I need from Tammany and the Democrats is help to expand my gambling businesses and protection for them. I've seen gambling palaces in San Francisco, and I want to build even better in New York. That's what you'd call an ambition, am I right?

Suzie had a mischievous glow in her eyes. "This man, Wood," she said, "told you Tammany takes care of its own. You should meet with him privately and tell him exactly what you need to realize that ambition."

John smiled and asked, will you help me make a list and write it for me?"

Suzie tilted her head and answered, "I have my price also, Mr. Morrissey. I'll take it in installments." She stood, dropped her robe, and led John to bed.

Twenty-Four

U pon his return to New York City, Morrissey hustled to his apartment at Irving House for a bath and a change of clothes. From there, he went to Belle of the Union. It was early afternoon, so Dad Cunningham was in the office, as expected. John knocked a coded signal, and his partner unlocked and opened the door. "Good to see that face!" Dad said as he closed and locked the door behind his friend. "How did you find things at Troy?"

Dad went to the bar and poured three fingers of whiskey into two crystal glasses before settling into matching leather chairs and touching glasses.

"I've decided what to do about Tammany and Wood, Dad."

"What's your plan, Johnny? I hope this one won't get me drowned, shot, or arrested." Dad would never let John forget about their California misadventures.

"I'll help get Wood elected. He promised they'd take care of me when he's mayor. That's fine, but I need a personal commitment from Wood before I gather our Irish for him. I'll be asking for three more saloon and gambling licenses for us, plus five more Irish precinct officers, and twenty more Irish police officers."

"What if Wood loses?" All Dad could think about was the potential loss of Belle of the Union.

"He won't lose, Dad, not if we get every breathing Irishman to the polls to vote for Wood – at least once!"

"I don't know how we can operate three more of these." Dad swept his hand to indicate Belle of the Union.

"We'll get partners. Johnny Lyng already wants to partner. There'll be others. The city's growing fast, and the money's going uptown. I'm going with it."

Dad burst out laughing. "Johnny, I don't have what our Irish parents called *misneach*! Not like you. You have more courage than any man ever breathed. If it's all the same, I'd like to remain your partner and manager here for the rest of my days."

The urge to argue was strong, but so was John's love and respect for Dad. He tilted his whiskey glass toward his partner. "To your health and happiness, Dad. Keep money flowin' at Belle of the Union. I've more news. Suzie and I'll meet Sunday with her parents. We've got father's permission to wed, but Mrs. Smith doesn't know. Suzie's gonna talk to herself this week. I'll be making it official with a diamond ring on Sunday, so I'll be needin' part of my share of our profits for it."

"Good luck to your Suzie, with that conversation!" Dad pretended to duck projectiles. "Have you lovebirds picked a date yet?" Dad rose and went to the safe.

"We plan on sometime in the summer."

"How much would you be needin', Johnny?" Dad withdrew a stack of currency and his ledger from the safe and brought them to his desk.

"Three hundred for the ring. Will that buy a big diamond?"

"How would I be knowing? Get a receipt for the ring. You're not to the altar yet, my friend."

John thanked Dad and promised to return before seven. Then, pocketing the cash, he headed south to 259 Broadway, where Charles Tiffany ran the city's busiest jewelry store. There, he waited for the proprietor to finish serving two shoppers.

"I'll be buying an engagement ring," John explained when Tiffany was free.

Charles Tiffany was good at sizing up his shoppers. Irishmen commonly had big dreams and thin wallets. "Do you have a design in mind?" he asked.

John looked through the glass display case below him and saw a ring with a brilliant, raised diamond and a host of smaller gems along the sides. "I favor that one," he said, pointing out the ring.

Tiffany smiled, removed the ring, and placed it on a gray cloth on the counter. "It is quite lovely, isn't it? I completed it last week."

"How much?" John couldn't take his eyes off the stunning creation.

"Two hundred and thirty," answered the jeweler, preparing to put it back, as he had done more than a dozen times in less than a week.

John counted the cash, saying, "Wrap it for me, please?"

On his way back to Belle of the Union, John crossed to Park Row and climbed the Empire Club's stairs. He bypassed the bar, where patrons nodded a greeting. He heard the buzz grow as he went up to Isaiah Reynders's office.

Rynders looked up from a stack of documents. "Well, I can't say I'm surprised to see you, Morrissey. Giving thought to helping Wood?"

"Matter of fact, I have, Captain. Can you schedule a meeting with Mr. Wood when you see him this week?"

Rynders looked puzzled and concerned. "Anything you need to discuss with the grand sachem, you can discuss with me, son."

"Wood can't win without the Irish vote, Captain. He knows that. The Democrats know it. You know it. My influence on the city's Irish is strong and growing. That's why you introduced me to your Tammany friends and Mr. Wood, and I appreciate it. You told me: *Power equals opportunity, and opportunity equals money.* I'll be needing to discuss certain conditions with Mr. Wood before I fly in to help."

Rynders was clearly furious, "Why should I request a meeting on your behalf, Morrissey? Tell me your 'commitments,' and I'll deliver them to Fernando."

"Thank you, Captain, but I'll speak directly with Mr. Wood. It'll be best for you and me if you make it happen."

Rynders rose and walked around his desk shaking his head, then extending a hand. "I think I'll regret the day I saved your life, young man," he said with a smirk. "You sure remind me of my younger self. You'll get your meeting with Fernando but be careful. It's a dangerous game you're dealing yourself into."

The Tammany chieftains met every Wednesday at midday. John planned to revisit Rynders on Thursday to get an answer. In the meantime, he visited Tom Petrie to thank him for Belle of the Union's support and decide if he would be interested in partnering in other locations. Petrie expressed his pleasure with Dad Cunningham's management and his share of the growing profits. "Sure," he said, "I'll consider new investments with the right partners, location, and terms." He would approach others, but that would wait until after meeting with Wood.

On Wednesday evening, with no telegram from Susannah, John was concerned and distracted. Every seat at his poker table was filled by eight o'clock. Three players ran up big wins and cashed out at two in the morning. In six hours, John had lost more than two thousand dollars for Belle of the Union. When he went to the office with the depleted bank, Dad counted the balance twice before looking up at his dejected partner. "We're up a thousand for the day, despite your bad night, Johnny. Let's have a quick whiskey, then get sleep. You'll get it back tomorrow."

John returned to Irving House and went to bed but slept little that night. There were so many unanswered questions. Would he place the ring on Susannah's finger this Sunday? Would Fernando Wood reject the demands he planned to make? Would Rynders undermine his efforts? Should he defend his championship belt to stop all the talk? Would Susannah object to another prizefight? He was exhausted when Thursday morning arrived.

After breakfast, John proceeded to Park Row to call on

Rynders. No patrons were in front of the building at the early hour, and only a few were in the bar. John went to Rynders's second-floor office. The door was closed and locked. He glanced up the stairs and considered heading to Rynders's private residence but resisted the urge. Instead, he waited, pacing the hallway until he heard footsteps descending the stairs. There was momentary surprise on Rynders's face when he saw John. That gave way to a grimace.

"Why, Johnny, here we are again, and I believe I know the reason." Rynders removed a key and opened his office door. "Please join me."

Captain Rynders moved from window to window to let the morning light fill the office, then went ahead to his desk and sat. John stood across the desk. He removed neither his overcoat nor top hat. "Did you make a meeting with Wood?"

"What you consider being direct, young man, can be considered impertinent. In case you don't know that word, it means fucking rude." Rynders swept his arm around as far as he could, pointing from left to right. "All these wards are mine. Tammany made me a chieftain because I control the votes here. I don't care if you're Irish, German, Jewish, or Negro. All I care about is votes. I agree with our grand sachem that you can help with the Irish. Wood will meet you next Wednesday. Be at the Hall at ten. I'll be joining you. Wood insists. Now, get out of my sight."

At Belle of the Union, John went to the office. Dad opened the door with a smile and a telegram in hand. After entering and locking the office door, John said, "Read it, please."

Dinner Sunday at four. I've spoken with Mother. She will not oppose. STS.

Dad smiled, folded the telegram, and handed it to John.

"Good news?" he asked.

"The best, Dad."

Twenty-Five

S usannah dreaded the unavoidable discussion with her mother. Having assured John that confirmation of their important Sunday dinner would arrive via telegram no later than Wednesday, it was now or never. She wished her father could be home for that conversation, but he would not return from New York until Friday evening.

Mr. Warren and his wife, Beatrice, were delighted with the quality and progress of their four children's education. On this Wednesday, however, Beatrice noticed how distracted Susannah appeared. "Is all well, Susannah?" she asked as the young tutor fastened her coat and tied her hat.

Susannah was surprised that the usually reserved Mrs. Warren would ask so intimate a question. "Yes, I am well, thank you, Mrs. Warren." She was not. Her heart was full of dread. She considered saying more, baring her troubled soul to someone before facing her mother, but this was not the time, and her employer was not the person.

"Your children were wonderful students today," Susannah assured Mrs. Warren. "It is a privilege to instruct them." She offered the best smile possible, exited the Porte-cochere, and climbed into the hansom cab for her ride home.

David had agreed to distract Addie after dinner so his sister could have private time with their mother. With the table cleared, Susannah went to Mrs. Smith and placed a hand on her shoulder. "I need a private conversation, Mother. Would you join me in the parlor?"

Mrs. Smith turned to her daughter, took her hand, looked into her eyes, and said, "Of course."

As they walked to the parlor, Mrs. Smith did not release her daughter's hand, squeezing instead. She quietly closed the door and led Susannah to the couch.

"What is it, Suzie?"

"Mother, I'm in love. I wish to marry, and I want your approval."

"Has the man spoken with Captain Smith?"

"He has, Mother. Father will consent, but only with your blessing."

Mrs. Smith held and squeezed both of Suzie's hands as her eyes filled with tears. "I have known of your relationship with Mr. Morrissey, darling. I have hoped that it would run its course and prayed that you would not find yourself with child. Your father and I have had discussions about your intentions. We do not keep secrets regarding our children's welfare. We know marrying an Irishman and a Catholic will expose you and your children to severe prejudice, and to marry one as notorious as your Mr. Morrissey is a reason for greater concern." She stopped to wipe the tears she couldn't hold back.

Steadying herself, Mrs. Smith continued. "Your father and I know you very well, Suzie. To stand against your betrothment would alienate you; we are sure. We do not wish to lose you. If you persist with the marriage, we intend to be here for you and Mr. Morrissey and, if so blessed, with your children." With that, Aldine

Smith could no longer constrain her emotions. She leaned her head into her daughter's neck and sobbed.

When John's train arrived at Union Station in Troy midday on Sunday, he took a hansom cab to his family's apartment. He assumed everyone would be home after church and preparing for Sunday dinner. He was right. His sister, Catherine, answered the door when he knocked. She shrieked and threw her arms around John's neck. The other girls came running and dragged their brother into the house.

Over the giggling and shouts of joy, Tim Morrissey's voice rose. "Lasses, stand aside now, and let at me boyo!" The girls cleared a path for their father. "Johnny, we were not expecting you."

"Is Ma here?" John asked. "I've news for the family."

"Well, let's go find herself." Tim led a procession of his children to the kitchen, where Judith was busy at the stove. She didn't turn as her family entered the room. "Ma, your son has arrived with news." Tim waited for a response. Getting none, he raised his voice. "Judith Morrissey, you'll be joining your family; you will!"

Judith wiped her hands on her apron, turned, and glared at her husband. "I'd be preparing your meal. Your son can share news if he's quick about it."

Tim blushed and took a step toward his wife.

John took hold of his arm and whispered, "No, Da." John looked around at his sisters' faces, offering a smile to each. "I've come to say I plan to marry."

It took seconds for the fact to register, then his sisters renewed their shrieking and shouted questions over each other.

"One at a time," John insisted with a laugh. He answered in turn. "Yes, she's from Troy. Susannah Smith. She's eighteen. Troy Female Seminary. Yes, Hannah, she's beautiful, indeed."

Tim said, "Congratulations, laddie. I'll be fetching a drink to cheer your good fortune." He headed to the cupboard for the whiskey and glasses.

"Is she Catholic?" Judith's question brought silence to the family.

"No, Ma." John knew what was to come.

Judith looked at her only son, clenching her fists. "Then you're not to be married in the Church? Are your children not to be saved by baptism? Is this why I brought you to America, where we're hated?" Judith's rage was building. Her eyes bore into her son. "Leave this house, John Morrissey, and don't be stepping foot here again."

"That's enough!" shouted Tim. "Johnny's our son and will always be, and the brother to these lasses. Hold your bitterness, woman!"

Judith's violent temper could be on display at any moment. John knew it was time to leave. His father and sisters trailed behind as he retreated down the stairs. John shook his father's hand on the front steps, promised to supply details about the wedding, and hugged each of his sisters. He could not look back at their tearful faces.

John needed to shake off his mother's rejection while hoping his evening with Susannah's family would go far better. When his hansom cab rolled to a stop in front of the Smith family home, he got out, paid the driver, took a deep breath, and stepped toward the house. As he climbed the stairs, the curtains in the bay window parted. Addie stood there smiling and waving. John waved back and knocked, and David appeared within a minute.

"It's good to see you, John." David offered his hand. "Susannah will be down presently. Father's in the parlor. He just chased Addie back upstairs. Let me take your things, then please join Father."

John thanked David, handed him his topcoat and hat, and followed him to the parlor.

"Well, Morrissey, last time I saw you, we witnessed the *Empire*'s sinking, if I'm not mistaken." The captain stood and offered his hand to his former deckhand.

"Yes, sir," John said, thankful for the warm reception. "A tragic day, sir. She was a grand ship."

"Well, Suzie asked us to gather for dinner. My daughter, it would appear, is determined to become Mrs. John Morrissey. Mrs. Smith wishes to speak with you and Suzie about your plans. The ladies will join us momentarily." Captain Smith leaned closer. He looked for and held John's eyes. "Before Aldine and Susannah join us, I'll share my concerns privately. I'm not without experience in the rougher aspects of life, though nothing compared with your experiences. A father never wishes to see his daughter or grandchildren live in fear or want. Suzie imagines a peaceful and prosperous life with you. I think she's naive. It will be hard, I'm afraid, for you to escape your past."

John held his soon-to-be father-in-law's gaze and nodded. "It's true I've known nothing but fighting, sir. I was raised in the worst conditions and with no proper guidance. Your daughter was the first to believe in me and insists my real strength lies here," John pointed to his chest, "not in my fists. She, sir, has the real strength."

Captain Smith leaned back in his chair. "Suzie is indeed strong. She'll test your heart and courage; I have no doubt."

John smiled and nodded. "You and Mrs. Smith will see I can care for Susannah as you would want. I've got a good business in New York and opportunities for more. I've got powerful friends there 'cause I'm the boxing champion and hero to the Irish. Best of all, sir, I've your daughter beside me. She makes anything possible."

Captain Smith smiled, leaned forward, and offered his hand. "I've said my piece and will not stand between you and Suzie. I've seen your better qualities firsthand and wish you the best. Mind that temper, Morrissey, and the drink."

As he shook the captain's hand, they heard Mrs. Smith's voice from the head of the stairs. "Addie, I told you to remain in your room. Now, up here!" Addie made no noise in her bare feet as she rushed back to her room.

Captain Smith rose, went to the doorway, and called up the stairs. "Aldine, would you and Suzie join us in the parlor?"

Both men stood waiting for Mrs. Smith and Susannah to join them. The women could not have been more lovely as they entered the parlor. Susannah wore a silk bodice and matching skirt with layers of pale-blue and white alternating stripes. Her hair was parted down the middle, topped by a small bonnet secured by a red bow tied under her chin. Aldine was equally breathtaking in a silk taffeta ensemble of pink and purple vertical panels. Her hair was the identical color to her daughter's, though straight and tied back. Her bonnet was larger and more ornate than Susannah's, with velvet, feathers, and glass beads. They stood in the parlor entryway, enjoying their effect on the men.

"Will you invite us to sit?" Mrs. Smith smiled at her husband, who, seemingly, had lost his tongue.

"Of course," he stammered, indicating the oversized couch. "Please be comfortable."

After Mrs. Smith and Susannah were seated, the men returned to their chairs. John appeared as stunned as the captain. Susannah had that now-familiar tilted head and smirk as she stared at her betrothed, waiting for him to find his voice.

John pulled his gaze away from Susannah to address her poised, stunning mother. "I'm honored by your invitation to dinner, Mrs. Smith." It sounded rehearsed, which it was. He blushed.

Mrs. Smith had no desire to prolong his agony. She looked him in the eyes and said, "Since you intend to marry our daughter, John Morrissey, a seat at our table will always be yours." She did not smile.

John looked from her to Susannah and replied, "Yes, Mrs. Smith, I do wish to marry Susannah, with your blessing, of course."

Susannah reached for her mother's hand and turned toward her. A tear began to slide down Mrs. Smith's cheek. She fought through her emotion and addressed John. "I have concerns about the proposed marriage. I have discussed those with Suzie and Captain Smith. I have prayed daily for the wisdom and compassion to support our daughter, who is as strong-willed as her father. She insists you are the right man to help her realize her ambitions. I hope that's true, Mr. Morrissey." Mrs. Smith turned again to Suzie before continuing. "It's useless to resist Susannah's will, as you'll discover. I will welcome you into our family, pray for you daily, and do my best to support you and my daughter in your marriage."

After glancing at Susannah, John, suddenly choking on emotion, turned to address her parents. All he could manage was, "Thank you, Captain and Mrs. Smith."

"Good, then," said Mrs. Smith, rescuing her future son-in-law. "Dinner's prepared, and it will get cold. Shall we adjourn to the family table?"

Mrs. Smith placed her hand on Captain Smith's elbow as they left the parlor.

Susannah hurried to John, threw her arms around his neck, and whispered, "I love you, John Morrissey." She took his hand, and they followed her parents to the dining room. On cue, David and Addie came downstairs.

"Please wait, children," Captain Smith said, "before taking your seats. We have an announcement." He waited for the family to settle behind their chairs. Addie rushed to stand next to Susannah and grabbed her hand. Mrs. Smith stood beside her husband, biting her lower lip. "You know our guest, John Morrissey. Mr. Morrissey wants to marry Susannah. Your mother and I gave our blessing. Mr. Morrissey has something to say to your sister before all of us." With a mischievous grin, Levi Smith nodded at John.

Susannah placed a reassuring hand on John's forearm as he reached his free hand into his vest pocket. His hand was shaking as he removed a tiny box from which he withdrew the Tiffany ring. Then, holding it between two fingers for Susannah to see, with his voice breaking, he said, "Susannah, I hope you'll wear this ring and agree to be my wife."

Susannah raised her hand to her mouth. Addie jumped up and down, shouting, "I knew it! I knew it!"

Susannah smiled at her little sister. "Yes, you did, Addie." Then, to John, she promised, "I will wear this ring as a sign of my commitment. I will forever be proud to be Mrs. John Morrissey." She took the ring and slipped it onto her finger. It fit perfectly.

After dinner and the Smith children's enthusiastic embrace, John rented a carriage, and he and Susannah went for a slow ride north along River Street through Lansingburgh and back. The bride-to-be kept holding the gorgeous ring close to her face to see it in the moonlight. "It's the most beautiful ring I could ever imagine, John. It's fit for an empress!"

John Morrissey felt an enormous weight lifted when Susannah Smith placed the ring on her finger. He could not, however, forget her parents' words. Susannah was risking much to marry him. He was sure he could provide the material things she would want and need. Yet, his notoriety and the world of violence he inhabited would be a threat to her happiness and peace of mind. At least in the near term.

Captain Smith was right; it would be hard to move beyond his past. There were obligations to the Dead Rabbits, and the support of Fernando Wood would set him against the nativists, who already marked him as a major threat. Also, demands that he defend his championship never stopped. John hoped, in time, he could escape his past, but his marriage would not put an end to threats. How much, he wondered, would Susannah tolerate in the interim?

Susannah sensed her fiancée was troubled. She couldn't see his face in the closed cab, but she could feel the stiffness. She whispered, "Care to share your thoughts with your future wife?"

John took Suzie's left hand and ran his finger over the edges of the engagement ring. They rode silently for minutes, passing grand houses on the Hudson. Susannah was about to repeat the question when John said, "Well, Suzie, I've never been a husband, and I'm afraid I won't get it right."

Susannah leaned across the seat, placed a hand gently on either side of her fiancé's face, and stared into his eyes. "Don't worry, John," she said, "we'll learn to be husband and wife together. I have no doubt." Touching his chest with the palm of her right hand, she added, "As long as this strong heart pulses, John, I know that you will fight for what we want and need." She took his right hand and placed it over her heart. "As long as this heart pulses, I will dream with you and grow with you."

"Yes, Suzie, so long as this heart beats, I promise I'll fight to be the man you deserve."

"We're just beginning, John, and we have so far to go." Shifting her gaze to her fiancé, she tilted her head, smiled flirtatiously, and whispered, "If I remember correctly, Mr. Champion of America, we're off to a very fine start."

To Be Continued...

Acknowledgments

Francis Joseph Baillargeon, Sr., 1920-2004, is the my father and inspiration for this series of books. For decades he remained focused on capturing and sharing the extraordinary story of a near-forgotten local hero. Bringing John Morrissey's story into public consciousness was a burning passion. The series is dedicated to his memory.

Dr. Fred Harvey Harrington, 1912-1995, served as President of the University of Wisconsin-Madison from 1962 to 1970. As a young historian, Dr. Harrington became fascinated with John Morrissey, also spending decades collecting valuable information to inform a biography. While he never completed that effort, he did leave volumes of notes and nine draft chapters of a biography upon which the author has drawn liberally.

Thank you Jonathan Starke, author, professional editor, and former boxer, for providing the line editing services that added the necessary "punch" to the extraordinary tale of ambitions and grit. Thanks to Stacey Smekofske of Edits by Stacey, who took the manuscript, turned it into an elegant finished product, and guided it through the daunting publishing process.

I am so grateful to Annelise Joy Farquhar, my granddaughter, is the creator of the beautiful cover art for this series. And to Sierra Farquhar, another talented granddaughter, and professional photographer who took my portrait.

Thank you Richard and Denise Borden who indulged their brother as enthusiastic listeners to version upon version of audio drafts. Their encouragement always gave this insecure author the confidence and motivation needed to move forward.

And most importantly, thank you Pat Baillargeon, my spouse of fifty-five years, who believed in this project for decades and provided emotional support and patient and critical editing throughout the writing journey. Like John Morrissey, my life would have been far less productive and rewarding without her by my side.

About the Author

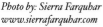

Frank Baillargeon is proud to offer this first installment of a 3-volume series of historical novels based on the life and times of John and Susannah Morrissey. He is proud and fortunate to have been invited by his father into the Morrisseys' world. It was a rare opportunity for a father and son to share and celebrate every large and small discovery.

Photo by: Sierra Farquhar
www.sierrafarquhar.com

Before his father died, he was determined to pull John Morrissey's wife, Susannah Smith Morrissey out of the shadows of the story and place her in the central role she deserves. It was their individual and shared ambitions that drove them, against all odds, to rise to the pinnacle of financial, political, and cultural success in mid-19th century America.

The author grew up on Van Schaick Island in Cohoes, N.Y. "The Island" as we know it, is formed by the convergence of the Mohawk and Hudson Rivers. It was across the Hudson in 1833 that two-year-old John Morrissey arrived in America and began a less than promising life. It was that proximity to the Baillargeon family's hometown that attracted Francis, Sr. to Morrissey's story.

Today, the author and his wife of fifty-five years live in Eagle, Idaho. They were blessed with three children and have nine grandchildren. Frank earned a B.A. in American History from the

University of Rochester. He retired in 2018 after forty-three years as an executive and consultant in the photographic industry.

f facebook.com/FrankWritesHistory

Coming Soon

Volume II and Volume III
of John and Susannah's story.

The Morrisseys

Made in the USA
Columbia, SC
03 December 2022